D0169626

The Urbana Free Library

To renew: call 217-367-4057
or go to "*urbanafreelibrary.org*"
and select "Renew/Request Items"

THE AVENUE
OF THE GIANTS

Marc Dugain

THE AVENUE
OF THE GIANTS

*Translated from the French
by Howard Curtis*

Europa
editions

Europa Editions
214 West 29th Street
New York, N.Y. 10001
www.europaeditions.com
info@europaeditions.com

Copyright © 2012 by Editions Gallimard
First Publication 2014 by Europa Editions

Translation by Howard Curtis
Original title: *Avenue des Géants*
Translation copyright © 2014 by Europa Editions

Library of Congress Cataloging in Publication Data is available
ISBN 978-1-60945-200-1

Dugain, Marc
The Avenue of the Giants

Book design by Emanuele Ragnisco
www.mekkanografici.com

Cover illustration realized from a photo © tiero/iStock

Prepress by Grafica Punto Print – Rome

Printed in the USA

To Florent, Héloïse, Roman
Kamil and Emmanuelle: my joy.

To Bruno Jeanmart, psychoanalyst and
philosopher, my oldest friend. This book
grew out of our belated discussions.

To be is to be cornered.
—E. M. CIORAN, *Drawn and Quartered*

THE AVENUE
OF THE GIANTS

1

She does what she does every month, plumps herself down on the chair facing him and takes a dozen books from her bag, most of them hardcovers. He glances through them quickly, then puts them down on the table. She gives him a thin smile but doesn't look him square in the face. For years she's avoided giving him a straight look. She's always turning away her eyes, or lowering her head, which has given him the opportunity over the years to see the bald furrow in the middle of her skull grow wider. She has long hair and it's hard to tell when it's clean. Even when it is clean, it doesn't look it. She must have been reasonably pretty once, though it's hard to make out her former beauty beneath those bloated features. He's just as decrepit, but he has a good reason for it, whereas with her, well, you wonder. He likes the woman, though. In fact, he's come to the conclusion that he likes her because he feels nothing for her, neither love nor hate. Sometimes she irritates him. He resents her for being the only visitor he ever has. He resents her for all the others who never visit him, which is a bit unfair, given that there aren't any others, not anymore. He's perceptive enough to have noticed that for some time now she's had something to tell him. But what? He has no idea. He can just feel the unexpressed words hanging heavy in the air. It's beyond simple shyness. She's never really natural with him. She's always playing a part. Not very well, so that often her voice is out of step with her expressions. Sometimes she seems all lit up, sometimes completely exhausted.

She has big, flaccid breasts beneath a wrinkled throat. In a woman who must be in her sixties, he doesn't find that very attractive. But he's grateful to her for not making him fantasize. You don't fire up an engine with no gas.

"Did you talk to the newspapers about what we mentioned?"

She takes a while to reply. Nothing unusual in that, she always takes a while to reply, as if she felt the weight of responsibility on her.

"Yes. A whole bunch of newspapers on the coast. They're int—let's just say they're intrigued. They're thinking it over. But I think it's feasible."

Her eyes start moving around again. He could punch her in the face when she does that, but deep down he doesn't really want to. He imagines the damage it would do, while she continues talking, every word seeming to apologize for coming out of her mouth. Her mouth is small for a face that size. She must have Indian blood. Not fresh blood, blood that goes back to the beginning of the century, when they were put down.

"You realize they'd be taking a risk . . ."

"You mean having me as a literary critic?"

"Oh, no! They'll form their own opinion about that. It's more about whether or not to reveal who you are. And if they don't say who you are, they might be blamed one day. At the same time, they think that if they do reveal your identity, they might create quite a stir. Get a lot of media attention . . ."

He nods distractedly as if he's lost interest in the conversation. He's always acted like that. It's a way of getting one over on the people he's talking to. Then he changes his mind and says, "I've read plenty of critics in my life. I don't see how they're any better than me. I've read 3,952 books since the beginning of the Seventies. And I read each one carefully, you can't argue with that. Now, does that give me the right to have an opinion about literature? I think it does."

"They told me they were thinking of you more as a reviewer of mysteries."

He makes an effort not to show his irritation in order not to scare her, because she's easily scared. "They must think they've hit the jackpot. Tell them I'm not interested in mysteries. Not one bit. Too conventional, too clichéd, just a whole lot of stupid puzzles."

For a while neither says a word, looking elsewhere. There's nothing to look at in this room, so they each stare at the opposite wall. He's already had enough of her, but he controls himself, he doesn't want her to feel it, it isn't her fault.

Abruptly, he says, "You can tell them that figure. 3,952 books since 1971. And if you want to make them laugh, tell them I'd only read a single book between when I was born in 1948 and 1971. I read it three times. Can you guess what it was?"

"The Bible."

"No, *Crime and Punishment*. That's one hell of a book. The best book ever written, in my opinion."

He can see it in her eyes—she's wondering if he's joking. She has a straight, pretty nose and eyes of an unusual color. But she smells of fear the way a corpse smells of death. A generalized fear of life. She smothers herself in patchouli to conceal it. That must deceive a lot of people. Not him.

He takes another look at the books she's brought him. He discovers the odd one out.

"What's this? A children's book?"

"It's a proposal. They realized there were no recordings for children. And there are lots more blind children than we think."

"Did you do this on purpose?"

She starts to melt like an ice cream in the sun. She wipes her forehead with the back of her hand. She doesn't understand what he's talking about.

"You probably don't know my grandmother used to write children's books," he says softly, to reassure her, because she's turned disturbingly red. "But that's not the most important thing. Can you imagine me recording CDs for children with my voice? They must be a bit desperate to have come up with an idea like that. And it's a massive job to put yourself in the place of a child when you were never given the chance to be one. I don't have that gift."

She quickly goes on, "Nobody's had as many awards as you for reading. It's you the publisher wants, I mean . . . that we want."

She thinks she's flattering him. He's too old for that, although he's proud of his awards.

He promises her he'll try, it doesn't cost anything and everyone will be happy. He doesn't mind making compromises. It may seem a stupid thing to say, but he gets a real pleasure from compromise. He's convinced that if everyone agreed to meet halfway, conflicts would be avoided. He often says that in his sermons to the guys. Once the idea of compromise has taken root in your mind, violence loses out. Even if you have no intention of meeting halfway, make just one step toward the other person and you've put violence behind you. He isn't going to argue about the question of children's books, it's agreed, he'll try it. If he didn't, he'd feel as if he was giving in to the past and he never wants to do that again.

"Good critics understand that the way an author treats his subject is more important than the subject itself. That's the real adventure of literature. What's the interest in typing thousands of pages just to say what you have to say? I've heard so much crap talked about people who didn't deserve it. When I read what Mary McCarthy or Henry Miller wrote about Salinger, never looking below the surface, I wonder how relevant their judgments are, or even if they're trying to avoid admitting how mediocre their own writings are. That makes me so mad sometimes! I won't even go into what I read about Raymond Carver. Of course now he's a classic, worthy to be spoken of in the same breath as Chekhov, but I was there when they said he was too minimalist. He had to die, of course. All these people prefer mummified corpses to the living. Well, let them do what they want, but as for mystery stories, they can forget about me, got that? It's a minor genre, completely beneath contempt. Even the seediest of mysteries can't convey ten percent of the reality they're supposedly portraying."

He says all this without raising his voice. He very seldom raises his voice. His fits of temper are contained within an airtight chamber. When he's angry, he's the only one who knows it.

"If you really don't want the children's book . . . "

As far as he's concerned, the matter's settled. Why is she still harping on about it? He's known lots of people like her, people who can't take a single step forward without looking behind them.

"I told you I'll read it."

She gives a pitiful little smile. She glances at her watch and smiles again to free herself of his insistent gaze. She thinks he's going to lash out at her, whereas in fact he's simply tired of staring at the wall behind her.

"When will you be back?"

She seems suddenly relieved. "In a month."

He could stop her from coming. He'd only have to ask the prison authorities. She could just drop the books in for him and go. He has the power to do it, that's for sure, but it would be an abuse of that power. Sometimes, he feels a kind of muted anger at the thought that the only woman he'll ever see is this airhead who looks like a cornfield in the rain. He's sure she does drugs. She's the kind of person who, for breakfast, has a joint in one hand and a cup of coffee in the other and forgets to eat. She probably sips soda all day long, and eats only the occasional hamburger dripping with grease. In all the time she's been coming to see him—at least thirty years now—he's grateful to her for never telling him anything personal about herself. He couldn't have stood that. It's hard to explain, but he'd have taken it badly. He can accept a professional relationship, nothing more. He keeps an eye open to seize on any liberties she might take, and she knows it. She's never made a false move yet.

It's time to finish. "Can you bring me a CD next time you come? I'll tell you straight off, I don't have anything to pay you with."

She's only too happy to please him, so she nods convulsively.

"All right, then," he says, getting to his feet. "Skip James. As many of his songs as you can find. But especially *Crow Jane* and *I'd Rather Be the Devil.*"

She promises as she stands up. It's a bit hard for her to get out of her chair. It's probably all that fat, weighing on her knees. He turns his back on her, raises his hand in farewell, lowers his head to get through the door, and leaves the room, adjusting his glasses as he does so.

A man who's respected enjoys a number of small privileges. One of his is that he's allowed to fetch his mail himself. The warden gives it to him with a smile. He'd like it if he only had to deal with guys like him. Not a day passes that he doesn't receive a letter. You don't know what a pleasure it is to open your mail and be sure you'll never receive bad news. He receives two kinds of letters. The most frequent are thanks from his listeners. They haven't written them themselves, they dictate them to relatives. They thank him for the careful way he reads the books. His performances, some say, are worthy of the Actor's Studio. He appreciates the compliment, even though he doesn't like actors. He doesn't trust people whose job is to be someone else. Sooner or later, they end up not knowing who they are. Empathy isn't his strong point and he thinks it's better to admit that rather than pretend, but all the same he has good feelings for the blind people who listen to him. He can imagine how terrible it must be to be blind, especially in the United States, the country with the most beautiful landscapes in the world, although of course, fortunately for them, those who are born like that don't know what they're missing. Apart from the blind, he receives letters from female admirers. They're often quite racy. They always send him photographs of themselves. Passport-style photos or full length portraits. Some actually pose in the nude, poses that go from the mildly erotic to the totally obscene and pornographic, with close-ups of their private parts. He finds that disgusting. The letters that come with them are often crazy, and he prefers not to talk about them, they present an image of humanity that's too depressing. To be honest, they make him think of crows perched on the guardrails of a highway, looking greedily at roadkill, waiting for a gap between the trucks roaring past to go peck at it. The prison authorities never open his mail. That's why these photos get through to him. He keeps them on his shelf but, quite honestly, he never looks at them. Sometimes he tears them up. About ten years ago, at the turn of the new century, a woman wrote declaring her love for him and asking him to marry her. She enclosed a photograph with her letter, a poor-quality one but good enough to see that on her more or less average face—you couldn't really call her pretty—her ears, nose and tongue were pierced with rings of different sizes. He showed the photograph to someone who'd recently arrived, who told him that a lot of people had those kinds of piercings now. He hesitated for about half an hour before making up his mind to reply to the woman, who lived in Reno.

I don't know why you're so interested in me. I never had any intention of getting married, let alone now. From your photo, all I see is a vulgar woman, punched full of holes for no reason. I don't know what you imagine in your madness and sickness and I don't want to know. I'm not the man I was thirty years ago, and that man wouldn't have loved you any more than I do. This is the first and last time I'll be answering any of your letters, we aren't from the same world, get that into your thick skull once and for all.

He never heard from her again.

2

The day Lee Harvey Oswald stole the limelight from me, there was nothing in that part of the Sierra Nevada to indicate that it was November. The country around my grandparents' farm was bare, but the trees on the hill opposite didn't change color in the fall. The day had started like so many others. I'd masturbated twice in my bed before getting up. An old trick for starting the day feeling calm. I'd only just finished when my grandmother started yelling for me to get up. Then she'd come into my room without knocking. I just had time to put the blanket over me. In a voice that was trying to be friendly, she said without even looking at me, "It's a really nice day, you should be up and about." I didn't take it badly, not like that one time when I thought I could kill her because she'd burst into my room uninvited when I was two seconds away from coming. I'd never before felt such violence inside me. I got up in the end, but later. I can't remember if it was a weekday or a weekend. It wouldn't be hard to check, November 22, 1963 is a pretty memorable date. Three days before, I'd celebrated my birthday with her and my grandfather. She'd baked a cake that tasted like cold plastic. The old man had unwrapped his present with tearful eyes: a Winchester Henry .22 caliber rifle. "To hunt rabbits and moles," he'd said, putting his hand on my arm. His hand had seemed very old and very lined, even though he was only seventy-one. He was a good man but I didn't like him because he was like a little dog around my grandmother. She was always giving him orders like

you'd give to a farm boy, though in kind of a democratic tone
so as not to humiliate him. And the old man would obey.
Whenever he saw me looking at him with contempt, he'd
lower his eyes and give me a pitiful little smile that meant,
"What else can I do but obey the woman I used to love?" But
anything would have been better than that slavery. "It's .22 caliber, Al, you know the principle. High velocity, fast penetration, but too small for big animals, they'd only suffer terribly."
I was left with rabbits, moles and a few hares. My grandmother
had leaped to her feet and said with that air of superiority she
was so good at, "If I see you firing at birds, I'll take that
Winchester off you and burn it." You wish, old woman!
There's nothing dumber than shooting rabbits. There are lots
of them, they huddle against the hedges thinking they're hiding, and when they take off they're never really in a hurry.
Whereas bringing down birds, any birds, now that's a real
sport, except when they're perched on a branch, of course. I
was surprised by the gift. My grandmother had apparently
objected to it on the grounds that, considering my abilities, I
didn't work hard enough at school. What could I do with my
abilities? Intelligence tests had shown that I had an IQ higher
than Einstein's. And with all that potential, I never did better
than average. My grandmother thought that was a waste and
she hated waste. There was no way you could leave food on
your plate, leave the light on in an empty room, leave the faucet
dripping, use too much toilet paper when you wiped yourself,
or not have the highest grades in every subject at school. She
was hysterical at the thought of it. She was always having problems with her uterus. It was her favorite topic of conversation
apart from her children's books. I never read any of her books
because by the time I started living in her house I wasn't a
child anymore, and anyway I didn't have the slightest curiosity
about what she wrote or illustrated. I assume it must have been
incredibly dumb. Cysts appeared regularly on her uterus like

threats, and were immediately eliminated with a simple operation. She kept count of her operations the way other people count their medals. I never could stand the high opinion she had of herself because of those recurrent tumors, or that childish need to be recognized as a brave woman for facing a disease that wasn't at all dangerous.

I hadn't yet tried the Winchester. I'd put it down on the table at the foot of my bed, in the middle of my schoolbooks. It was a light weapon with a matte black barrel. It drew me to it, but I didn't dare touch it.

That morning, November 22, I went down to have breakfast. My grandmother was cleaning the sink. I could tell she wanted to take me to task for not getting out of bed when she first told me to but was holding back. We looked at each other for a moment or two. Then she asked me what I was planning to do with my free day. The school had organized a rafting trip and I'd gotten myself excused as usual. I was having a bad day, one of those mornings when my usual lack of desire combined with a feeling of suffocation. "Why don't you go hunting? The rabbits are eating all my vegetables." It was as good an idea as any other, even though I had no desire to please her. Then she added, "Five cents a mole, ten cents a rabbit," as if I were mercenary. The family pet, an old English setter, all skin and bones, was already wagging his tail at the idea, in spite of his rheumatism. I went back up to my room and methodically loaded my weapon, fifteen small bullets that you slipped into a chamber under the barrel. Then I cleaned my teeth and washed my armpits with cold water. I put on my father's military jacket, the only item of clothing I was attached to, the only one that made me look like more than just someone who was too tall, who made people wonder if the sky was his limit. At the age of fifteen, I was already three inches taller than my father and I wasn't exactly happy at the thought that I was quietly heading for seven feet. I couldn't get through a door without bending and wherever I went people turned to stare at me. Sitting in class, I was the same size as the teacher when he was standing, and the looks everyone gave me were the kind you give a strange animal. Sometimes I dreamed about being short, about being picked on by those who were bigger than me and attracting some kind girl who'd take pity on a mistreated boy. But nobody ever dared pick on me and the only reason the girls sometimes stared at me, stifling their giggles, was because they were wondering if the size of my dick was in proportion with the rest of me. I didn't make that up, I overheard a conversation like that one day in the corridor during recess. I never received any kindness from my classmates. They all regarded me as someone apart, tall and mysterious, and the big glasses I wore because I was short-sighted didn't make contact any easier because you could barely make out my eyes through the thick lenses. Everything came easy to me at school and when I saw those dumb jocks sweating blood over a simple equation, I felt nothing but contempt for my classmates. Most of them talked only about rafting, lived only for rafting. What interest could there possibly be in shooting the rapids at breakneck speed and risking drowning? I never understood that. The principal, Mr. Abbott, always looked at me in the same disappointed way as my grandmother. He couldn't understand why I was wasting my talent. He even called me up to his office on the second floor to tell me that. His office was like an explorer's cave. It was said that Abbott sometimes slept there rather than go home to his wife. It had gotten to the point where she was convinced he had a girlfriend. Abbott, a girlfriend, can you imagine that? But that was none of my business. It was hard for someone my size to find a place to sit in that little room of his.

"You know, Kenner, that you have a way above average intellect, so what's wrong?"

It was a really embarrassing question, which in my opinion didn't call for an answer.

"I don't know."

"Do you realize what you could become if you really applied yourself? What are your plans for the future?"

"The future?"

I smiled, for the first time in a long time, and pushed my big square glasses further up my nose, which was something I always did before I spoke—still do—then said, "I've never thought about the future, Mr. Abbott. There's something in me that tells me I don't have one."

"But you must have ambitions, Kenner? Don't you?"

"Ambitions?"

I had to force myself to answer. Not so much because of the question. It was rather that, seeing that runt with his faded bow tie, who sometimes slept in this shack to get away from his wife, seeing him there in front of me I didn't think he had the right to talk to me about my problems, let alone try to solve them.

"You aren't the person to talk about what I should or shouldn't do, Mr. Abbott."

He adjusted his bow tie. "And why's that, Kenner?"

I looked at him intensely without saying anything, without moving. He started shifting from one leg to the other, and I saw his face fall. I was sitting there between him and the door, barring his way, motionless and silent. When I saw him start sweating, I decided it had lasted long enough, and I got up and went out. He never again tried talking to me about my future. I think he must have given instructions to the other teachers, because none of them ever tried talking to me about it either.

Who can you talk to about the boredom that overwhelms you from morning to night, that saps your will insidiously to the point where any action you want to take is stillborn? I never made a single friend during the two years I spent in North Fork. I never wanted to talk to anybody, and that must have been so obvious that they all carefully avoided me. I knew

I was occasionally the target of malicious gossip but I didn't care. I didn't care what other people thought of me, I didn't care about their playacting or their humdrum little lives in this town that claimed to be the best place in California. The Vietnam War was just starting and I'd gladly have enlisted in honor of my father, who was a distinguished veteran of World War II. But I had a visceral fear of physical violence. Every time a fight started at school, I thanked the Lord that my size kept me out of it. Faced with the smallest little punk who'd made up his mind to beat me up, I'd have chickened out.

My fantasies about girls were my only link with that community. A space where I could be free, a no-go area. I did what I wanted with them in my dreams and nobody could say a word about it. Fantasies rule the world. Most people who make love aren't really thinking about the person they're having sex with, I'm convinced of that. I took my ability to fantasize as a sign of superiority, because in my dreams I could lay any woman I wanted, teachers, pupils, the pretty ones, the ugly ones I found a way to cast a spell on, and, without their knowing it, I gave them the kind of thrill that no creature of flesh and blood could ever offer them. I saw in all these girls' eyes the embarrassment they felt because I'd had them for such a long time. My fantasies were enough for me. It never occurred to me to want to sleep with a girl for real, not only because I knew it'd be difficult for me to find one who'd agree to it, but because it was a matter of control. In my fantasies I controlled everything, but what might have happened in real life? Anything might have gone wrong.

With Ava Pinzer it was different. There was a connection between us from the start. She was also very tall. Not as tall as me but too tall for a girl, over six feet, which made her unusual. It took us a whole three months before we spoke. When we passed in the corridors of the school, from my height all I saw was her, and all she saw was me. I'd never have taken the first step. Neither would she. We sometimes smiled at each other in a kind of conspiratorial way. The reason I finally made up my mind to speak to her was that she already had her driving license and her parents had brought her an old midnight blue Dodge to get home, because they lived quite far from North Fork and the school bus didn't go all the way there. She still had to walk four miles after the last stop, half of the way on asphalt, the other half on a dirt road that led to what had once been a little gold prospectors' town where only one house in five was left now from its glory days. All that came out the first time we talked. On the way out of school, we'd found ourselves pinned up against each other in the crush and she'd started a conversation. She wasn't pretty and she wasn't ugly, which suited me fine. She had quite a big nose and big feet but overall she was quite feminine. I hate masculine women. I'm even more uncomfortable when I see a mannish woman than when I come across an effeminate guy. A masculine woman makes me panic. Ava—her parents had called her that because of Ava Gardner—had a German name, like me. That should have brought us closer together but we didn't give a damn. I didn't know much about my family background and she didn't know much about hers either. That would have meant her finding out why her parents had ended up in a backwater like that and she didn't really want to. On my side, I remembered that before my father had joined Special Forces during the war, the military police had thoroughly investigated his origins. That didn't necessarily make his name more acceptable, especially as, in the Sixties, nobody was particularly interested in Germany. Since nobody dared to make fun of me anyway, I hadn't suffered because of my name. Her parents liked me right from the start, they thought I seemed a safe choice for their daughter. Plus, next to me, she looked quite small, which made her more feminine. They were good people, both of them. Her father had just retired from the Forest Service and her mother had a long, calm face. They cultivated a strip of earth around the house, which allowed them to be more or less self-sufficient when it came to food. They asked me to stay for dinner several times but I didn't want to. I knew they belonged to some kind of church, so saying grace might go on forever and at the time I wasn't crazy about that kind of stuff. I wasn't an atheist, far from it, but I couldn't stand anyone talking to me about God, I found it obscene. Ava was like me. She lived without any real aim. She had no particular motivation. She hated sports, but she didn't mind taking long walks around the area where she lived, up on those dry hills covered in low grass and fir trees, where you sometimes caught sight of a bear or a stag. We didn't talk much and I liked her for that. She was levelheaded, unlike all those vain girls who attended the school and bored the boys to death with their dreams of beauty contests. She often drove me home and, unlike her parents, who were so considerate to me, my grandmother would give her a contemptuous nod of the head. My grandmother wasn't good at talking to men and was silent with other women unless it was in her own self-interest to make conversation. Even when we were together, Ava and I could be as solitary as ever, because there was nothing at stake.

I broke up with her on a day like any other, just a week before the famous November 22. We'd set off on a long, silent walk and I wasn't feeling well. There was a weird kind of buzzing in my head that was stopping me from enjoying the peace of the country. It started raining, a sudden heavy downpour that beat down on the ground, which was all dusty from the long dry autumn. We took refuge in a wooden cabin that must have been used as a shelter by gold prospectors in the previous century. The door was open, and banging in the wind. The interior was clean in spite of being neglected. There was a wall seat up against one of the little windows, forming a corner with a wooden table. We sat down to wait for the rain to stop.

After sitting side by side for a moment, she put her hand on my thigh. I didn't know how to react. Seeing that I wasn't moving, she brought her hand closer to my crotch and at the same time offered me her lips, just to do things in the right order. I couldn't kiss her, it was impossible. I sat there paralyzed while she stroked me. Nothing happened. Absolutely nothing. She suggested we undress but I found the idea ridiculous. I let her open my flies and take my dick out. She took it in her hand like it was a robin that was just knocked itself out by flying into a window. The bird didn't come back to life. It was as if the connection between my mind and my body had suddenly snapped. She looked at it for a long time without saying anything. I could have wept, but I had too much dignity for that. I moved her hand away, gently but firmly, buttoned up my pants again and left without turning around. We went back down the mountain, one behind the other, without saying anything. Outside her parents' house, I waved her goodbye and set off alone on foot. I felt like knocking my head against the trees lining the road. I had realized that everything that was real was forbidden to me and I hadn't the faintest idea why. For the few days remaining until November 22, I carefully avoided her at school.

3

After loading the Winchester I put on my boots, although I still didn't know if I wanted to go out. The old dog started turning around and around outside my door, I could hear his claws on the floor, and I knew the old woman would soon appear and yell at me for letting the dog back in the house, as if that was my fault. I went downstairs, followed by the mutt, who almost went sprawling twice, the stairs were so polished. I never understood how a woman who claimed to be an artist, writing and illustrating books for children, could be so fussy. For me, only people whose heads are in a mess are obsessed with keeping everything spick and span. Real artists don't care if things look tidy or not. I went out without saying a word, with the dog waddling along close behind me.

There wasn't a breath of air and my footsteps echoed on the ground. I went past my grandmother's vegetable patch. She'd given it a good watering and the earth was black. There were three rabbits. I saw them before the dog scented them—his sense of smell was pretty much shot. I aimed at them, twice, without firing. It wasn't that I felt sorry for them, but I couldn't care less about making my grandmother happy. Some kind of bullfinch landed on the roof of the toolshed. I aimed and fired and didn't see anything anymore. I don't know if I got him. The black earth brought back all the anger I'd been feeling ever since I'd ended up in this place four months earlier. I thought about my father and I had tears in my eyes. I remembered the only moment of deep joy in my life, when I'd traveled from my mother's house in Helena, Montana, to see my father, who was living in Los Angeles. I'd hitchhiked all the way, thinking I was going to the promised land. I'd spent hours in cars, with good guys mostly. I'd had to listen to their stories in return for the ride and I'd pretended to take an interest. I'd sometimes waited for hours in a deserted place for someone to give me a ride. And then I remembered one of the worst moments of my life, I won't say the worst, because there were lots of them.

My father had come into my room, in his faded little wooden house surrounded by a tiny, bare garden below a road leading to the busiest highway in L.A., a highway that goes everywhere and nowhere. From my room you could hear the roar, a deafening noise I'd somehow gotten used to, even though I'd come from a state where the slightest sound seems like an insult to the Lord. The summer was starting to wear people down. The mixture of heat and pollution might have seemed stifling to some old guy with asthma, but it suited me just fine. I hadn't yet raised the blinds, but a bright light was already filtering in under the edge. I wasn't too sure what I was going to do with my day. I'd gotten up feeling like shit because I'd hit the booze the night before, and I went in the kitchen to look for something to settle my stomach. I dug into a big bowl of cornflakes. I searched desperately for coffee, but there wasn't any, and I couldn't be bothered to make some. I went back to my room. The house seemed empty. Usually, when they went out, my father would look into my room and tell me where he and his new wife were going and when they'd be back. I didn't give a damn where they went or what time they came back, but it had become a convention between us. And now there was nobody in, and that got me shook up. I thought I'd been abandoned like a poor mutt the family's gotten tired of having around. The previous night's bender must have increased that fear. So I rushed into my father's room. I didn't even think to knock. I threw the door open and there was my father's wife, standing stark naked in front of the wardrobe mirror. She had her back to me, and her curly platinum blond hair was tumbling over her thin shoulders. She had one hell of a nice back, only slightly spoiled by the cellulite that made her hips a little bumpy. Nostalgia isn't exactly my thing, but when I think about it now, I tell myself it was the first and last time in my life that I saw a naked woman alive. I could see her face in the mirror, although I was more focused on her breasts. Her eyes were popping out of their sockets and I closed the door again before she could say anything. I must have been eyeing her up for a while, otherwise my father wouldn't have made such a fuss when he got back. But there wasn't only that incident, he told me I was upsetting her with my heavy silences, that she never felt safe when I was alone in the house with her, as if there was a threat hanging over her.

"What threat?" I asked.

"I don't know, a threat. You can't stay here, don't you understand?"

What I understood was something completely different, something we didn't want to talk about because I wouldn't have been able to and I didn't want to hurt him. As far as he was concerned, the only witness to what my mother had made him endure was living under his roof, and he was afraid I'd tell his new wife and she'd lose confidence in him, start thinking he wasn't a real man. But I'd never have played a dirty trick like that.

"I feel fine here."

"You don't show it, Al. No, really, we can't let you stay."

I knew he wouldn't change his mind and I didn't want to get in an argument with him, that wasn't the way things worked between us. Of course, according to him, nothing was settled but I could see that this month with him was going to be the last.

I heard him call my mother on the phone while his new wife was out at the hairdresser's. He was pale and twitchy. What I gathered was that my mother didn't want to take me back and that was fine by me, I'd have run away and taken my chances on the road rather than go back to Montana. They agreed to send me to stay with my grandparents—my father's parents—in the Sierra Nevada. Now I come to think of it, every time they agreed on something, the result was a disaster.

I put my Winchester down next to me in the living room, sat down, took off my boots, and put my head in my hands. I wasn't shaking and yet I had the feeling I was. I felt strange. I'd done something stupid, the kind of thing you do when you're a teenager. It's an age when you like to see how far you can go. I say that now, I didn't think it at the time, because I wasn't thinking about anything. It was cold now, because my grandmother was mean with the heating. I thought to go raise it a notch, but then I'd have to go back past a place where I never wanted to set foot again. If I left the house, it was the same problem. So I switched on the TV. Waiting for it to warm up, I went and raided the kitchen. I emptied the cupboards of everything I thought I could eat easily. I took a six-pack of beer too, I deserved it. My footsteps echoed strangely, I'd never noticed that before. I took the cap off a bottle with my teeth because I'd seen people do that in movies, and I lay down full length on the couch, hanging over at both ends. I didn't stay long like that. I stood to turn up the volume on the TV. Someone had shot the President. What I found amazing about the news was that a guy had actually done something like that. The news they were giving out mentioned a lone gunman. I couldn't get over it. An ordinary guy had had the strength to decide in his own head, all alone in his corner, "I'm going to shoot the President of the United States." I guessed thousands of men had had that idea before him, but he had done it and, incredibly, he had succeeded. I didn't yet know how far he'd succeeded, at that point they were saying only that the President was seriously wounded. I was green with admiration and envy. Envy because this guy was going to steal the limelight from me. It was supposed to be my day of fame but, even in the local rags, that was all they were going to be talking about. How could something like that have happened to me? I continued listening to the various reporters and commentators getting really worked up, and knocked back beer after beer. By the sixth, I'd kind of changed my mind. I thought it was a good thing that Kennedy had been killed that day, I might pass unnoticed, or they wouldn't be so mad at me, or whatever. To be quite honest, I was starting to chicken out slightly.

After giving up on the idea of shooting rabbits, I'd left the farm and headed for open country. I could hear my grandmother hollering because I'd walked out past her garden. Her voice worked on me like an electric shock. I followed part of a neighbor's fence, a fence he used to keep in a fine roan quarter horse that fascinated me with its slim head and muscular rump. I aimed at it with my Winchester, just for the pleasure of aiming at such a big animal. I climbed the hill and started to feel out of breath. My grandmother was still yelling, enjoying hearing the echo of her own voice. I only weighed about 250 pounds at the time, but it was still a weight I had to drag. The dog was following me with his tongue out. I finally reached a point where there were no more houses, no signs of life at all. I sat down against a tall pine that leaned toward the west. There, the old woman's voice caught up with me. The dog lay down a bit further on. He never lay down next to me. He was looking at me with his glassy eyes. I should have felt calm but even in those wide open spaces I felt enclosed, and just thinking about it started up a storm inside my head that was worse than all the hurricanes in Alabama. I stayed like that for a good half-hour, long enough for my anger to subside, throwing pieces of wood at the dog, who didn't get up to fetch them. I went back down by another path, longer but less steep. I've never been very steady on my feet, I guess because of my rapid growth, and I'm always scared of twisting my ankle. I didn't get back onto level ground until I was near my grandparents' house. Seeing it from a distance, I told myself that a lot of people would have liked to live there, not far from a nice quiet lake, just a few miles from Yosemite National Park, where I've never set foot. When I got to within a hundred yards of the house, I saw my grandmother. She was outside the window of her room, with her back to me to avoid having the sun in her face. She was bent over an easel, painting. Painting what? I assumed an illustration for a children's book. She sometimes also painted nature scenes just for herself. I never understood why. I told her that once and she took it badly. I advanced toward her, my head pretty much empty. I felt the stirrings of annoyance at seeing her again but no more than that. There were only about twenty yards between us now. She must have heard the sound of my boots on the dry earth. She didn't turn. Inside me I was saying, "Turn around, come on, turn around." Why did I want her to turn around? I didn't know. The only thing that crossed my mind at that moment was: "I'd really like to know what it feels like to kill your grandmother." That's the kind of ridiculous idea that teenagers have, except that usually they don't go through with it. I got to within about ten yards of her, cocking the Winchester as I slowed down. She still hadn't turned around, even though she must have recognized my footsteps, because they were so heavy and so determined they couldn't be confused with anybody else's. I took aim and shot her in the back of the neck. She collapsed onto her easel, taking it down with her as she fell. I approached her. She was lying on her stomach and in that position she looked a bit grotesque. She was almost certainly dead, but I didn't hate her so much that I wanted her to suffer, so I fired two bullets in her back, in the area of the heart. There couldn't be any argument about it now. I left her there, while the dog looked on in dismay. Then I went inside the house. There was no chance now that she'd yell, "Al, take off your boots and put on your slippers."

Once it had been established that Kennedy was well and truly dead, I didn't know what to think anymore. Not only had the guy who'd killed him been incredibly successful, but he'd cast a giant shadow over what I'd done. My feeling of being famous had faded away during the afternoon and now I was confused. I thought about taking to the road. But I knew that wouldn't get me far. A guy like me, more than six feet tall, calls attention to himself. I could take my grandfather's car and take off but it was the kind of station wagon that guzzled gas and I didn't have any money. I searched the whole house. It amused me to put myself in my grandparents' place and imagine where they might have stashed their savings. The old man didn't trust banks enough to leave all his money in them. What with the farm and his work for the Department of Public Roads, he must surely have put aside a tidy sum. I started by going and taking a look at his wallet. It was inside his jacket pocket. I didn't feel good about doing that. When my grandfather came back from his shopping, I'd find myself in one hell of a dilemma. Either I let him find my grandmother's body with all the pain and resentment that would cause him, or I executed him too. I know that after a month or two he would have seen my grandmother's death as a liberation, but like any good slave he was also in love with his chains.

As the car was coming up in back of the house, I came to the conclusion that I was going to cause him a terrible amount of pain and I couldn't bear that. I saw him moving along the little track with that smug air that he had. He gave me a little wave to tell me he was pleased to see me, then slowed down some more to enter the garage. Once parked, he got slowly out of the car, stretched, then walked to the trunk and opened it by lowering the tailgate. He was tempted to turn to ask me for help but I didn't give him time. I shot him twice in the back. Those words of his came back into my mind: "Be careful, Al, with that kind of caliber, don't shoot at big animals, it wouldn't kill them, it'd only make them suffer, unless you get them in the head." I rushed to him. He'd fallen to his knees, his head on the tailgate of the car. I shot him twice in the head. He was dead. I walked back outside to calm down. Killing my grandmother had taken the edge off my anger, but killing the old man made things worse again. Just then, the dog arrived to distract me from my dark thoughts. What was going to become of that poor old mutt now? He went and vaguely sniffed my grandfather's body, then gave me a cautious look and dropped onto the concrete floor of the garage. I wondered again what I was going to do with him. "Shit, Bobby," I said, "I can't solve every problem in the world." I was expecting at least a gleam of gratitude in his eyes. Nothing. I went back outside.

My grandfather was already starting to get stiff when I decided to go through his pockets. The banknotes I found in his wallet would keep me going for three or four days on the run, and the food that was still in the trunk of the station wagon would have been enough for three people for a week. Most of it wasn't fresh food, which was a stroke of luck. But I didn't feel up to wiping the blood off the car if there was any. Not that it disgusted me but it was kind of like a superstition. I pulled at my grandfather's body to get him away from the car. I had never held him in my arms like that before, and embracing that cold body made me uncomfortable. I moved him over to a red and green plaid blanket he used to lie down on when he inspected the underside of his car, and laid him down gently. I resumed my search of the house. It didn't take me long to realize that the ideal place to hide the stash was the shack in the yard that had been used as a john until my grandparents invested in a new indoor toilet. The dough was in an iron box stuck inside the S-bend. Nice little wads of bills all set aside for a rainy day. But then the thought that I was going to steal them and that people might think I was the kind of deadbeat who'd kill his own grandparents for their money made me really uncomfortable. In the end, that thought was stronger than anything else. So I went back in the house and got the phone book and looked up the number of the county police. I hesitated for a moment then dialed the number. A woman answered. I asked to speak with the sheriff.

"What about?"

"It's personal."

"I don't think the sheriff has time for that right now, son, you know the President's been assassinated?"

I said, "Why, do you think the assassin would be likely to hide in a dump like this?"

"How can you say that? Aren't you proud of where you live? Carry on talking like that, son, and let's see where you end up!"

I don't know who she was or what exactly she was doing in the sheriff's office but I'd really riled her by criticizing the area.

"What do you want?"

"Could you ask the sheriff to call me back?"

"Who is this?"

"Al Kenner."

"How do you spell that?"

"K, E, double N, E, R."

"Where from?"

"Wolf Creek Farm, seven miles north of North Fork."

"Does he know you?"

"He'll remember me."

I was sure he did. My grandfather had a .45 in his night table and I knew. My grandmother knew that I knew. Whenever she left to go shopping, she would put the .45 in her pocketbook so I wouldn't be tempted to try it. So one day, I'd rung the sheriff and said, "I'm calling to let you know that a sixty-five-year-old woman driving a 1959 Ford station wagon is hiding a .45 in her pocketbook and she's planning to hold up the Chase Manhattan bank just outside town on the way to North Fork. If you don't do anything, don't say I didn't warn you. I know what I'm talking about, I'm her grandson."

The old lady had found herself surrounded by half a dozen police cars as she drove into the bank's parking lot. They'd pinned her up against the door of her car, with her hands up. She'd had a lot of explaining to do at the station house. They let her go in the end without revealing their sources—the cops like to make you think they don't need informers. She'd suspected it was me, but I denied it, saying, "You think I have time to waste on dumb stuff like that?"

"What do you want?"
"I want to tell him I killed my grandparents."
"I'll tell him."
She hung up. She must have thought it was a joke. It isn't easy to convince someone that you've just committed a murder on the day the President of the United States is assassinated. I put myself in the woman's place. Even if the President had been killed by a lone gunman, there was nothing to say the gunman wasn't working for the Communists. Maybe she reckoned we were close to a nuclear war and was more worried about her ass right then than about a couple of old folks who were going to die sooner or later anyway.

In any case, I'd thrown my bottle into the sea, and I was feeling better.

8

I was going to hit the road and take advantage of the wide open spaces without feeling suffocated this time. I got my things ready. I pulled my grandmother inside the house by the feet, without looking at her. She was as stiff as a tree trunk. I loaded my things in the car, plus a little bag where I put all my shirts. I took with me all the beers that were left and two bottles of whiskey in case the nights were cold. I also found a camp stove and some saucepans so I wouldn't have to use fast food joints, a few blankets and an old military sleeping bag left there by my father. I also took all the rolls of toilet paper in the house, a toothbrush and some soap. I was good and ready. Once I'd gotten the car out of the garage, I closed all the doors but left the shutters open. Then I set off. I hadn't gone a hundred yards before I turned back. My Winchester was still inside the house and that wasn't a good idea. The second time, after half a mile, I smelled kind of a familiar smell in the car. It was the dog. He'd taken advantage of the door being open to get in. My first thought was to take him back to the farm, then I told myself I'd abandon him somewhere when I had the chance. A south wind raised the sand from the track that led to the road. I started the windshield wipers. The country was trying to trap me. When I got to the crossroads, I headed due north, with a single idea in mind: to cross the state line as soon as possible and take advantage of all the confusion over the Kennedy assassination to slip quietly away. The north led to Canada. Of course, from the Sierra Nevada, Mexico was closer.

But I couldn't speak Spanish and I wasn't attracted to the country. From what I knew of it through westerns, the men looked cruel and degenerate, and as for the women, they didn't say much, they were there either to be raped or to cook for those drunken brutes. The advantage of Canada was that they spoke English. I'd spent the first fifteen years of my life in a border state, Montana, and I wouldn't feel out of place, even though I've never liked Montana. In theory, I'd have run less risk of being picked up if I went east. But I'd have to get over the mountains first and in that season there was a good chance I'd be turned into a snowman. If I did make it over the mountains, I'd find myself in the state of Nevada, which isn't famous for its hospitable climate, and I didn't want to end up stuck in the desert, out of gas and dying of thirst. So I was going to head northwest and get close to the sea to avoid the worst of the winter. I already had a plan in my mind, which was to sell the old man's station wagon as soon as I could, keep part of the money to see me through the trip and buy a big motorbike with what was left. I had a feeling the journey was going to go well. I didn't feel like a fugitive, more like a guy who's taking a last vacation before starting a job that isn't likely to be a whole lot of fun. I never for a moment imagined I was going to get away with it. I just wanted to breathe fresh air before I had to face whatever was in store for me: a life sentence, maybe even the electric chair. They fried a whole bunch of people in those days, it was worse than mosquitoes hitting a halogen lamp on a summer evening when you're engrossed in a mystery story. In general, they didn't kill anybody underage, except with the time a trial and everything else takes, by the time they decided on the final sentence I wouldn't be a teenager anymore. I say that now, but I don't remember thinking about it so clearly then. I've only ever been afraid of two things: physical confrontation, which was pretty rare given my size, and myself, and that second fear poisoned my whole fucking life. But what

I did, I probably had my reasons for doing. Being afraid of the consequences of my actions was pointless.

On the radio, all the news was about the assassination of the President. They'd tracked down my hero. Superman had actually gone to ground in a movie theater after shooting Kennedy. The self-confidence of the guy! He's just shot the President and he goes and calmly plants himself in a red plush seat, lights a cigarette and watches Humphrey Bogart threatening to beat up a guy twice as brawny as he is and you know the guy won't bat an eyelid because it's Humphrey Bogart he's dealing with. When he comes out of the theater, a cop comes up and tries to arrest him, and, without a moment's hesitation, he opens fire on the guy like in a comic strip where the dead never really look dead. They cornered him in the end. He was a guy who had worked for the Reds, there was no doubt about that, but they seemed to think the Kennedy assassination was his own idea.

Anyway, I drove until two in the morning and stopped near Mount Shasta, on the shore of a lake. I didn't see any roadblocks or any isolated police cars. If they really had thought my phone call was a joke, then the weekend would pass peacefully and nobody would notice a thing. My grandmother had driven everyone away with her mean temper and nobody ever paid them a visit. She had ordered the old man to put the mailbox at the end of the track so that the postman couldn't stick his nose in their business. Unless there was certified mail or a special package, he had no reason to come up to the farm. Anyway, I'd shut the gate, a sign that people weren't welcome. I lowered the backseat and settled down to sleep, but even so I was forced to lie curled up and the floor of the station wagon was damned hard. I threw the dog out because I didn't want his smell in my nose or to wake up feeling nauseous. I fell asleep from exhaustion. Images of the two dead bodies kept flashing through my mind. I was angry with myself for leaving them on the ground like that, there's no nakedness more absolute than death. I could imagine the scene a few days later when they were found. By the time dawn came up over the lake, I was soaked and I told myself that I'd do better from now on to sleep in motels until I got to the border, I could afford it. I took two doughnuts from my provisions and started off for town, leaving the dog behind me. He was taking a piss when I drove away. In this part of California, I thought, he'd easily find a family to take him in. I waited for a while for the bar I had my eyes on to open. A guy like me, first customer of the morning, people remember something like that, but what the hell, I hadn't chosen to live as a fugitive. I ordered two big coffees. Seeing the size of me, the waitress wasn't surprised. She was in the mood to talk. An event like the Kennedy assassination does that to people.

"When I look at Mount Shasta early in the morning with the sun coming up, it doesn't feel like anything could really happen to us."

Mount Shasta stood out against a clear yellow sky. It was one hell of a size.

"You staying around here a while?"

"No, I'm going to Los Angeles to see my father. In fact, I need to call him, do you have a phone?"

She pointed to a booth at the far end of the room, between the toilets and the cigarette machine. Passing the machine, I bought a pack of unfiltered Lucky Strikes. My father was out, it was his wife who answered.

"Can I tell him to call you back?"

"No."

"Aren't you at your grandparents' farm?"

"No."

"What's going on, Al, is there anything we need to worry about?"

"You personally, no."

"So what shall we do?"

"I'll call back in half an hour."

I hung up and went and finished my second large coffee, which had cooled down quite a bit even though the waitress had served it to me boiling hot. If there are two things capable of getting me riled, it's lukewarm coffee and boiling hot coffee.

"This fucking coffee's cold!"

She hadn't expected me to react like that, I could see it in her eyes. She started to get scared. "Stupid bitch!" I thought. "If you think stripping you naked and having you behind your counter would be enough for me, you're kidding yourself."

My eyes must have said the same thing because I thought she was going to turn to jelly. Then I smiled and she regained her composure.

"Where can I find a car lot around here?"

She told me there was a guy who had a lot on the edge of town and I was relieved to know I'd soon be able to get out of there. The half hour seemed long. I was starting to regret calling my father. I couldn't back down, his new wife would let him know anyway, he'd call the farm and, when nobody answered, he'd alert the whole county and that wasn't what I wanted. It had to be done differently.

After another coffee the girl had quickly made me, one that wasn't either lukewarm or boiling hot, I went and called again.

"Dad, I have good news and bad news. The good news is that I killed grandma. The bad news is that I also killed grandpa. I swear it was only to spare him the pain of seeing grandma dead."

There was a long pause, more than a minute, then my father recovered enough to say, "Goddammit, Al, what have you done? I can't believe it, I can't believe it . . ."

He kept repeating that without being able to stop.

Then he stopped. After another silence—all I could hear was his breathing—he started up again.

"You're completely crazy, Al, completely crazy. Goddammit, look what you've done to our lives!" Then he gave kind of a hiccup and said, "Tell me it isn't true, tell me you didn't do it. Why, why, Goddammit, why?"

"Why? I'll tell you why, dad. Because I had to. Because you should have done it. I did it for you. I'm sorry for the old man, I never planned that. Nothing was planned, but it had to be done."

In the silence that followed, he recovered a little. After all he was a man who'd fought with Special Forces.

"Where did you put the bodies?"

"I left them where they were."

"And where are you?"

"I'm on the road."

"Where?"

"On the road."

"Have you told anybody?"

For a brief moment I thought maybe my father and I could work something out together. We clean up the scene of the crime, we say the old couple left for a trip to Alaska in a motorhome they bought for cash, we dump the bodies in the middle of a forest, they're found three-quarters eaten by grizzly bears, and everyone says, "Too bad."

"I hope you called the police."

"They had other things on their minds with the Kennedy assassination."

"I'd have preferred it if you'd killed that son of a bitch instead of my parents but Goddammit, Al, how could you have done a thing like that? You killed my parents and they're going to kill you. You've killed everything that came before me and after me."

"My sisters are still around."

I thought that would console him.

"Your sisters are like your mother."

But that wasn't the problem.

"Do you plan to turn yourself in?"

"Yes, but not right away. I'd like to go for a long ride, get a bit of air in my lungs, because I might not get another chance. If you can just hold off for a while . . ."

"But I have to tell the police, Al, and they're going to come after you. I hope you're not planning to resist arrest?"

"No, Dad, you know me well enough, you know I'm not violent. I'm going to give myself up, but I'm not ready yet. Tell them it's a matter of days, a few days. It's the first time I've had a chance to breathe out here in the wild, don't you see? If I wasn't planning to give myself up, I'd never have called you. In fact, what concerns me is making sure grandma and grandpa are buried. I didn't have the guts. Don't leave them like that out in the open. The old man doesn't deserve it. I feel a hell of a lot better for telling you. For doing it and for telling you. You can't imagine what a weight that is off my back."

"You're completely crazy, Al, your mother warned me. I'm calling the police and then I'm getting in my car and driving out to the farm. I don't know where you are, but turn around and come back."

"I will come back. Only not right away. I need to get some air in my lungs before the gas chamber."

"There's no gas chamber if you're underage. Do you still have the weapon?"

"Yes, it's the Winchester the old man gave me."

"You're not going to kill anybody else, are you, Al?"

"Anybody else? What for? I have to go now, Dad, sorry again to disturb you. I won't be long."

I hung up. With the emotion and everything, we could have talked for hours. On the other hand, it was a hard thing for him to come to terms with. It's the kind of thing that takes a while for you to get it into your head. And there was no point arguing about it. During my call, some locals had come in for their morning coffee. They gave me weird looks, but no worse than the way people usually look at a stranger, especially when that stranger's a whole lot taller than they are. The conversation immediately turned to the Kennedy assassination. There were those who were all cut up about it and others who said openly that the son of a bitch deserved it. Conversations about subjects that don't concern folks personally never last very long, everyone puts in their two cents without much interest and the others don't really listen and then they all go back to talking about their local concerns. These guys were getting ready to hunt deer the next morning and Kennedy had been a deer like any other. I sensed they wanted to include me in their conversation, so we talked about rifles. They asked me where I was from, because people don't usually get into a deep conversation before they know who they're dealing with. I said I was studying Indian civilizations in Vancouver and that I was on my way down to a conference in Berkeley and I'd come by way of Mount Shasta because my father used to come down here in the summer and camp on the shores of Lake Siskiyou. My thick glasses made that seem pretty credible. Anyway they couldn't argue with it. The waitress was looking at me furtively as she cleaned her counter and I could see she was a bit cagy toward me since my fit of anger. The conversation fizzled out like an old campfire—people doesn't have so much to say to each other. The reason they fizzle out is because the alcoholics have taken over. I left the bar and went back to my car.

9

I followed the girl's directions. Yes, there was a car lot three or four miles along the highway. I'd expected something fancier, this was more like a scrap yard. A big yellow dog with a black collar was standing in the way, barking fit to tear its vocal cords. As soon as it saw me unfolding myself from the car, it changed its mind and sloped off, looking annoyed. The owner of the lot looked more like a farmer on the label of a can of insecticide.

"I have a station wagon to sell, I'd like to exchange it for a motorcycle."

A deal like that meant he'd end up having to pay out money and he didn't seem happy about the idea.

We walked to the car. He walked around it, glanced inside, then wiped his hands on a cloth he took out of his pocket. He went and sat inside, moved the seat forward about three feet, gave me a knowing little smile, and set off for a little ride around the yard. That seemed to convince him.

"No problem about the car. If you want a bike, I can let you have an Indian Chief. It's the only bike suitable for someone your size, unless you want to ride with your knees dragging on the ground."

He was pleased with his joke and started laughing very loud. The Indian was on the other side of the garage. A wonderful bike, the kind I'd always dreamed of riding. A thousand-pound monster that made a big Harley-Davidson look like an exercise bicycle. It was red and white, with gleaming paint and chrome, wrap-around fenders, tires with white stripes, and a light brown leather saddle with fringes. I'd have had to work for years to afford a bike like that. While I was going into ecstasies over it, the guy looked through the papers for the car. Then he came back to the bike.

"A 53 model, one of the last bikes they made, in fact the serial number is five figures. 1,300cc twin engine, hydraulic forks. You could go around the world on that, son. I'll let you have it for the price of the station wagon."

I had no desire to argue. I know what happens when an argument doesn't work out the way I'd like it to. Once past the point of no return, my anger has to come out, directed either against myself or against the other person. Most often it's against myself and then I need days to get over it. I didn't want to spoil a moment like this. I left him a fair amount of my grandfather's provisions as an extra, the Indian's saddlebags couldn't take everything. When I got on the bike, the guy looked at the two of us in astonishment.

"How much do you weigh, son?"

"Around two hundred and sixty pounds."

"Look at that, the bike hardly moved when you sat down on it. Be careful on narrow roads, you can easily get trapped in the ruts." He checked that the fringed leather saddlebags had been properly greased. "Never let them get dry, them or the saddle. Grease them with neatsfoot oil every week, especially if you keep it outdoors."

Just when I thought we'd said everything, he added, as if changing the subject, "About the station wagon, I think I'm going to wait a while before I put it on the market. Something tells me that might be best." When I didn't reply, he went on, "After this Kennedy assassination, there might well be another depression, like the one that made my parents leave Arkansas in '31. And when things go bad, it's always cars that take the brunt of it. Now look, make sure you don't mix up the gas switch and the oil switch on the right half-tank. That's the worst thing that could happen, you'd mix up two gears and then . . . Anyway, have a good trip."

He hadn't finished what he was saying when he was already going back into the garage and getting back to work.

I was about to leave when I suddenly thought of something. The Winchester was still under the back seat.

"I forgot something!"

When I took the gun out of the car, he didn't say anything at first, then gave me a sly look and said, "During the war, military motorcycles were fitted with a holster where you could put an assault rifle. Unfortunately, I don't have one and anyhow, if you rode with that, you'd have cops on your tail like mutts after a bitch on heat. I advise you to cut it. If you ever need to use it, you won't be able to shoot far anyway, it isn't a hunting gun. We'll saw off the barrel, it'll fit nicely in a saddlebag and nobody'll know."

Grabbing the Winchester, he strode to his work bench, where he had a vise. He fitted the rifle into it and carefully cut off the barrel with a saw.

When he'd finished, he handed me the rifle. "If the cops stop you with that, tell them you think you're Josh Randall in *Wanted: Dead or Alive*, he has the same kind of gun."

I'd seen the show and the only thing Steve McQueen and I had in common was the gun. Maybe the bike too, but I wasn't sure. Later, coming across a photo of him before he died, I saw that he rode the same bike as me.

10

As I rode toward Oregon, a state where more people are killed by pumas than are murdered, I told myself I'd have liked to be in the police force, because when you came down to it I had nothing against law and order. But I suspected that after what I'd done, they wouldn't welcome me with open arms.

I passed a few cops zooming by on their Harleys. They looked as if they might be looking for a gray station wagon even if they weren't. I rode all day on side roads. My size, and my unusually low center of gravity, made me leave that endless straight line running across country, used by truckers, and keep to the winding road that leads to Crater Lake. The higher I got, the colder I felt, in spite of the things I bought as I went: a wonderful horsehide jacket, sheepskin-lined gloves, trapper's boots. The V-shaped twin-engine hummed reassuringly, while all the time my thoughts were running off in all directions at once. I felt like phoning my mother and explaining why I had done what I had done. She must know by now. My father must have called her. I suppose she'd pretended not to be surprised even if she was. "I told you the kid would end up a murderer." From that point of view, she was right, she'd never stopped shouting it from the rooftops as if she expected me to give credence to her prophecies. But I wondered all the same if her joy at being proved right would be stronger than the drawbacks of becoming the mother of a criminal. She was the one who had carried a killer in her womb, and she'd never be able to deny that. My mother, who was so bossy and lectured everyone else, thinking everyone was beneath her, had raised a homicidal teenager. I couldn't have made things any worse for her. I had turned her uterus into a repeating rifle, and that gave me a real kick—a kick that only faded when I thought about the future and how complicated everything was going to be.

I stopped at the top of a pass. The highest point was a summer vacation hotel by the side of the road. It was closed right now. A track on the right led off to Crater Lake. I left it and followed the main road as far as an intersection, where I turned left to get back toward the 101. There were some little vacation cabins alongside a stream. I spotted one that was more isolated than the others and decided to stop there. I shoved the door open with my shoulder and was afraid the rest of the structure would collapse on me. The interior was clean and tidy. I lighted a fire in the little stone fireplace, praying it didn't snow during the night. I knocked back a bottle of whiskey as I made myself something to eat on the fire. Feeling only slightly drunk depressed me. The wind rose just as I lay down with my eyes closed on a hard bed, all curled up to stop myself going over. There's no such thing as silence or noise in the country. It isn't like in a town, what you hear always calms you down, as long as you trust life in the wild. I thought about my grandparents. I wondered where they might be now, if there was the slightest chance that anything remained of their carcasses, which must be decomposing while waiting for my father to show up. If their souls were on their way to heaven, I hoped they wouldn't meet up there, I hadn't killed my grandfather down here for him to have to put up with the old lady's tantrums for all eternity. I took stock of the situation. I didn't know when I was going to give myself up, but I didn't want it to be before the funeral. The altitude and my tiredness got the better of me, and I fell into a deep sleep. I was just starting to have nightmares when I heard noises outside. I thought at first the cops had come to arrest me, then I realized bears must be prowling around the saddlebags on the bike, which I'd left full of food. I went out with my Winchester in my hand and saw two coyotes running off with their tails between their legs. It was impossible to get back to sleep after that. Early in the morning, I felt dazed, the whiskey had gone to my head. A guy knocked at the door with a cup of coffee in his hand. He was out of sugar. I gave him some. But that wasn't enough for him, he had to talk. It's often like that in this country. People look for solitude for some reason and then take it out on the first civilian who shows up, spouting off at him for hours. He told me proudly that Kennedy's assassin had himself been shot down coming out of a station house or someplace like that. The killer's name was Jack Ruby. He had murdered my hero. That made me sad. The guy who was talking to me lived a bit further down, and made a living doing odd jobs as a park ranger. I must have seemed strange to him, with that habit I have of always thinking about two things at the same time, which means I sometimes take a long time to answer. It's always the subject that's stressing me the most that takes precedence. Especially as I couldn't give a damn about his life, which was really nothing special. If it had been, it would have bored me just as much. When he tried to find out a bit more about me, I clammed up, except that clams never look as mean as I apparently do when I've decided a conversation has gone on long enough. He apologized for disturbing me and walked away, but turned around several times. Something must have bothered him about the way I was behaving. I sat down on the two broken half-logs that served as front steps and looked at the motorcycle. I didn't have any desire for anything anymore. I searched inside myself for something I really wanted, but nothing came. I left the cabin, closing the door behind me as best I could—I'd made a hell of a mess of it when I arrived. The Indian Chief started up again right away and I set off again in the direction of Canada, knowing perfectly well that I'd never reach the border because I didn't want that any more than the cops did. Riding slowly down onto the plains brought me back to life. As I took the big turns, the cool air energized my mind. I started cutting across those turns, hoping that a car or a truck would come along and put an end to a life that had gotten off to such a bad start, you couldn't expect anything decent from it. But I didn't see anyone.

Once I was down on the plains, I accelerated. The rise in temperature justified that. After a few miles, I came to an industrial town where freight trains were waiting to be loaded. Big guys with hard hats and thick beige gloves were bustling around the wagons. In the distance, chimneys were belching thick gray smoke laboriously out into the sky. The main street was slowly waking up. This town was so damned orderly, it gave me the blues. I was tempted to drive straight on through, but I didn't have enough gas. I found a gas station on the main street. An old guy, with bow legs as if he'd ridden a tank truck as a child instead of a rocking horse, carefully put out his cigarette and served me.

"Nice bike!"

I didn't answer him. My answer would have been lost anyway, I wasn't looking at him.

"They stopped making them in '53, didn't they? A pity, they should have kept right on."

"Where's the sheriff's office?" I asked.

He stretched out his arm. "But you won't find him there right now. He was called up into the mountains. A park ranger who gave his wife a thrashing with the flat of his ax. Not a pretty sight, they say, though nobody's seen her yet. Booze is bad for some people. But one of his two deputies must be in the office." He glanced at his watch, which had a crack in its face. "Should be opening up soon." Then he looked at me as if I was a giant sequoia. "I don't think I've ever seen anyone as tall as you, son."

What kind of answer can you give to that?

I paid him and kept on along the main street to the sheriff's office. It looked more like a post office, and the American flag waving timidly outside wasn't exactly new. I stayed outside for a minute or two, riding slowly up and down on my bike, not sure what to do. Finally I shut off the engine.

When I went in, I didn't see anybody there at first. But then I saw a blonde woman with a round face peeping up over the counter. She smiled at me, with the same inane smile Clark Gable has in all his movies.

"What can I do for you?"

I put my helmet on the counter with my gloves inside and opened wide my leather jacket. "I'm here to give myself up."

She laughed. "Give yourself up? They after you for speeding?"

"No, for a double murder."

She peered at me to see if I was serious. We continued in the same lighthearted tone.

"In this county?"

"No, south of here. North Fork, Sierra Nevada, California. The police in Fresno should know all about it."

"How?"

She still wasn't quite clued in.

"My father probably told them. In fact, he must be there by now."

"All right, take a seat, I'll get in touch with them. Until I get confirmation, I can't arrest you."

"Then I'll go buy a doughnut. I'll be back."

I picked up my helmet and gloves and went out while the blonde woman watched me openmouthed.

I slowly got back on my bike and set off down what was left of the main street at the legal speed. As I rode I calculated what I was prepared to pay society for the double murder of my grandparents: the average of the years they still had to live.

Fifteen and nine out of a life expectancy of eighty years, divide that in two, you got twelve years. Twelve years in the can, I'd be out at twenty-seven, that seemed pretty reasonable, my grandparents weren't worth more than that.

The cops found me as I was sitting on the steps of a timber warehouse on the edge of town, sipping a watery coffee and eating a doughnut. I was lost in thought, envying all those guys who could get up every morning and do the same job all their lives. The two deputies, a man and a woman, got out of the police car. They both had their hands on their guns, which I thought was pretty pathetic. I wanted to take my bike back to the station house and for them to show me a sheltered spot to park it. I was sure my father would come and pick it up. They didn't look too sold on the idea. "Why would I be turning myself in if I was planning to run away," I said, "can you tell me that?"

The argument seemed to convince them, and I was able to take my bike to the police garage. Then they read me my rights. After making a few phone calls, they took me to Fresno. We stopped on the way in a one-horse town where I spent the night in a cell with two drunks. They never stopped talking and laughing about nothing. When I'd had enough, I told them I was there for a double murder and needed some rest. They moved away from me and I didn't hear another peep out of them. We set off again at sunrise. In the car, we didn't say much more than we had the day before. The two cops were talking about all kinds of dumb things and ignored me except when I spoke up. I needed to focus my attention on something. The woman cop was my target. I fantasized about her all through the ride, imagining all kinds of things I wouldn't have done to her in reality. Basically, sexual fantasies I needed in order to feel I was still alive.

12

W hen we arrived, a few photographers from the local rags were waiting for us. The two cops posed next to me like Hemingway standing by a six-foot-long swordfish he'd just fished from the sea. I thought it was dishonest of them to claim they'd caught me when I'd given myself up. They took me to the lieutenant in charge of my case, who was drinking coffee with his legs up on his desk, examining photos that had nothing to do with my grandparents.

In the long corridor that led to him, I felt like a bear being paraded by its trainer to a crowd of bloodthirsty onlookers. All the cops and secretaries in the place were staring at me. The lieutenant greeted me with a weak smile that was more sorrowful than vengeful. He led me into an interrogation room. He took some photographs of my grandparents' bodies from a file with my name on it, and spread them in front of me.

"This is what you did."

He was expecting me to look away, but instead I took the pictures one by one. The old couple hadn't changed much since I had left them. A bit stiff, a bit more wrinkled, nothing more than that. I was struck by how much a corpse contradicts the idea of life after death.

"Why did you do it?"

I took a deep breath, which may have made him think I was getting ready to make a long speech.

"I wanted to see what it'd be like. For about two weeks I'd been wondering what it'd be like to kill my grandmother. It was an obsession. I'd think about it, then it'd pass. It'd come back even stronger than before, then disappear. And when I was doing it, I stopped thinking about it, the fact of doing it was what mattered more than anything else. For the old man, it was different, I never wanted to kill him. It was the circumstances that forced me to do it. He was too dependent on her. Letting him survive the old girl would have meant condemning him to suffer for the rest of his life."

"Did you think of the harm you were doing them, the harm you were doing your father?"

"To be honest, I had to kill my grandmother and I didn't really care whether it was right or wrong. When it came to the old man, I felt bad about it and I still do. But talking about my father, I did him a service. And even though I'm not sure why, I think it was a great service. Of course, he's in shock, as you are, but in a few weeks, when the emotion's died down, the positive aspects of what I did will come to the surface like the body of a drowned man, sorry for the metaphor. Where *is* my father?"

"In the bar across the street. He doesn't want to see you. Not for the moment. He's going to have the bodies taken to Los Angeles, and he told me he'll come back when he has some idea what we're going to do with you."

"You should keep an eye on him."

"Why?"

"He has a tendency to drink whenever anything bothers him. And he can drink a lot. You've seen him so you know he's as big as I am."

"We contacted your mother."

"And?"

"She says she isn't surprised. She's says you've had it inside you for a long time, that you once cut the head off a cat."

"If every teenager in this country who's cut the head off a cat killed their grandparents, you could close the retirement homes."

"Anyway, she doesn't want to come, she's waiting to see what the justice system decides."

"And what will it decide?"

"You'll be examined by an expert. Because you're under sixteen, he'll have to determine whether or not you're responsible for your actions. Then the California Youth Authority will have to decide what it wants to do with you, put you in prison or in a psychiatric hospital. It's all a bit vague to me, it's the first time in my career I've had to deal with two murders committed by a minor. Why did you give yourself up?"

"Because I had no reason to keep on going. I like driving for hours at a time, I can even drive all night. And then I feel this kind of a big slowing down inside me. I've always been kept indoors. But when I'm free and in the open air, after a few days I feel dizzy and I realize I'm not meant to be free like that. And yet I'd be ready to kill anyone who tried to take that freedom away from me. That's what I did with my grandmother. Killing her gave me forty-eight hours of freedom."

"Do you think it was worth it?"

"Yes."

13

He's already been sitting there for a minute when the door opens and her puffy face appears. She's breathing heavily. She's loaded down. By herself, by what she's carrying, by everything.

"They make me sign that form every single time, that's what delayed me."

"What form?"

"The form saying I won't sue the prison authorities if you attack me."

He laughs. "If I attacked you, you wouldn't be suing anybody anymore."

She doesn't think that's funny, or if she does, she doesn't show it.

"An FBI guy came and questioned me once, and I made him think I was going to strangle him. He called for help, but nobody came, they were changing shifts, it was lunchtime. He told me he was armed, I said you couldn't come into a prison armed, even if you were FBI. He started babbling about the martial arts he practiced and, when he saw I wasn't impressed by that, he pissed in his pants. By the time they came to get him, there was a big wet patch between his legs. You should have seen this muscular little guy in his black suit, white shirt and black tie, with his neat crew cut, walking with his feet turned in to hide his shame. The guards got a big kick out of that. They know how peaceable I am."

He's already looked through the pile of books she heaved onto the desk between them when she says, "Happy birthday!"

"How do you know it's my birthday?"

"Because I was born the same day as you, four years later."

She starts to blush as if apologizing for this coincidence.

"You mean you're fifty-nine. That's what I thought. Outside, being a year older means one year less to live, one year less to get bored, it's not quite the same. I'm not going to read all these."

"You do what you can, as usual it's just a suggestion, but they're so used to how fast you are . . ."

"I've started writing."

"Writing?"

She starts to tremble.

"I'm not being offered a job as a critic, so I started a novel. An autobiographical novel. You think there might be a publisher who'd be interested?"

"Writing?" she repeats.

"Yes," he says irritably.

"You're planning to tell the whole story?"

"That's the question. I won't agree to being published unless they take my book in full."

"I see, it's just that . . . "

"It's just nothing. Do you know any publishers?"

"I know a few."

She seems terribly upset all of a sudden. That happens often. She's too emotional. Not just emotional, unstable. Now she seems to have given up the will to live. He sees people like that every day in this prison. If she's going to come here and be the same way, he's going to tell her to get lost. This thing about his book seems to have really knocked her for six. He doesn't know why, but it's really knocked her sideways. So he decides to strike while the iron is hot.

"I've asked to be transferred."

She's completely disoriented. "Transferred where?"

"To heaven, but they turned me down. No, seriously, I've

asked to go to Angola Penitentiary in Louisiana. It's likely to take a while, because a prisoner at Angola the same age as me, also a lifer, would have to make the opposite request. My religious record has impressed the warden at Angola. He's a religious nut and he likes to have converts in his prison."

"And when would that be?"

"Tomorrow, in a month, in ten years, never."

"But you won't have anyone to visit you there."

"What difference does that make?"

She doesn't reply, simply lowers her head.

"After all these years, I sometimes wonder what keeps me going. Reading, now writing, contributing to the understanding of serial killers. I heard that in Angola the prisoners work on a farm with horses. I have memories of horses from my childhood in Montana. They're pretty much my only good memories. There's something more human about horses than about people. I never wanted to escape this life. I cut my wrists twice, but just to watch my blood flow, like a little boy watching a dirty river flowing near his house. Getting out of prison has never motivated me either. I put in a request for parole, but when I went in front of the board, all I could find to say was: 'I don't think you'd be making a terrible mistake if you release me, but you can never be sure.' I like to see you. But you only come once a month. Whereas down there I'll have the company of horses every day, don't you see? And every year there's a rodeo. The prisoners mount bulls and mustangs in front of their families and paying customers. This money finances their extras for the year. But it's the main event I'd really like to take part in. Four prisoners sit around a table in the middle of the ring and play poker. They have to concentrate to follow the game because the stakes are high. After a while, a really mean bull is let out into the ring and heads straight for the table. The last guy to stand and run gets all the stake money."

They only see each other half an hour a month and, after five minutes, they have nothing more to say to each other. She's an ex-hippie, he's sure of that. She still has the smell and the tired, twisted hair. Those young people haven't aged any better than the Vietnam veterans. At least, at the time, their eyes lit up, even if that light came from LSD. Sometimes he thinks about all those girls who advocated free love, who fucked lots of men just to prove that they could, that they didn't belong to anyone in particular. He never even took advantage of that. They disgusted him. A drag on a joint, I open my thighs, I close them again, I don't know the name of the guy who just shot his load into me, but I belong to the brotherhood of man. That's the program. Nobody knows whose the children are, but that's fine, that way they're everybody's and therefore nobody's. He hated that generation. All that's left of it now are people like Susan who think they're broadminded even though their minds are shrunk by dope. A psychiatrist he knows would have said that they lived through a kind of collective schizophrenic episode, involving split personality, constant hallucinations, catatonia, marginalization, in other words, a whole series of symptoms that would eventually have made these schizophrenics normal if they had ever grown up. She's sweating. Even without moving. She lives in a state of insecurity, that's why. It isn't about weight. He's 360 pounds, and he never sweats.

"Books for blind people and all that bullshit, I'm not convinced that's the main reason that brought you here. But I'm going to be frank with you, I don't want to know the reason, though I know that if you're hiding it, it must be stronger than anything else. I don't give a damn about it, Susan. We have a professional relationship, for a specific time, and it's perfect like that. I like your visits, but I could just as easily do without them. After you, there won't be anybody to come and see me, but what the fuck do I care? You're my only female contact in a world where all I see is guys who jerk off eight times a day. hoping to forget the walls of their cells. But if I have to do without you . . ."

She lowers her head, giving a pathetic half-smile that fades immediately. She must be wondering if she should cry. She doesn't dare. He examines the pile of books and reads the cover copy. None of them appeal to him. Most books don't, that's the general rule. He eliminates three books that are too thick. When a book's too long the reader gets lost, even if he's blind. He stands and stretches.

"Try to mention my book to a publisher, you'd be doing me a big favor. So long."

He turns one last time before leaving the room.

"If they agree to transfer me to Angola, I'll write and let you know."

14

The shrink at the hearing gave his diagnosis: paranoid schizophrenic. I was about as impressed as a guy who doesn't have a ticket hearing the winning number in the lottery. The presiding judge didn't seem very impressed either. The hearing lasted a quarter of an hour. The shrink read his notes in a monotone voice, which he tried to vary by occasionally going faster. He didn't seem very comfortable. He said I was psychotic, confused, unable to function, a danger to society and to myself. He added that the treatment that might possibly cure me of my disorder would be long, very long. His conclusion was that I should be found not responsible for my actions.

As the judge was listening to this litany with one ear—I guess he'd closed the other to save energy—I whispered to my court-appointed lawyer that I thought this conclusion was ridiculous. I wanted to claim responsibility for my actions. He made a dismissive gesture and whispered, "This is your only chance to ever see the light of day again, son." I just had to grin and bear it.

I had spent an afternoon with the shrink. That was all the justice system could afford for a guy like me. He was obsessed by the "trigger" that had led me to do what I did. He wanted to know if before I killed my grandmother I'd heard voices or if I'd had the feeling that superior forces had taken possession of me. "I'd been thinking about it for several weeks. I knew it was bad, very bad even. I never for a moment thought I was committing an act that society would excuse, but it was a necessity, a matter of survival. It was her or me. If I hadn't done it, I'm sure I'd have killed myself in the next few days. I swapped her life for mine. And I didn't feel all that guilty about swapping an old woman's life for a teenager's. I also did it for my father. I'd have liked him to have the courage, then I wouldn't have had to do it."

We didn't talk much about my childhood. He'd heard enough to form an opinion. He returned to the subject of my grandmother.

"Did she beat you?"

"No."

"Did she humiliate you verbally?"

"No, not really."

"So what did you have against her?"

"She was stifling me."

"And do you think that was reason enough to kill her?"

That was where I must have seemed confused to him. I couldn't organize my thoughts well enough to explain how they'd developed. I wasn't sure they'd followed any kind of logic. All I remembered was the conclusion. But I was the one who'd made the decision, not someone else, not a voice from some other galaxy.

There was kind of a desolate atmosphere in the courtroom, with it being early in the morning and the building being overheated. Everyone was numb. The judge sneezed several times before he declared me not responsible for my actions and put me in the care of the California Youth Authority.

I could see in his eyes how relieved he was to be able to wash his hands of my case. He went out without looking at me, thinking of the hot cup of coffee waiting for him in his office.

The board ordered the same stuff as the court. A whole bunch of shrinks and social workers paraded in front of me and asked me all kinds of questions about my life, as if they were planning to write my biography. According to my lawyer, who had read their reports, there was no consensus among the shrinks in my case, and they even disagreed completely with the conclusions of the shrink at the hearing. But in the end they agreed on the fact that I wouldn't get the appropriate treatment in prison, and that it would only increase my guilt feelings. I didn't have any guilt feelings, but maybe they didn't give the same meaning to the words.

The few weeks I spent in prison waiting for my fate to be decided didn't leave me with any particular memory. I was expecting to find it claustrophobic but it was O.K. You can feel locked up outside and free inside, it all comes down to your state of mind. I was well treated and my fellow prisoners left me alone, seeing I wasn't doomed to rot in the same hole as they were. I could sense they respected me because of my size. The thing a new convict always thinks about is the fear of getting fucked in the showers. Unless the guy had a firemen's ladder between his legs, I didn't see how I was running any risk of that. I didn't become friends with anybody. It's not in my nature and I didn't see the point.

All the same, by the time I left there, I was a little tense. Because of my sense of decency, it'd been several weeks since I'd been able to find any release for my sexual tensions. Relieving yourself with other guys around is degrading, although I realize you get used to it after a few years. In the car transferring me to the state psychiatric hospital in Atascadero, I looked out the window and saw pretty girls full of life walking all carefree on the street, and I felt like crying. It was nostalgia for something I'd never known. Emotion was soon replaced by desire. Not the desire to possess them, but something more complicated that I dismissed from my mind. I sank back in my seat and thought about my bike. Maybe I'd get it back one day, though I was sure the battery would be flat. Suddenly, I started getting the jitters. I was scared I might really go crazy. I didn't want to go there anymore. I started to prefer prison. I remembered stories I'd heard about normal people institutionalized for some dumb crap they'd done, who'd come out with their brains wiped as clean as the deck of a ship. I asked the two officers who were taking me what things were like at Atascadero. They replied that they didn't know too much about it. According to them, it was a place where they protected the citizens of California from all kinds of crazy people. I also asked them what kind of patients they had there. The one who was in charge smoothed his mustache and told me that as far as he knew a third of them were criminals and two thirds were guys who were so out of it, they wouldn't harm a fly. The other cop, who hadn't said anything up until now, suddenly blew his top about all these sons of bitches who were locked up at the taxpayer's expense and who they pretended to treat, as if you could treat evil. He turned and gave me a contemptuous look.

"You think a guy who killed his grandparents is going to turn back into a model citizen one day? Do you really think that, boy?"

I'm sure that if I hadn't been wearing handcuffs, he wouldn't have added "boy." But he didn't faze me. "I had my reasons for doing it."

"That's what makes you a nut, that you could think you had good reasons for killing your grandparents. They're going to keep you in there for years to teach you to regret what you did, but the evil is in you. You've gone over to the other side, it's too late now."

He lighted a cigarette and lowered the window on his side.

"You know, I'd like to believe they could cure you. But you can't cure crazy people. If a dog bites a kid, you can never trust that dog again, even if a minute later it rubs up against you and wags its tail. You might as well get used to it. You crossed a line. Personally, I wouldn't kill you for that. But I wouldn't let you out of there."

15

We'd been in open country for a while now, driving past fields where black cows were grazing. From a distance, the hospital looked like a big birthday cake topped with cream and plumped down on a tablecloth that's too brightly colored. The ice had started melting on the side. As we approached, the cake got bigger, the high walls surrounding it too. There were coils of barbed wire all the way along the perimeter wall. I didn't see any watchtowers, but the whole place looked like one hell of a prison. Two male nurses, who must have thought they were big men before they saw me, came and fetched me from the administration block. They took me to see a pleasant but firm lady and stayed with us while we filled in a form that was meant to give them all the information they needed about me. I asked her if I could have visitors. She nodded then told me with an apologetic air that they'd contacted my father and my mother so that they could be present when I was admitted to the hospital, but neither of them wanted to have anything to do with me for the moment. She tried to sound reassuring. It was often like that, she said. With time, things got ironed out.

"You have to understand them. Not only did you kill, but you killed members of your family, your father's parents. It's going to take time for them to think of you as part of the family again. Your psychiatrist may want to meet with them, so they'll have to come here eventually. But don't worry about that for now."

She dismissed me with a smile. The two male nurses escorted me to my room. We must have walked nearly half a mile to get there. Everything was high, long and narrow in that hospital. The corridors were endless. In the section for non-criminal patients, we passed guys who were strolling around freely. Many looked like victims of an accident of birth, with foreheads low down over their eyebrows or huge dome-shaped heads. The only light came in through small windows high up in the walls, which didn't improve their appearance any. Not a single one looked at me. They were in another place, a place I guessed you didn't come back from. Some were twitchy, others waddled like hens. I would never have done them any harm, but frankly these people with their wandering brains made me nauseous.

The high-security wing was more like a prison than a hospital but at least the criminals looked normal. The few I passed anyway. At that hour of the afternoon, most people were in their rooms. Mine was as narrow as a trouser leg. There was no room to move between the closet and the bed. There was an unbarred window high up in the wall, which would have been out of reach for any ordinary man. The nurses apologized, saying that nobody had warned them of my size. They left me there for about half an hour, then came back and took me to a room that wasn't much bigger but where I could at least turn around without bumping into the walls. When I saw that the toilets were outside, I realized I wasn't here to be punished even though, apart from a few details, it was hard to tell the difference from a federal prison. And anyway, when you're alone in a room, you get a new perspective on things. It may seem like a contradiction, but I started liking this room as much as I'd liked the wide open spaces at other times. There was something reassuring about it. Through the window, which was six feet from the ground, I could see a strip of meadow in the distance, though it was mostly hidden by the wall and the barbed wire on top. I lay down on my bed and stayed there for about two hours, looking up at the ceiling and not thinking about anything, but feeling weirdly safe.

I couldn't spend years in this hospital sleeping curled up. I called a guard and showed him that, quite honestly, I was about a foot longer than the bed. The uprights were solid and there was nothing you could do about it. He promised he'd have a look in the storeroom to see if there was a medical bed that might do the trick. I waited for dinnertime. I put on the uniform that was used for the most dangerous patients, which I'd found folded at the foot of my bed, and when the hooter sounded, a guard came and opened the door for me. Each inmate had to keep his distance from the others. We marched to the canteen, where we lined up in single file in front of steaming vats filled with food that was all mashed up so that it could be eaten without a knife. I chose a seat at random. It's always risky to do that in prison. There's always a guy or a gang that claims it. But here, there was no feeling of aggression. Nobody played the tough guy, there were no gangs trying to lay down the law, people looked at you without seeing you. Killers classified as mentally ill are fiercely individualistic and withdrawn. I'd even say, after the long years of experience I've had of them, that they're scaredy-cats. Direct confrontation terrifies them. They resort to violence only when they're sure they can lord it over a weaker victim. But I didn't know that at the time. How could I have known? The other patients just stared at me, mostly out of the corners of their eyes. My size impressed them. Not so much the size itself, more the idea it must have given them of how I was when I was in action, when that famous "trigger" was pressed. Every one of the inmates who sat down next to me tended to ignore me, except for one guy pushing fifty who stood out because of his refined manner. He kept giving me these furtive smiles and winks as if we were accomplices. In what, I had no idea. I wondered if he was gay, even though I was never the kind of teenager people like that fantasized about. I noticed two or three really scary-looking guys, especially a man in his fifties who looked like a weird cross between an Indian chief and an Irish truck driver. His head was so big he'd have given a hat maker a heart attack, and his eyes were big and black, but what made it worse was that he was cross-eyed. The food was okay. Better than in prison, but then it could hardly have been worse. Nobody talked to me, though I could sense that some of them were itching to say something. They must have been curious to know what I was doing there at my age. A short, skinny guy, so ugly you'd have thought his parents had made him like that deliberately, sat down opposite me. He kept fidgeting on his chair and grimacing, and every thirty seconds a kind of contemptuous grin came over his face. He was bald, but not bald the way people are when they're losing their hair. His hair looked as if it had never really grown, as if something had discouraged it. I could see he wanted to talk to me, but nothing came. After each attempt he stroked the top of his skull. The touch of foam at the corners of his lips made me feel nauseous, and I stopped looking at him so that I could finish my dinner in peace. When I don't want to meet someone's eyes, all I have to do is stare straight ahead of me, which puts me a long way above their heads. To use a military metaphor of my father's, when I'm under fire I camouflage myself as the air. It's a trick my father, who wasn't much shorter than I was, often used. I saw him do it whenever my mother started screaming as if she was possessed. He would stand there with his arms folded, leaning against a wall, his eyes fixed straight ahead.

I resented the fact that he hadn't put in a single appearance since my arrest. My mother was another matter. She must have been really angry. I'm sure she didn't want to take time off because she'd have had to tell her office colleagues why. I wasn't even sure she'd talked about it to my sisters. Or else I can imagine the conversation. The two girls come home, one from work, the other from school. My mother is sitting peeling potatoes. Fat is sizzling in a frying pan. They say hello without kissing. My mother's new guy is in the living room. He's reading the newspaper in the warmth, in his slippers because, without slippers, she wouldn't have let him in the room. I couldn't describe him to you, I'd already left when he took my father's place. It didn't take her long. My mother needs to get laid at least twice a day even if she never looks the guy in the face. Anyhow, that's my analysis, based on a whole bunch of clues I gathered over the fourteen years that my parents slept above me on the first floor. But what she most needs is to yell at the guy as he's zipping up his pants that she didn't have an orgasm because he's an ignoramus, a deadbeat who doesn't know how to pleasure a woman—until they start all over again. Anyway, my sisters come home. Without looking up, my mother says, "Your brother killed your grandparents." My younger sister, who has the brains of a halibut, must have asked straight out, "Which ones?" even though she knows our other grandparents died a long time ago and we never knew them. As for my older sister, I can just see her saying, "Son of a bitch!" as she opens the refrigerator to look for something substantial she can wolf down before dinner. By the time she's found her snack, the news has faded from her mind. Nothing ever affects her. I've never seen her either happy or sad and, even when she's being mean, you sense she's forcing herself, that it doesn't come naturally. As for being nice, that requires too much imagination, she can't grasp the concept.

When dinner was over, we filed back to our rooms. The guard locked mine. I asked him where I could get something to read. He told me he would do me a favor and, just this once, bring me a magazine with my medication, but that I'd have access to the library the next day. The magazine and the medication arrived half an hour later. I didn't ask what the medication was for. I assumed it was to treat the sickness that had led me to kill my grandparents. I was only on the third page of the magazine, leering at Marilyn Monroe's ass—she'd been dead for more than a year and a half, but that didn't make the picture any less sexy—when I felt my eyelids grow heavy. The nice little fantasies I'd been preparing for myself couldn't resist the sleeping pill I'd been given and I slept without any nightmares, which was something that had never happened to me before.

When I woke up, I felt weak. All the same, before breakfast I instinctively cut out the photo of Marilyn Monroe, folded it, and put it in my closet. The meal was even more silent than the day before, although two or three of the patients seemed as wound up as toys. The others started staring at me again. My age intrigued them. I was the youngest by far. Once I'd finished my coffee and the revolting doughnut that went with it, I was taken back to my room to wait for my first session with the psychiatrist. I fell asleep again as if I had years of sleep to catch up on. A male nurse came and woke me, and although I was unsteady on my feet I followed him into a room that looked like a police interrogation room with a glass partition for the staff to look through to make sure the doctor wasn't in any danger. I sat there for a moment without doing anything and ended up falling asleep again with my head on the table in front of me and my arms dangling. A nurse immediately woke me.

16

When the shrink came in, he told me I could sit down. I said I was already sitting and he smiled.

"We won't always be in this room. It's just to see if you behave yourself, which I don't doubt you will."

I could tell from the start that he was a kindly man. Kindly, that's the word. He looked at me for a long time, trying to see past the reflection in my big glasses to my eyes.

"A terrible thing happened to you. We're going to try to put that right, so that you'll be able to get out of here one day. Is that what you want?"

My brain was working in slow motion. "What am I supposed to want?"

He smiled again. "To get out of here. Do you want that?"

I hesitated. "Right now, I'm not too sure."

"Do you want to go back to the same life as other young people your age, a normal life?"

By now my brain was working again. "It's obvious you don't know how those so-called normal people live. Of course I want to get out of here. But not if it means becoming as dumb as they are."

"Your file says you're exceptionally intelligent, Al. To be honest with you, I've never had to deal with anyone as intelligent as you. I'm impressed. I'll try to be equal to the task. You know, I'm very pleased to be treating you. But your intelligence will never be worth a damn if it doesn't adapt. Right now, that unusual intelligence of yours has no direction. You'll leave here the day a board decides you're no longer a danger, either to yourself or to society, and that you've shown a real ability to adapt."

"But I'm not a danger to society. I killed my grandmother because she was stifling me and I blamed her for what my father is. As for my grandfather . . . "

"I know all that. You're telling me you're totally responsible for your actions. I don't want to hear that. Especially after telling me you aren't sure you want to get out of here. That's the kind of contradiction the two of us have to tackle. We're going to meet every morning. In the afternoon you'll have to do a real job with other inmates. In a few weeks, if I consider it feasible, you'll be able to resume your studies. Tell me what you like doing in life, your hobbies."

That isn't the kind of question someone like me finds it easy to answer. He sensed my hesitation.

"Motorcycles. I like to ride motorcycles and feel the wind in my hair. That's when I feel good. Apart from that, I used to like shooting. I guess I'm going to have to give that one up."

"I guess so. What else?"

"Nothing else."

"There's nothing else that interests you?"

"How can I explain this to you? Every time something interests me, I quickly get tired of it because these bad thoughts come along and screw things up. They dominate everything and I can't go any further with what I wanted to do."

"I see. That's something we'll talk about some more another time. But for example, you can't read a book right to the end, is that it?"

"That's it."

"Then let's make a deal. Get a book from the library and force yourself to read every day, without thinking about anything else. Ten, twenty pages, whatever you can manage. Try to put these bad thoughts out of your mind as best you can.

You'll get out of here the day the doctors are convinced that you're the one who decides what you think. Do you understand?"

"I understand." There was a question I was dying to ask. "Tell me, what's a paranoid schizophrenic?"

He looked at me for the longest time, scratching his chin. "Why do you ask that?"

"That's what the expert in court said I was."

"Ah, yes, I see. Don't worry about that. It's just psychiatric jargon. Nobody's too sure what a schizophrenic is. To cut a long story short, it's anything that isn't normal, apart from a few very specific illnesses. But most people who kill are normal. Maybe you're normal after all, Al."

"If you find out I'm normal, will you send me to prison?"

He could see I wasn't afraid of that.

"Oh, no, son. You don't quite grasp the subtlety of the system. If you'd been seen as normal when you did what you did, you'd be in prison for the rest of your life. But if you become normal again here, that'll mean you've been cured. Let me give you a piece of advice. Keep your distance from the other inmates. Try not to make friends with them. They have a lot to take from you and not very much to give."

He stood up and gave me a friendly pat on the shoulder.

"I'll see you tomorrow. In my office this time."

Sorry, I didn't think to describe him. That's me, I don't care what people look like. Most times, when I look at them, I don't even see them. But I can imagine the way they see me. Behind his square glasses with their black frames, Leitner had very blue eyes. The kind of blue that doesn't fade with the years. He looked old enough to have been twenty at the time of the Normandy landings. He didn't seem like the kind of shrink who drags all the misery of human abnormalities around with him, or the kind who deals with crazy people to convince him-

self he's better than they are. No, he seemed more of an optimist, someone who could see things in perspective. Outside
the hospital, he probably lived a normal life. He looked the
kind of person who'd like to get into his convertible and drive
for hours along the coast—though I didn't know if he earned
enough to afford anything very special as a car. I find it hard to
define what I felt after that first session. In general I don't feel
anything. Sometimes I don't like someone in the sense that I
feel an instinctive threat. I often despise people I meet, because
that's the way I am, I've seen so many people who were completely lacking in intelligence, people I just found pitiful. To
cut a long story short, Dr. Leitner didn't seem to want to do me
any harm.

I went straight to the library, which was like everything else
there, long, narrow and high. I wonder what the architect who
designed that hospital could have been thinking. In two seconds, I realized the librarian had been there a long time and
would be staying for a long time to come. It gave me the jitters
to realize that psychiatry isn't an exact science and not everybody is cured. I saw myself in fifty years, pale-faced like him,
my hair in clumps, bags under my eyes, and I could only hope
that Leitner knew his job. The male nurse who went with me
greeted the librarian by name but he didn't reply. He was taking books out of a carton and sorting them into two piles under
two different signs, one yellow, the other red. One book
seemed to be a problem, he didn't know which pile to put it in.
When he finally got around to asking me what I wanted, he
stared at my uniform, the uniform that indicated I was a criminal. He pushed his glasses up onto the bridge of his nose and
set off between the stacks. He came back with a copy of *Crime
and Punishment* and put it down in front of me, like a grocer
presenting some cheap produce.

Why do people write? Often because some hidden vanity makes them proud of their own misfortunes and they decide to share them with the rest of mankind because, deep down, they're too much of a burden to bear alone. I also think a lot of people write because they don't get any support from their family. Worse still, it's often their family that's the root of all their troubles. Having readers gives them the feeling they're not so alone, without the disadvantage of having to rub shoulders with well-intentioned but tiresome people. Often, too, they write to leave something of their poor little lives behind them when they're gone. But why them rather than someone else? So the book gets published for no particular reason and goes straight into the garbage can of boredom. But I know why I write. I just want to reconnect with the rest of the human race.

Dostoevsky is something else. I plunged straight in, lying down on that narrow bed that was too small for me. I held out for about twenty pages before the bad thoughts overcame me. Sometimes I get carried away by them for hours and lose all sense of time. Sometimes they end with a violent orgasm. Sometimes I fall asleep before that happens, calmed by the thought of the pleasure they might have given me.

17

Leitner could have been one of President Kennedy's men. He had the relaxed manner, the self-confidence, the fashionable glasses and the steady gaze of those Democrats who were sure they could change the world. His light beige Baracuta jacket gave him a casual look. In other words, he was just like all those people my father hated more than anything since the Bay of Pigs. My father couldn't forgive them for leaving his brothers in Special Forces to die on a beach in Cuba because pretty boy JFK hadn't had the guts to order air support during the landing. In all the time he'd been a soldier, he'd never seen a betrayal like that by a Commander-in-Chief. That a rich kid sitting comfortably in his oval office with his cigar in his mouth could have decided to sacrifice this country's elite—that was something he'd have to pay for one day, my father would say when he played poker with survivors from his regiment who, like him, had stayed in Helena after leaving the army. His three pals agreed, of course, and sometimes went even further in their comments about that son of a bitch and the torments he'd suffer in hell.

In the first few months of my therapy, Leitner never talked to me about my grandparents. Whenever I got on to the subject, he'd assume an absent air, as if it was a minor concern. Their deaths and the circumstances surrounding them weren't his priority. At our first session, he established the rules of the game. He asked me if I played chess. My grandfather had taught me the basics. I hadn't shown him much gratitude, shooting him in the back and then again in the head, but you can't argue with the facts. Just mentioning my grandfather in this connection disturbed me. I told Leitner I was really sorry I'd killed him. He made an exception to his rule by asking me if I felt empathy for him. I wasn't too sure what empathy meant. He explained that it meant putting myself in his place and feeling what he suffered. The question surprised me. How could I put myself in his place? How can you put yourself in the place of a dead man? A tenth of a second before the shots, he's an old guy taking shopping bags out of his station wagon. What can he be saying to himself: "Did I forget anything from the list my wife gave me? If I did she's going to bawl me out. Mind you, she'll find an excuse to bawl me out anyway, that's the way she marks her territory." Maybe he's also thinking about lunch and looking forward to opening a bottle of his favorite beer, or else he's looking forward to the gardening he's planned for the afternoon. Or, another possibility, he's worrying about me, thinking my father landed them with one hell of a problem when he sent me to them, or else admitting that my grandmother is really too hard on me, that he ought to tell her, but he doesn't have the guts, and anyway it's none of his business, the only thing that concerns him being that the old woman he's been living with for fifty years has no reason to get all worked up and poison yet another day of his retirement. A tenth of a second after thinking this, he's dead and gone. So I asked Leitner, where was there any room for empathy? You can only feel empathy for somebody who knows he's going to die. My father used to say that watching his buddies die in Italy had been less hard than watching them watch themselves die. "I swear to you, Al, in their eyes they were begging for their mothers. They were like helpless kids." But for the old man, my grandfather, there was no time between his last thought and his death. I must have convinced Leitner, because he didn't pursue it. He just laid out the chess game in front of us on a stool. I took advantage of that little pause to ask him what he did on weekends. I could sense he was reluctant to answer a patient about a personal matter. But his reticence didn't hold out for long. "I've just bought a 1957 Harley-Davidson and I ride it along the 1." I couldn't get over it. He realized he had scored a point.

"What model?"

"The XL Sportster."

"What color?"

"Two colors, cream and matte gold."

"The first 900cc engine with an overhead valve. Transmission in the engine casting."

He must have sensed the touch of excitement in my voice. "You sound like a real enthusiast."

I thought this over and said, "Interested. I'm interested. But an enthusiast, no. I imagine an enthusiast is someone who's carried away by a subject. No subject could carry me for long, I'm too heavy, it'd get out of breath. I'm very happy to talk about bikes with you right now, but if we went on too long about them, I'd end up getting bored and want to change the subject. Do you see?"

"I see."

All the same, I told him about my trip on the Indian Chief before my arrest. I also told him about the bike my father had brought from Camp Harrison to Helena before the end of the war. A 1934 single cylinder. I added that I'd really like to get it back one day if I left this hospital, not forgetting my Indian Chief, which must have been rotting in a police depot. I wouldn't give up. I asked him straight out if he couldn't pick it up for me, seeing as how I didn't know anybody else who could do it. He told me that might be difficult, but he promised he'd see what he could do. We sat there for a good long while, talking about bikes and the wide open spaces. I told him I missed both of them, but what hurt me the most, so much that I sometimes cried about it, was to think that I was better off locked up in here. I told him how, when I was eleven or twelve, my mother had forced me to work as a blacksmith's assistant on a ranch twenty miles from Helena. A horse's feet are like the hands of a woman, they tell you a lot about their owner. He knew a fair amount about the subject too, seeing as how his grandfather had raised quarter horses in northern California, not very far from Mount Shasta, the very place where I had swapped my grandfather's station wagon for that wonderful Indian Chief. I said that made quite a lot of things we had in common. Of course the big difference between us was that I had killed my grandparents and he hadn't, I was sick and he wasn't. What I didn't mention obviously—it would have seemed a bit obscene—was that, to judge by the ring he wore on his ring finger, he must have a wife at home and maybe even kids. Whereas, even though I wasn't much more than fifteen, something deep inside told me I never would. I saw the impossibility of it all rising in front of me like a grizzly bear in a forest in Alaska. Not that it made me feel sad. Any more than a homosexual realizing he'll never see a vagina in his life. That's the way it is, why fret about it?

We started playing chess and he explained the rules of the game. Not the rules of chess. He told me it was a good idea to talk between moves and take all the time I wanted to make them. A game could last an hour or a week, he didn't care. During that time, I was supposed to tell him about my life, the whole of my life. From time to time, he might decide to interrupt and tell me a story that had a connection with my problem. And then, as a guarantee of his goodwill in this adventure we were going to share for the next few months, he agreed to pick up my Indian Chief from the Oregon State Police, that is, if my father hadn't already done it. To cut a long story short, two months later he told me, a tad annoyed, that the bike had been sold to cover some of the legal costs of my case.

18

Imagine you're a novelist, how would you tell your story?" I'd never read a novel all the way through for the reason you know. But all the same I'd started a good few, often more out of curiosity than anything else and, I admit, to convince myself that plenty of books weren't worth the effort of going any further. I'd noticed that Americans novelists often started with their family background. As if you couldn't talk about a tree without mentioning the roots. I asked Leitner if I had to follow chronological order and he was categorical: "You're under no obligation of any kind." All the same I did what everyone does. I moved a pawn and we were off. He had a notebook by his side but he didn't use it often. I told him that when I was a child I'd had plenty of time to think about life and death for reasons I would go into later. I know people are adamant that the two things are completely different, and you can understand why. Even when I was a kid, I was fascinated by how much adults prized life and how scared they were of death. Even the most religious of them. I remembered one of our neighbors, a nice woman but so fat her children sometimes had to take her around in a wheelbarrow. She was really religious. An evangelist pastor often visited her. She had what you'd call a pretty crummy life—no money, no husband, restricted movements, three young kids including a daughter who was autistic—and she couldn't even take a quiet breather because she breathed like a bull. Sometimes in spring, when the weather started to get better, her kids would put her out in the garden. She'd stay there for two or three hours without doing anything. On the other side of the fence, we'd try to stay out of her field of vision because she'd collar you and inflict these endless monologues on you. One time she caught me by chance and kept me there for a whole hour. Caring about other people was too much for her, but contemplating the disaster of her own life was an inexhaustible topic. She told me about her fear of death. Because I was only about eleven, she must have thought I wouldn't understand what she was talking about. "I'm afraid of nothingness, Al, whatever my life is like down here, it's better than nothingness. There's nothing after death, we're supposed to have a soul that makes us different than the rest of the universe but the flies eat it in a few days." As she was speaking, a big black fly landed on her damp, greasy skin. That fly gorging itself on that grotesque woman was the perfect image of an unequal struggle. She kept trying to chase it away, but her gestures were too slow because of how heavy her arms were. That fear of death ruined her life, and I was the only person around her who could understand her. I thought maybe I should kill her, to relieve her suffering, then I told myself it was none of my business and anyway nobody would realize I'd acted out of generosity. I'd gotten this far with my story when I started to feel incredibly weary. Leitner was surprised.

"I won't go so far as to say that I envied that woman for being afraid of death, which is something I've never felt, but I did sense that it was a potential source of pleasure. No more than that."

I started again as if nothing had happened, changing the subject to the size of my father's feet.

"My father looks like John Wayne. He's a lot taller than Wayne, but from his face you'd say they were brothers. You can see they're both good, brave men. Above all they walk the same way. I wondered why for a long time before I discovered they both have small feet for their height. For example

I'm seven feet tall and take size 14 shoes. My father was about 6' 10" and only took size 8. Can you imagine size 8? It's like walking on stumps."

I could see that Leitner was pleased with how talkative I was. A patient who speaks without being asked is certainly better than the opposite.

"My father killed more people than I did. At least thirty, and he never even boasted about it."

"But it was for a good cause," Leitner said. "Someone once wrote that the state has a monopoly on the legitimate use of violence. I also killed people, Al, in Normandy in 1944."

He didn't seem any prouder of it than my father.

"You think that, in two years, I could enlist for Vietnam?"

"Why would you want to do that?"

"Maybe killing with the blessing of my country might rehabilitate me. That's how my father started. He'd stolen a motorcycle near Los Angeles and cussed the cops who came to arrest him. They found out he was kind of a deserter, because he'd run out on his job in a factory making war planes. He'd been working as an electrician at McDonnell, installing electrical systems in B-25s. He'd had an itch to take to the road and so he decided to take some time off. Since he couldn't afford a Harley, he stole one and rode up the 101 as far as Olympia. He hadn't been planning to cross the border or anything, but because they suspected him of desertion, they gave him three years. A few weeks after he went inside, he was offered the chance to join one of the Special Forces brigades that used guys like him. That's how he got out of prison in Los Angeles. The military police took him on a train to Helena. My father said that when he arrived he thought Fort Harrison was like a movie set. Rows of wooden huts on a vast flat plain surrounded by threatening mountains. Most of the men stationed there had been in trouble with the law, but he soon found out that none of them had committed a murder or a serious crime.

They were just petty crooks, street fighters, and my father liked them. Because of his size, nobody ever thought to cross him, but I remember him telling me about his gut fear of violence. He was so afraid, he'd vowed to overcome it, convinced you couldn't live a decent life if you're always scared. That bunch of roughnecks eventually knuckled down to training. It was meant to turn them into an elite troop, one of the most highly skilled commando units in the United States Army. A winter spent climbing the Rockies, skiing down between the trees, learning to fly light planes and use all the guns under the sun made them fit for duty. That was all my father ever told me. I know he was sent to Italy. But too many of his buddies died and he'd lost any desire to boast about his experiences. But to me, he was a hero, there was no doubt about it.

"I never really liked Montana. The winters there are colder than the grave and the summers are incredibly hot."

I'd gotten this far in my story when I realized I was going to checkmate Leitner.

19

My mother was born on a farm in Montana and grew up there with her three sisters. I never knew my grandparents on my mother's side, they died in an accident at the end of the war. My grandfather was of German descent, from somewhere in Bavaria. It was his grandfather who had left Germany for Montana. My grandparents died because my grandfather was drunk. He'd downed something like ten pints of beer that day. They went off the road at a hairpin bend and the car did about twenty somersaults before coming to a halt. It happened a few weeks after my parents met one Saturday night in a bar in Helena. He was there with three of his pals, two of them war veterans like him. They'd been knocking it back and my father felt attracted by this tall woman. She was just over six feet, and normal men shied away from her because of her height. I think my mother made a beeline for my father because the chance of meeting a man eight inches taller than her, who'd make her look a tiny little thing when he had his arm around her, wouldn't come along again in a hurry. My father didn't have any particular type when it came to women. You try to keep things open, and you end up sleeping with a woman who's the spitting image of your mother."

Leitner laughed out loud when I said that.

"Where did you get that rule from?"

I thought hard for moment or two, but couldn't find an answer.

It's true, though. Both my mother and my grandmother

were tall women who bossed their men about once they'd nailed them. I saw the way my mother was with her new guy. After my father left, I thought she was going to go crazy from the loneliness. Then she met a bank clerk. You should have seen how she talked to him at the beginning. I was forced to hear their conversation from my bedroom in the cellar. She'd say a whole bunch of nice things to him, and then she'd do a striptease and tell him to take her like a bitch. I don't know if he took her like a bitch or not, all I know is that the ceiling above my head shook like a wooden bridge when a train's going over it. Once she'd hooked the guy, though, she wasn't the same woman anymore.

I was surprised to learn that my mother had been relieved when her parents died. She had admitted that during one of the many quarrels she'd start with my father as soon as the door of their bedroom closed behind them. She got frustrated because she couldn't get a reaction from my father, so she told him that her own father used to feel up his daughters. Alone on his farm in Montana with five girls, the old man must have lost his marbles. My mother never let him, but her youngest sister had had to take it all. Even let herself be sodomized, my mother said. I didn't know what that meant at the time, and I just had to hear my father say, "Quiet, the boy will hear you," to rush straight to the dictionary. The definition there was pretty obscure, as if the dictionary people were embarrassed having to define the word, but I understood that it was a more animal kind of penetration . . .

"I don't think that kind of penetration is so common in the animal world, Al, it's quite specific to our species and the way it exercises power."

He must have had the passing impression that he'd gone a bit far in his explanation to a boy of sixteen, but I immediately saw it was wiped out by the certainty that he could talk to me like an adult.

The way I'd placed my queen, Leitner had only one solution: to castle. But I knew that within three moves he was done for.

When my mother married my father, she'd married a hero who had made her pregnant with my older sister. She found herself living with a two-bit electrician in a nothing construction company, who spent his free time hunting and playing cards with his buddies. He'd play poker, always with the same guys, Bruce Gaberty and Andrew Stamp, two Special Forces veterans who, like him, never reminisced about the war. My father needed to have them near him, even if they didn't talk. I mean, they did talk, about lots of other things, but never about the war. When Jo Benford, the fourth guy, started in on the subject with all the talkativeness of a guy who's done three years in a cushy desk job at HQ, he'd run straight into a conspiracy of silence. They played every Saturday evening in the cellar, next to my bedroom. In general, they joked a lot but when all at once everything stopped, it was because Benford had mentioned the war. The cellar was the one place my mother allowed them to play cards. The house belonged to her. She had bought it with her share of the proceeds from selling my grandparents' ranch after their accidental death. At least two or three times a day, she'd be sure to mention that it was her house, which was kind of humiliating for my father. And she never let a day go by without reminding him what a disappointment he was to her. She wanted to leave Montana, she wanted him to go back into the aeronautics industry and climb the ladder rung by rung so that they could have a real social life in a nice house on the west coast. My father would answer that he wasn't ready to leave Montana, that he needed its wide open spaces to survive. "To survive what, you dumb-ass?" And when he didn't reply, she'd go right on, "If I'd known I was going to marry a crybaby, always mooning over his dead buddies, I wouldn't have come anywhere near you, I'd have given you a wide berth, I wouldn't have given you three children, I wouldn't have sacrificed my ambitions." My father never reacted to her insults. The only times I felt he was starting to boil over was when my mother would go up to him, looking like she was going to hit him. He'd be rooted to the spot, and he'd look down at his feet, just his feet. And I was dying to tell him, "Lift your head, Dad, lift your head, damn it." But he'd stay there without moving like a little boy waiting for his mother to calm down. She never dared hit him, though. She was quite capable of doing it, but she had no idea what he might have done if he was pushed to the edge. The reason he left one morning without warning was to stop himself killing her. He'd held out for twenty years without raising a hand to her. He'd preferred to avoid her. I'm even more convinced he would have killed my mother if she'd raised her hand to him in front of me. In front of my sisters, she might have gotten away with it, because my father was no fool, he knew my sisters were just a couple of stupid bitches. Whereas I was the only person he loved, even though he found it hard to show it. I often felt that he was kind of ashamed he wasn't a better father. He wasn't a happy man, that's for sure, he really wasn't a happy man. Hard to say what was bugging him all that time. He gave the impression he lived with ghosts that hardly ever left him alone.

I sensed that Leitner was really pleased but that he wanted to slow me down, that everything was going too quickly, that by pouring it all out in one go we might break the most fragile part of it. To give him a way out, I checkmated him. He couldn't get over it. I'm sure it was the first time he'd ever been beaten by a boy who wasn't yet sixteen. A convict had thrashed a civilian. Instead of taking it bad, I could see he was delighted. The man had a deep respect for intelligence, even though in my case you could say it was a little bit depraved. And then he must have had it up to the neck with all these guys he had to deal with every day who never said a word. He took off his glasses, wiped them for the longest time, and then put them down on the table.

I remember that moment distinctly. It's engraved in my memory as one of the few moments of real joy, enthusiasm and hope I've ever had the luck to experience.

The session was almost over but Leitner wanted to know how my reading had gone.

"What book did you choose?"

"Dostoy—"

"*Crime and Punishment*. I know, that's the book the librarian loves to give the new arrivals in your wing. Did you manage to concentrate?"

"I think so."

"And the bad thoughts?"

"They waited."

"Can you say something about your reading so far?"

"A couple of sentences stuck in my mind. 'At that time, he didn't yet believe in the reality of his daydreams, and merely let himself be tantalized by their despicable but seductive audacity.' And then, a bit later: 'Despite himself he had become accustomed to considering "the despicable dream" as an undertaking to be realized . . . ' That's well expressed, isn't it?"

Leitner smiled, made a note, then looked at his watch. We had gone well over the time allotted for the session.

"The passage about the alcoholic in the tavern too. My parents both drink, but not so they become different people or collapse or anything like that. I'd say when they drink they become just a little bit more themselves."

20

A t first, nobody came and sat down next to me at lunch. It was as if the other inmates were trying to keep me at a safe distance. Stafford had been eyeing me hesitantly for a while. He finally stood up and came and sat down. He was holding his head up high, trying to make himself look good. He was between forty and sixty. What made me think it was more likely sixty was his wrinkled neck, with folds of skin hanging down like on a chicken. It was obvious he wanted to make friends with me, which is the kind of thing that immediately puts me on the defensive. I just sat upright on my chair and looked straight ahead. He ended up tugging at the sleeve of my uniform.

"Don't you want to talk, son?"

I took my time, shoveling a big spoonful of mash into my mouth and slowly swallowing it. Then I looked down at him and said, "Talking's the easiest thing in the world. Everybody talks, everybody shoots the breeze, you think it's never going to end."

He nodded. But not once: ten times, twenty times. And then he asked me what I was in here for, in a low voice as if it was a state secret. When I told him I'd bumped off my grandparents, he seemed doubtful and even disappointed. He'd been expecting better.

"How old would you say I am?"

I paused before answering. Seeing all the effort he was making to be nice to me, I said about fifty.

He started laughing like a man possessed. "I was born a year before the start of this century."

That was an easy calculation to make. I remembered Leitner's advice. None of the guys in this wing were really a danger to me, but I had nothing to gain from making friends with these perverts. I had nothing in common with the rapists, the crazies who didn't distinguish between a woman, a man, a child or a goat as long as they could bang it. At the thought that I could be confused with guys like that, a dull anger rose inside me. That was the best thing they could do if they really wanted to make me feel guilty.

I went back to my room. At that hour I was supposed to be taking part in a group session but they didn't yet know which group to put me in. I stayed on my bed for about an hour and a half, reading. I lay on my back, looking up through the skylight at the sky. It was the same blue sky every day, flecked with high white clouds. I was gradually getting into my book. I'd held back a little at first, but then let myself go.

A guard interrupted my reading to take me to the laundry. It was at the other end of the hospital, and to get there you had to go down a mile of corridors painted piss yellow. I knew a lot depended on that laundry. That was where they would judge my aptitude for work, and therefore my suitability for rehabilitation. I'd dirtied my own linen, now I was being asked to wash it, which seemed logical.

Two thousand sheets passed through the laundry every week as well as at least a good thousand uniforms of different sizes, not to mention the underwear. It was a huge piece of organization. Some inmates were in charge of collecting the dirty linen, others of stuffing it into big industrial washing machines, others of drying, folding and redistribution. Along with the kitchens, it was the activity that required the most manpower. There were two or three patients on the management side of things but you could tell they were just there to support the other supervisors, who all came from among the guards. After all, apart from me, and I say this in all sincerity, all the men being kept there were really sick people. You could understand that, when it came to such serious tasks, they weren't entrusted to patients. It was my intention to change all that. At least until I entered the laundry, where I thought I was going to faint. The smell of washing mixed with the damp of a Turkish bath reminded me of the washroom in the house in Montana. I felt so bad I almost turned right around again. My determination to prove I didn't belong in this community of crazies made me change my mind. The only way I could still show that I'd been sane when I committed those two crimes was to behave at all times like the normal man that I was. At that precise moment, I'd happily have spent twenty years in prison as long as they recognized that I'd been responsible for my actions.

I had killed the old lady because of that screechy voice of hers that started up every time I got any further from the house than a limit she'd set arbitrarily, which corresponded to that part of the land she'd completely domesticated, apart from the moles and rabbits. The worst of it was that I didn't even have any desire to get away from that fucking house. I felt suffocated when I did. But that she should forbid me to do something I didn't even allow myself, that was something that required a drastic solution. I have to admit when I fired, I wasn't thinking about all that. I really wasn't. I don't know if it's true that I have a higher IQ than Einstein, but I have to admit that I didn't spend a lot of time thinking during the first part of my life, I was too busy struggling with thoughts I hadn't initiated. When I started thinking again about these things, surrounded by the detergent smells of the laundry, I was filled with an inner anger. At times like that, I could kill someone, but I didn't see who, so my anger abated in a few seconds. The guard who had brought me introduced me to one of the laundry managers, who took his time explaining my job. I remembered the little jobs I'd done when I was younger. The people who'd employed me then were always surprised by how quickly I picked things up. I'd helped a blacksmith on a ranch, I'd branded cattle, and I had sold newspapers on a busy street in Helena in the middle of winter, where it was so cold you could hear the sinister sound of the rocks in the mountains cracking. To toughen me up, my mother had forbidden me to wear gloves. I must have been about eleven. I remember an old man who made a detour to buy a paper from me on the pretext that, in the condition I was in, the news had to be fresher than a fish frozen on a line. My mother always said my father's approach to bringing me up would turn me into a girl. That was when she was sober. But when she was drunk, she'd scream at him that he was turning me into a big fat fairy. I could never understand what my weight had to do with my future situation. My hatred of Montana was certainly born out of that time when my mother made the climate even harder to bear. When it was cold, she made sure I got even colder than anybody else. She'd send me to school in a shirt with an unlined linen jacket, with no gloves and no hat. Waiting for the school bus became an ordeal. If someone ever told her off about it, she would reply that I was never sick, unlike those kids who wore too many thick clothes. In the hottest part of the summer, she'd take advantage of the heat to give me really tiring chores to do.

I never knew what homosexuality was until I got to that hospital. A few months after my arrival, when I was already in a position of responsibility in the laundry, I caught three guys indulging in that kind of thing between piles of linen in the storeroom. I had the impression that one of them hadn't totally consented, so I went in and broke it up. They all left in different directions, without a word and without showing any shame. This episode didn't arouse anything in me, either desire or revulsion.

My first job was folding the sheets. There were ten of us at work, in teams of two. My partner was a sad-eyed old man who smiled all the time. He wasn't very tall, and he had a bald skull lined with blue veins. When the folding was done, he came toward me with a ridiculous little dance step. I think he was a friend of Stafford, the guy who'd tried to befriend me. This guy was as crazy as Stafford was—apparently—normal. I felt bad when he told me he'd also killed his grandparents at my age, well before he was arrested for raping minors, a charge he denied because, according to him, not only were these minors consenting but they had provoked him. The medication was having an effect on him, you could see it by his sunken eyes and his complexion, which was sometimes paler than a corpse. I took things in hand when I realized that it was taking three times longer than necessary to carry out our share of the work. I pushed him along a little. He must have thought about hitting back but my size and his medication stopped him in his tracks. Over the next few days, he behaved with me like a stray dog that's latched on to a new master. I was quite proud of my ascendancy. It's thanks to him that I decided never to take the pills I was handed every night before they turned the lights out.

I was open about that with Leitner, I told him I didn't want to end up like all those ghosts wandering around the hospital. He assured me that the only purpose of the molecule I was being given was to relax me and to avoid panic attacks linked to my guilt for what I had done.

"I often felt guilty in the past, but that was when I didn't know why."

He didn't want to make a big thing out of the medication, and he left me free to take it or not. But the question of guilt seemed to be on his mind.

"Don't you ever feel sad about your grandfather?"

"I've tried, but I don't see any reason to be sad. Why do you ask me that?"

He lit a pipe, which I'd never seen him do before and which didn't suit his face, passed his hand through his hair and then said, evasively and with a touch of mockery, "My job is to ask questions, lots of questions. I don't always know why I ask them and I never know when the answer will come. Sometimes it comes when I'm least expecting it. You see, when you tell me about your grandfather, I think about another grandfather. I didn't know him but I took an interest in his life. This was a man who lived in the Midwest and took care of his grandson when he was a child. The child had been abandoned by his father, and his mother didn't see much of him because she drove a truck and was always on the road. Then she took up with another man—a good man—and the boy went to live with her. He'd become a disturbed teenager. One day, for no apparent reason, he killed his mother and her new husband. He was later sentenced to death and executed. His grandfather wasn't present at the execution, he died a few days later, of grief. Do you think the boy should also have killed his grandfather to save him all that pain?"

"I think there was only one person he should have killed, that son of a bitch his father, who abandoned him. And anyway there's no comparison, my grandfather never took care of me. To be honest, I didn't know him very well. He bought me a Winchester .22 for my birthday, but that wasn't to please me, he just wanted to use me to kill pests, because my grandmother was obsessed with the moles and rabbits. The farm stretched over about a hundred and twenty-five acres, but she was obsessed with the twenty thousand square feet of garden she'd planted around the house. If I'd believed that my father really cared about his parents, I might have thought twice about shooting them. I'm sure he was shocked but now he doesn't care. I know I scare him, but I'm sure he doesn't hold it against me. He's killed people, he knows what it's like, he knows sometimes you have no choice, if you don't want to die yourself.

And why would I have swapped my life for the old girl's? Why? To get back to the young man you talked about, I think you have to be really crazy to hit the wrong target like that. He must have lost his mind."

"And you, Al, do you have the feeling you lost your mind at some point?"

"Send me back to prison if you like but I've never lost my mind. I have to tell you, Dr. Leitner, it makes me sick that I wasn't sent to prison. They simply dismissed me with a wave of the hand, like I was some poor kid who wasn't responsible for what he did. It's the same old story, you know? My mother looked at me like a horse looking at its own shit, my sisters saw me as an obstacle between them and the refrigerator, my grandmother as her whipping boy and my grandfather as the person who was going to cause him problems with his wife. After living through all that, there were reasons to feel guilty, to tell myself I must really be a monster for everyone to treat me like that, even though my father tried to reach out to me whenever my mother let him. You see, I know a hell of a lot about guilt. So when I say I have no reason to feel guilty for what I did, I'd like people to accept that."

Whenever Leitner's eyes became even bluer than usual, it meant he was really worried. "There's no question of sending you back to prison, Al. My objective is to allow you to re-enter society sooner or later, when we think you're no longer a danger to it. As long as you remain convinced you were right to kill your grandmother and relieve your grandfather of his life, everyone will think of you as a pathological case. We haven't known each other for very long, Al, but there's something in you that makes you likeable. Get it into your head, society will give you another chance the day you feel guilty for what you did, the day you have empathy for your grandparents. Without guilt, there's no civilization, Al, we become animals again. I already told you, only the state, in other words, society, can justify killing in the interests of the community. But society will always think of you as a criminal or a sick person if you give yourself permission to kill. It'll get rid of you one way or another, you can rely on that. Society normally has a representative in the brain of every human being, which sets the limits of what's admissible. Its representative didn't do its job in yours. You don't know the difference between right and wrong, I'm sure because nobody ever did right by you, or taught you. As a result, the border between the two is porous. I'm going to try to rebuild it, and you're going to help me in that direction. Your reason was altered by the way your family destroyed your emotional center. Reason and emotion go together, if one of the two gets disconnected, that's when the trouble starts. That's what happened to you. Now, tell me, you claim that what triggered your act was your grandmother's voice when you went beyond the garden. Why? Did that remind you of something? Or rather, no, let's look at it from another angle. You told me you sometimes felt a strong sense of guilt in your childhood. Guilt about what?"

I remembered vague but violent feelings of anxiety that grabbed hold of me at the top of the stairs leading up from the cellar to the first floor of the house, where the others were allowed to live. As soon as I entered all that light and space, I had the feeling I wasn't in my place anymore. There was an incredible amount of space around the house. I was really drawn to it, but as soon as I surrendered, I felt that anxiety in my limbs, along with a sense of suffocation.

As well as my parents' room, there were three bedrooms on the first floor, one for each of my sisters and a guest room that was never used, because there were never any guests. But it had to stay free. The upper floor was used as a loft. I sometimes went up there to hide.

The room where I'd been stuck since my birth wasn't as small as all that, although it's true that a child sees everything as being bigger than it is. In some ways, it was too big for a child. It occupied a good third of the cellar. I don't know if you can call it a bedroom, given that there was no separation between it and the boiler. A big gas boiler that was always on, because when it wasn't heating the house, it was still heating the water. It would come on every hour for a good fifteen minutes. Through its open firebox I could see the fires of hell spitting away. Although they taught us in catechism classes that God would decide at the end of our lives whether we were bound for heaven or hell, I had the feeling that when it came to me, everything had already been decided. I opened up about that to the priest who looked after the small Catholic community of Helena. He was tall, a good man, I guess, as far as I knew about goodness. He visited my mother one day when she wasn't expecting it. She took it very badly because she didn't like surprises. She was scathing at first, saying that even an envoy of God has to let people's know he's coming. The priest wouldn't let himself be intimated by my mother's size or her low voice, which was slurred by booze and tobacco. My mother thought he'd come to complain about my behavior in catechism classes, so before he could even open his mouth she told him that I was a child who carried evil in him. The priest replied that he doubted it, then came to the real point of his visit. She looked at him for a long time in silence, long enough to turn into an understanding and open-minded woman. She told him that putting me so close to the boiler was meant to remind me where I'd end up if I wasn't a better person. Before he could ask her permission to take a look, she apologized and said she couldn't show him my room, because I kept it incredibly untidy. Then she stood up and dismissed him without even offering him a cup of coffee. After he left I went off to hide because I knew she was going to bawl me out. But when dinnertime came, she turned on my father, and that overshadowed the anger she had intended for me. The following day I punished her. My mother loved cats. I think they're the only things I ever saw her love. She was proud of them because they won prizes at competitions. Toward my sisters, who were neither cats nor men, she had a kind of benign indifference, which consisted in letting them stuff themselves while pretending to encourage them not to eat too much. She had a long-haired she-cat, a highly prized kind, which she'd let breed. She had kept one kitten and sold the others. The day after the priest's visit, coming back from school, I found myself alone in the house. I grabbed the kitten. It clung to my hands with its little claws as if it had an idea of what was in store for it. I was torn between the pity it inspired in me by its innocence and an uncontrollable need to punish my mother. But into the boiler it went. I really enjoyed it when my mother sat in front of me, gave me one of her pitiless stares, and asked me what had happened to the kitten. I didn't look away but didn't say anything, savoring the silence. She was tempted to beat me to get me to talk, then she gave up and poured herself a glass of scotch. That was the first and last time I incinerated one of her prize kittens alive. Six months later, I cut the head off of one of them, buried the body and kept the head in my room in a box for bicycle tire repair patches. I don't know how that box got in my room when I didn't have a bicycle. My mother regularly searched my room. She'd go through it from top to bottom like the guards in prison—nobody knows what they're looking for but they must know. She came across the box with the kitten's head rotting in it and started screaming. At first it was anger, then despair at the fact that she'd given birth to a torturer. But as so often, the worse her anger got, the more she distanced herself from me. She never came and screamed in my face. Curiously, this event brought me closer to my sister, the younger of the two.

At this point, I'll take a pause in my story. All these things I'm telling you may not be an exact reflection of what I told

Leitner. A sixteen-year-old kid, even one as advanced as I must have been, doesn't give up his secrets easily, doesn't have confession in the blood, you understand. There were times he really had to drag it out of me, times when my memories came out in such a jumble that he had to make an effort to reconstruct them chronologically. What I liked about Leitner was that he didn't judge me. I never heard him make a moral statement about any of my actions. The story of the decapitation did startle him, though, even though he must already have known about it because it was mentioned in the statement my mother made to the police after I was arrested. In it she'd said that she hadn't been surprised by what I did because I'd once cut the head off a cat. He stood up and started walking around his office. I noticed for the first time that the window of his office looked out on open country and that he never locked it even though it did have a lock. But I had no desire to run away. Even if they'd thrown open the doors of the hospital and rolled out the red carpet for me, I wouldn't have wanted to leave the place, because then I wouldn't have had anyone to talk to. By the time he sat down again, his face was all lit up with satisfaction, and what he was saying he was saying for himself.

"She makes you lose your head. She makes you lose your head, you cut off the head of what matters most to her. You make her lose her head. You're even. You start by throwing the kitten in the boiler. That's a straightforward reaction to the fact that she makes you sleep next to the boiler. But that's not enough. You cut the head off her cat and leave it in a box in your room, knowing perfectly well she'll find it sooner or later. Are you following me?"

I was following him.

"It's symbolic. You kill her cat and cut its head off, because you don't dare do that to your mother. Did you ever think about cutting your mother's head off?"

"No, never."

"Yet she's the one who makes you lose your head." He stopped to think for a while. "Up until that point, you're in control of everything. Things start to go wrong when you move to your grandparents' house. You don't know your grandmother well. How many times had you seen her before?"

"Twice."

"But did you feel close to her? Did you feel any affection for her?"

"I don't think I've ever felt any affection for anyone."

"Not even your father?"

"Oh, sure."

"Your grandmother reminds you of your mother. She's pretty much the same kind of domineering personality. It's no surprise your father married your mother. It's because she's so like *his* mother. And when he finally realizes that, he leaves her, he gets a divorce, because he can't stand the idea of sleeping with his mother. For you, your grandmother is the model your father married when he married your mother. Unconsciously, you blame her for your parents' marriage. Are you following me?"

I was still following him, although, in all modesty, I wasn't learning much.

"You blame your grandmother for your birth. The real responsibility is hers. What you can just about take from your mother, because she's your mother, you can't take from your grandmother. It's now that the idea of killing her takes root. What stopped you from killing your mother doesn't stop you from killing your grandmother. The door's wide open, all you're waiting for is the signal. The signal comes when you hear her voice as you're going beyond the limits of the garden. The limits of the garden remind you of that other place where you were kept under a kind of house arrest: the cellar. There's no question about it anymore. You have to act now. It's her or you. It's her life against your sanity. By killing her you're avoiding insanity. Which means you aren't insane. But you aren't responsible either because you were driven by an insane impulse. But you weren't performing some kind of charitable act either, Al. You can't take the law into your own hands, especially when other people's justice isn't capable of understanding your gesture and, in any case, like they say: 'Thou shalt not kill.'"

He breathed as if he had done the hardest part. He took off his glasses, held them up to the light to see if the lenses were dirty, and put them down in front of him. He moved back and stretched his legs.

"In our country, people are fascinated by their geographical roots. They'd be better off if they were fascinated by their psychological roots. The beginning of your story, Al, goes back a long way. What made your maternal grandfather a pervert ready to commit incest, we'll never know. But he's probably the reason your mother hates men. She could have kept her distance from them, but no, she prefers to get close to them so that she can grind them down. Your father got caught in her net because his mother had predisposed him to it. She'd hounded him all his life. As for you, you were her creature, her thing, she could do whatever she liked with you. You had to defend yourself against the crushing weight of that family tradition. How? By cutting the branches. It's a miracle you didn't put a complete end to that dynasty of perversion, Al. I've known cases where the youngest child killed everybody before killing himself. It was as if in some strange way he was trying to purge the whole bloodline."

He was silent for a while.

"Be prepared for the possibility that your father will have other children. Crossing his bloodline with your mother's was a disaster for him. His son ended up killing his own mother. It's like a pincer movement, cutting him free from both his parents and his offspring at the same time. You describe your sisters as dull creatures, so the war hero will have to start again from scratch to survive. I know it's a little brutal, Al, but you'll never see your father again. When he got rid of you in Los Angeles by sending you to your grandparents, he was starting to protect himself. He couldn't bear to have the consequences of his disastrous marriage right there under his nose. He knows it's not your fault, but seeing you suffocates him."

He stopped to think for a moment, as if something was bothering him.

"I'm sure you thought about killing yourself before you left for Los Angeles."

"Yes, twice."

"How many times did you think about killing your mother?"

"Also twice."

"Did you think about killing yourself immediately after planning to kill your mother?"

"Yes, right away."

Then he brought the session to an abrupt end as if everything had gone too fast. The chess game hadn't started. Satisfaction was written all over his face. I felt excluded. I wondered if understanding made any difference to my situation.

In the following sessions, it was as if all the essential things had already been said. But we continued to unravel my story. My relationship with the youngest of my sisters interested him. She would join me in private games. An old barber's chair stored in the house, we had no idea why, became a makeshift electric chair for us. We'd take turns in trying our forearms to the chair with electric wire. We used a transformer we found among my father's equipment to get the current moving and gradually increase the intensity. Pushed to the maximum, it sent through enough juice to knock back a bull. That way we tested our resistance to pain. The dial went from 1 to 6. Every time one of the two of us did something wrong that our mother found out about, we'd punish each other. The discovery of the mummified head of the prize kitten earned me a level 6 electrocution. We both knew I could withstand that intensity. The temptation was stronger than reason. I sat down in the chair, and my sister carefully tied my wrists. She held the transformer in her hands and I could sense the real pleasure that gave her. Suddenly, she started the current and I fainted. She took fright and immediately went up to see my mother, who just then was talking to some cops who'd come over to question her about a drunk-driving incident. She came down to the cellar, in no hurry at all, and seeing that I had woken up, said she was going to punish me. I had just been in the electric chair, what more could I fear? But she never talked about it again, as if risking your life on morbid games wasn't worth bothering about. She was more worried about that drunk-driving thing. She'd probably have to pay a heavy fine, and she was afraid for her reputation. She always liked to make out she was a respectable woman.

21

From session to session, Leitner seemed more and more confident about my case. A small panel met to decide on whether I could go back to school. I had to sit in on it and be ready to answer any questions they had for me. But they didn't have any, they were convinced by Leitner's presentation. The thing that bothered them was the possibility that I might be violent toward my classmates. Deciding on this was a big responsibility for them. What if they gave their consent and ten days after my admission I shot a dozen pupils just because I didn't like their faces? Leitner was categorical: "Al Kenner killed because of an uncontrollable impulse connected to his family history. Nothing predisposes him to kill outside this context, he doesn't want to and he has no taste for it." The other shrinks brought up the first verdict that had been passed about me, that I was a paranoid schizophrenic. "I don't think we can give a name to Al Kenner's case, or confine him to one particular pathology. I think he killed to defend himself against psychosis, in reaction to a totally destructive family environment. But he isn't insane, and he's of above average intelligence. He'll stay here until he's been taught not to kill any more of his family. I really don't see what would drive him to attack a person outside the family context. I've been working on his case for several months and there's nothing that would suggest that he's a true schizophrenic in the sense of constructing a fantasy world. I've seen a young man with a strong grounding in reality and a genuine ability to analyze his own actions. As for the paranoia, it can't be denied that he's distrustful of other people, which is understandable when we know how hostile they've been to him since he was born, but there's no persecution syndrome as such."

There are two ways to be cautious in life, either you do things cautiously or you don't do anything at all, and I could see that the shrinks were leaning toward the second solution. But Leitner insisted that the object of my incarceration had always been rehabilitation.

"Kenner has been away from school for nearly eight months. We can't afford to keep him out of education for much longer. The most terrible thing that could happen to a superior mind like his would be to be held back socially by a poor academic record. His intelligence needs to have something real to work with. If you leave him here, working in the laundry, he'll become the boss of it, that's for certain. And then? Don't forget he's only sixteen. This hospital has been of benefit to him so far, in the sense that he's become aware of himself and his mental chains. We're going to enter a phase where his incarceration, if it doesn't have an educational component, will become negative. The bad company he'll fall into here will win out over therapy. I'll even be very honest with you. If it were up to me alone, I'd release him within the next six to nine months as long as he's totally prohibited from seeing any member of his family"—"Or what's left of it," one of the shrinks, who'd been staring at me since the beginning of the hearing, said with heavy irony—"and in particular his mother. Whatever happens, I'm categorical about this, he must never see his mother again. Ever."

"But that's not the question right now, Leitner," retorted one of the members of the panel, who looked like a wise old Indian.

"Would you be prepared to sign a paper stating categorically that this young man is no longer dangerous?" asked another of the shrinks, who I'd twice caught dozing off and who'd only really woken up for the conclusion, which involved him.

Leitner said he would. The panel put the matter to a vote. They needed to be unanimous. I think one or two were tempted to postpone my going back to school, but they ended up giving their approval.

I went back to school three weeks later, which was how long it took for the paperwork to go through. A male nurse would take me there every morning and come to get me every evening, which made me look like some kind of big shot with his own driver. Seeing the California sky again was a bit dazzling at first. All those months of gloom and artificial light had affected my eyesight. The nurse wasn't very talkative on the way. Even though he was a big guy, with muscles straining at the buttons of his shirt, he must have been worried about whether he'd be able to overpower me if he had to. The cattle grazing peacefully in the vast enclosed meadows seemed unreal to me. The ride lasted a good twenty minutes, during which the thought of going back to the free world never crossed my mind. Leitner had given me the keys, but they weren't enough to return to society for the moment. Contrary to what he claimed, I felt quite capable of killing anyone who got in my way and tried to deny me as an individual, wipe me from the records of mankind, or persuade me that I had no purpose in living, because once again it came down to my own survival. I didn't want to talk about this with Leitner for fear of spoiling his optimism, and besides he should have known better than I did whether or not I was capable of responding to a trigger. It was an expression he used often, the final barrier between normal people and guys like me. He claimed that murder was present in us from our earliest childhood, symbolically at first, then often fantasized about. He talked to me for hours about the relationship between fantasy and the world of the insane, between fantasy and the triggers that pushed people to act. He took Vietnam as an example to show me that once the social taboo against killing was lifted, very few men were capable of resisting that freedom. He had his own special way of debunking murder, showing me how stupid it was, making it seem hateful to me.

For a long period, he let me ask him more questions than he asked me. The setting for our therapy sessions was always the same, his office and the little table where the chess game was set up. I'd never allowed him to beat me, and the more time passed, the quicker the games finished. We sometimes played three or four games during one session. Leitner never forgot anything. We both had the same kind of hypermnesia, which in my case made it possible for me to remember, for example, the exact color and shape of the buttons on my mother's blouse at any stage in telling the story of my dealings with her. I'm quite capable of remembering very precisely the smell of her breath when we talked and the kind of alcohol she was drinking—beer, whiskey, wine, martini— whether her makeup was light or heavy, whether her lipstick was contained within the outline of her lips or went over onto her skin and made her look, not like a woman, but like a clown.

Leitner would suddenly dig up major events I thought were buried forever. That was the case with what I had called the bad thoughts, which sometimes made it impossible for me to concentrate. He didn't know it, but these bad thoughts were still there, although they'd become less obtrusive since we'd talked about them. I realized then that naming something made it possible to partly defuse it. By lifting the taboo on talking about it, its essence gradually faded, a little bit like a perfume bottle left open. I was still uncomfortable, though, with talking about my bad thoughts directly. When I say uncomfortable, I had the impression I was stripping myself naked in the middle of the street on Halloween. Faced with the strange reticence that had come over me, Leitner did not insist. But I remembered that in front of the panel he'd talked about fantasy as a criterion for schizophrenia. I had good reason to want him not to ascribe symptoms like that to me.

"I talked about schizophrenia because that's how they classify things but I don't need to put a name on something to understand it. The human mind, with all its deviations, isn't like a pharmacist's cabinet where every plant, every cure is in a particular order. But what is it that's bothering you?"

22

I had to talk about that obsession in the end. It was something that had taken up residence in my mind, something that sometimes took it over so that I couldn't think of anything else, but I knew deep down that without it I would really go crazy, because it was the only way I could feel pleasure. Eventually, I came out with it.

I told him about the Fourth of July the year I turned twelve. A huge funfair had been set up on a field that belonged to the town. The inhabitants of Helena had come in their hundreds. My mother had finally yielded to pressure from my father to go there with the whole family. It was an opportunity for her to drink lots of beer, and that's what made up her mind. It was hot and humid, the way it often is in Montana in early summer. All the humidity comes up from the ground, and the sun beats down as heavily as lead. We parked some distance away and my mother wouldn't stop complaining because she hated walking. We saw a few people she knew, and when we did, it was if hypocrisy was second nature to her, she'd be friendly and sympathetic. In front of her colleagues from the town hall she went so far as to scratch my head with an affectionate gesture, and she never failed to mention my father's past in Special Forces when she introduced him. My sisters followed in their Sunday best, eyeing up every boy their age, as if there were going to be any who'd want two big lumps who waddled like penguins. They embarrassed me with their clothes, which were too feminine, I'd have preferred them to be dressed like men. My father and I walked behind, my mother in front with her two daughters on either side. My father said we should split up, but my mother wouldn't hear of it. She didn't want to face any more chance encounters, alone with her offspring, if she couldn't make up for that distressing spectacle with a mention of my father's war record. And how could she talk about that if he wasn't there? For once my father wouldn't give in. We finally did split up, arranging to meet an hour later in front of a big gallows-like construction that looked like a guillotine. We hung around the shooting range for a while. My father scored a clear round in front of a group of hunters who were amazed that anyone could shoot so accurately. Several of them asked him in which branch he had served during the war but he didn't reply. He simply scored another clear round on moving targets. And then another. Nothing could knock him off his aim. He finally tired of it and you could see on his face that he had paid dearly for the satisfaction of excelling like that in public. In the tests of strength, we were up against stronger competition. Size isn't everything, and a bunch of lumberjacks who'd come down from the mountains were able to push back the machine about a foot and a half more than he could. A storm had gathered above our heads and my father judged it was time to go to the meeting point. The three women were there, a few yards from the guillotine, not knowing where to look. My mother was pretending to be outraged. I wanted to see what was going on. I told my father, who told my mother, who refused. But my father wouldn't listen, you don't insult in public someone you've introduced as a hero. Behind the guillotine, the mountains looked closer, a sign that it was going to rain. I reckoned we had about fifteen minutes before the rain came down and the crowd scattered, and as I was looking at the sky, the carny who ran the guillotine introduced a very pretty young girl. I'd never seen a nicer looking girl. She had wavy blonde hair all the way down to her breasts, which were just staring to grow—she must have been my age. From where I was, I couldn't see her eyes but I couldn't imagine them any other color than bright blue. I saw lots of other boys around me who'd suddenly stopped their bragging and fallen silent, struck dumb by the sight of the girl, who was so lovely you just couldn't be vulgar around her. She kneeled and lay her head down, directly under the guillotine. The crowd moved forward, cutting off my view. Lightning flashed across the sky just as the carny started the mechanism, and the blade shone as it fell. It was hard to believe the girl wasn't going to lose her head, even though you knew it was all faked. That prospect released an orgasm in me, and I felt a kind of wild ecstasy in all my senses that I'd never known before in my short life. At the same moment, big drops of rain started hitting the onlookers with a noise like clapping. The crowd didn't panic but headed for the parking lot. I looked desperately around for the girl but she had disappeared.

That evening, for the first time, my father lost his temper about my being confined to the cellar. As my mother wouldn't listen, he threatened to call the police to report my mistreatment at her hands. My mother at last gave in. In retaliation, she made my father spend the night on the couch in the living room, but at least I was able to sleep in the guest room. I slept badly, missing my lair and the noises in the pipes I usually heard during the night. Early the next morning, my father ran away for the first time and nothing was the same as before between my mother and him. I mean, the balance of terror had shifted. He came back two days later, talking openly about divorce. But he didn't yet have the courage, and I like to think it was the thought of leaving me alone in my mother's hands that kept him from going for good. If he hadn't defended me like that, I mightn't have killed his parents to prove my gratitude.

Leitner took his head in his hands and stayed like that for the longest time. I could tell that my story had bothered him a

little. He asked me if since then there'd later been any particular triggers that gave me the desire to carry out that particular
act. Our relationship was too advanced for me to lie to him. I
admitted that two months later I'd wanted to cut the head off
one of my teachers, a woman who'd recently been hired and
who for some reason seemed very concerned about me. I
thought she was really elegant and stylish. One evening, I got
all my equipment together and walked to her house, which was
on its own in a residential area where there were no fences.
Her dog, which had been sleeping on the front steps, greeted
me and wagged its tail. I watched her through the curtainless
windows on the first floor. She was cooking with a green apron
tied around her waist and dragging sporadically on a cigarette
which she kept putting down in an ashtray. Through the windows I could hear some really lively modern music. Every time
she passed in front of a mirror on one of the walls, she checked
her hair and lifted it a bit. She was wearing tight-fitting jeans,
but her figure didn't have the same effect on me as her transparent eyes. She could have been walking around naked and
I'd still have searched out her eyes. From a distance, I saw the
headlights of a car coming toward me. I was hoping it would
go somewhere else, but unfortunately it stopped outside the
house. A good-looking guy got out and walked toward the
steps. I moved back behind a bush. She opened the door to
him without her apron on. She kept shifting her weight from
one leg to the other, I guess she was shy. The man seemed more
sure of himself. The door closed behind them and I went back
home. Had I been jealous of the man, had I wanted to kill him?
No, certainly not. With his physique and his age, I thought he
was the perfect man for a woman like that. No, really, the
thought of hurting him never even crossed my mind. Did I
think I'd have been capable of seeing my plan through? I don't
know, I don't think so, even though to be honest the closer I
got to her the more I wanted to do it. But it wasn't something

I couldn't control. Even if she'd been alone, I'd have been content to kick the idea out and go back home without any fuss.

Leitner, who often thought aloud, was trying to find a new explanation for my fantasy. "Making her lose her head" wasn't enough anymore. He was looking for some connection with castration, and with authority, but wasn't sure exactly what. The most direct question came when he asked me if I was able to achieve orgasm through masturbation without these decapitation fantasies. I had to admit I couldn't. We talked about the frequency of those orgasms. I said two or three times a day. Mostly it was to get a bit of peace and rid myself, at least for a moment, of those bad thoughts that took me over, as if to remind myself that I was a man of flesh and blood, that pleasure wasn't forbidden to me.

Leitner was more and more worried and I was more and more relieved. There wasn't a single corner of my mind that I hadn't revealed to him. I'd played the game through to the end.

"I'm grateful to you, Al," he said, putting his hand on my forearm. Then he stood up, filled his pipe and lighted it, and walked up and down his office. He threw open the window, which looked out on a vast lawn, the kind you see in college campuses. In the distance, on the other side of the road, you could just make out a meadow enclosed by fencing, where there were black patches that I assumed were cattle. That was all there was in that place, cattle and the hospital. The thought that this confession was going to keep me there a good while longer crossed my mind, but Leitner started muttering.

"A perverted defense mechanism against psychosis. The two of us still have a lot of work to do to get rid of these bad thoughts. I may have underestimated my task. That said, if we appeared before the panel again I'd say the same thing. I don't think that basically you are a danger to others. And certainly not to your classmates, who are only boys. Have you ever wanted to cut the head off a man, Al?"

"Oh, God, no. I think that'd make me want to throw up."

He laughed. And so did I, for the first time in my life, which amazed me. Then I felt a little sad again at the thought that he was going to do everything he could to take away those dark thoughts. What would I have left then? That was the question. Of course, I couldn't tell him that, but what would I have except those rides on my motorcycle? I know other men are interested in dozens of things. They have families, hobbies, a God, a dog, a house, a garden and lots of dreams that'll never come true. They can take any *Playboy* centerfold, fantasize over the girl, jerk off if they feel like it. They think their little lives are worth something, that faith will stop them dying really, that there's no beginning and no end. All I have is this fantasy, and a desire to take to the road that usually fades after a few miles.

23

I would look at Leitner when he sat there deep in thought and realize how dependent I was on him. I was like a vast haunted house where there's only one item of furniture left, and he was suggesting I help him move it outside and burn it. I was prepared to play the game on condition that he find a way to help me put in some new furniture. Was he capable of that? For the first time I had my doubts about him. Not about his ability to wipe the slate clean. But to rebuild something that would keep me alive through the years that separated me from death. I knew perfectly well what was hidden behind that fantasy, a cold desire to kill myself and have done with this fucking life that has no meaning, not even the one we try to give it. At that precise moment, I saw Leitner as one of those contractors who dig sand quarries in the mountains and promise their neighbors they'll fill them in again. They never do it, for the simple reason that they don't know how. And when they do it, it's to bury garbage or toxic waste.

I went back to school the next day, more somber than I'd been since my arrest. But nobody noticed. That's the advantage of never talking to anybody, everybody thinks you're grouchy rather than moody. I spoke to the teachers only when they asked me something. They were the only ones who knew where I came from and they had their eye on me. I'd have distanced myself even more from the other pupils if I could, I'd have liked to be there without being there. I wondered what we could possibly have in common. What can there be in common between a young man coming home from Vietnam and another the same age who's only ever seen war in the movies? A man who's killed is like someone living at a very high altitude, he gets old prematurely. I felt no more affinity with the people around me at that moment than I'd had with my classmates before my double murder. From time to time I wanted to boast about it, to rub my story in their faces, but I was afraid that wouldn't do me any favors. Especially as I really didn't have any reason to do it, given that all these guys were simple country boys. You should have seen what a hard time they had with their studies. Those who hadn't completely switched off had to make a huge effort to solve simple equations or say anything about a story by Edgar Allan Poe. If I hadn't been a little lacking in affect, as Leitner put it, I would have cottoned on to literature earlier. Apart from a few purely cerebral authors, you need a little bit of sensitivity to appreciate a writer. The finest writing I was given to read at the time was a story by Faulkner that was in the collection we studied in class, the story of an old maid who hides the dead body of her only love in her house.

As we're talking about literature, it was around this time that I got a letter from my mother, a bit like the one Raskolnikov reads at the beginning of *Crime and Punishment*. The parallel struck me because, in her letter, my mother also told me my sister was getting married. This was my older sister, the one I'd spoken to about as much as you might speak to a heifer in a corral. I couldn't get over it. Nowhere in the letter did my mother ask me what I was doing or how I was. It was the kind of informative letter people write when they have nothing better to do. My sister worked at K-Mart and was going to marry a guy who also worked at K-Mart, not just anybody of course. I understood from the letter that the guy was an idiot, but my mother couldn't stop herself from making up a brilliant future for him. He had twice been named employee of the year and would soon be getting a promotion and moving to California as assistant buyer or some crap like that. The guy must have been really desperate for sex to commit himself in front of God to fucking my sister until he died. My mother took the opportunity to attack my father, who had vanished from the face of the earth. She told me that one of her cop friends—as if my mother had friends—had made inquiries all over the place without finding any trace of him. She could understand him running away from a son who was nothing but a sick criminal, but how could he abandon his daughters like that? She didn't say much about her new husband, a plumber who was apparently very well-known. How can a plumber in a shitty town in Montana be well-known? She also wrote that if her son-in-law was transferred to California, she would go with them because she was starting to be tired of the climate and the mentality of the inhabitants around there, as if it wasn't her mentality too—she'd never in her life left Montana.

She didn't at any point express any joy at the thought that she'd be closer to me. She ended the letter by telling me she had phoned the administration of the hospital and they had told her, after consulting my therapists, that I might easily be there for another three or four years, which wasn't long enough in her opinion to become a normal boy again. In passing, she repeated her idea that even though she had been surprised that her son had become a criminal, the more she thought over the past, the more logical she found it that I'd done what I'd done. She didn't bother to develop that idea, but I'm sure the decapitation of her prize kitten was still eating away at her. She didn't want to end, so she'd added a PS where she asked if I had any regrets, not for what I'd done but for the shame and disgrace I'd brought to our family, an honest, respectable family, and how I planned to go about repairing the damage done to our reputation. Then she gave her own opinion of my case. No, I wasn't sick, and those who'd con-

sidered me sick had been quite generous to do so. I was simply one of the many incarnations of evil. In her opinion, an
exorcism would be more appropriate than psychotherapy. She
was glad the State of California hadn't presented her with a bill
for my incarceration, which would have added ruin to the
shame of it all. Then she attacked my father again, reminding
me of the number of times she'd told him that his upbringing
would turn me into a deviant. The reason she'd stuck me in
that cellar for twelve years was because she had suspected
since my birth that I was in league with the devil. She signed in
big legible letters, Cornell Paterson. Paterson must have been
her new husband's name. She wasn't so much boasting about
this new husband as showing how pleased she was to remove
Kenner from her name.

24

I n all those months, Stafford was the only guy I became friendly with. He was the one who had taken the first step. He had probably sensed that we were on the same intellectual level, even though I wasn't as old as him, or as well educated, and I certainly didn't have the same cultural knowledge. He was a kind of aristocrat. He had taught literature in one of the biggest universities on the West Coast. He'd been put inside for the rape of eleven of his female students and the murder of the last of them. He liked to talk about his past a lot. He had a high opinion of himself. He told me that when he was teaching, the co-eds were crazy about him. His charisma, his breadth of knowledge, his looks, all created an ascendancy over young girls, and even over young men, although he'd never been interested in men. Rather than seducing them, he preferred to rape them. He knew I'd done some hunting—I'd boasted to him of killing stags and moose even though I'd never killed anything but moles and rabbits—so he used this metaphor: "You don't eat the meat of an animal you've spent hours tracking the way you'd eat meat you bought ready-wrapped in the freezer compartment of a supermarket." The strange thing was that he thought raping his female students was less of a danger to his career than seducing them. If he'd seduced them, they'd have ended up bragging about it and sooner or later the dean would have found out and dismissed him. When it was a matter of rape, it was down to him not to be found out. In fact he never had been. He'd given himself up after the last rape because he'd killed the girl. He claimed it was involuntary. He had stopped her from breathing by placing his hand over her mouth and nose when she'd tried to scream. His great pride was that he had managed to rape all those girls without gagging them and without any of them ever screaming. He always wore a mask. He would get into their houses and, once their first panic was over, he managed to persuade them to go along with him without resorting to violence. He never ejaculated inside them, because he didn't think they deserved it and it was his way of proving that he wasn't acting under the pressure of some kind of animal impulse but was demonstrating a different kind of power. My God, the guy thought his sperm was holy! It wasn't so much possessing the girls that interested him, it was getting all the details right: the preparation, checking the escape routes, getting through the doors, covering his tracks. It was because he was so good at all this that he'd never been caught. He'd turned himself in because killing had never been his intention and he wanted to be given the right punishment for his sin. By a narrow majority, the panel of psychiatrists had judged him not responsible for his actions. He had been rotting in this hospital for about ten years. Knowing that I had become friendly with him, Leitner talked to me about him even though he wasn't his patient. He told me that in ten years Stafford hadn't made any progress because he was using all his intelligence not to be cured. He was obsessed with demonstrating his superiority over his therapist.

I had real responsibilities in the laundry. I was in charge of twenty guys, all of them older than me. But I couldn't make any more progress and I was starting to find the work routine. I'd always had a problem with routine. Repeating things in exactly the same way all the time was reassuring at first, but then it started to weigh me down and eventually stopped me from going on. Without routine, I felt a kind of inner panic.

Once the routine was established, the absurdity of all that rep-
etition brought on a sense of unease that might explode at any
moment. This was the point I had reached. Stafford was well
liked in the library, so I asked him if he could pull some strings
and get me a job there. He put himself back inside the skin of
a college professor and asked me what I had read. I passed
myself off as a specialist on Dostoevsky. That took some nerve
because I hadn't read anything except the first thirty pages of
Crime and Punishment, although I was planning to get back to
it soon. From now on, I was going to force myself to finish
what I started. My life couldn't amount to undertaking things
and giving up halfway. I realized that this syndrome was connected to my relationship with space, a reckless need to hit the
road immediately frustrated by my guilt at just taking off like
that. If Stafford had looked into it, he would quickly have realized that I wasn't a specialist in anything at all. But he didn't
give a damn. What counted was that, next to him, my size
would protect him from the aggressiveness of a few violent
inmates who would have liked nothing better than the opportunity to wipe that smug look off his face. I was moved to the
library a few days after making my request, supported by
Stafford and by the guy in charge of the laundry, who praised
my "remarkable sense of organization." There was a reason I'd
requested the library. I really wanted to start reading and learning as much as my brain allowed me. Deep down, I was toying
with the idea of learning all about psychiatry and eventually
knowing enough about the subject to understand myself. My
first object of study was Stafford. Thanks to him and the books
I read, I quickly became familiar with the question of perversion, and it didn't take me long to understand the role of the
father. One evening, while the other patients in our wing were
watching a football game on TV, Stafford started telling me
about his father, how mean and violent he'd been, his absolute
contempt for his son. Then he changed the subject completely

and recommended I read Kafka's *Amerika* but without saying why. I've never read it, so I'll never know if there was a connection, even a distant one, with his father.

I grew closer to the chaplain of the hospital, who'd heard about my good behavior. He was a glum-looking priest of about fifty. There weren't many Catholics among the inmates. His first question was about my motivation. I told him I'd been born under the sign of the devil and about the Satanic rituals I'd performed, either alone or with the younger of my two sisters. I was forced to tell him that if God existed, he had completely forgotten me. I had never seen Him manifest Himself or show any kindness toward me. But I believed in Jesus Christ, not as the son of God but as a guru of the human race. He asked me if I thought I would believe in God one day. My answer reassured him, because I was so positive in my attitude. We agreed to spend two hours together every week.

Like a snake shedding its old skin in a hostile desert, I didn't want to be a hostage to my childhood anymore, or to wake up with an erection after an obsessive dream. These periods of optimism were followed by periods of black pessimism. I imagined I'd never get away from them and that one day I'd lose control. This thought first made me morose, as if I was doomed never to escape my destiny, and then downright depressed. I was a victim of what Leitner called the zombie syndrome. I had the impression I was already dead while continuing to live mechanically, without any of my senses giving me the kind of joy that would prove to me that I was alive. I had the feeling that death was imminent, almost natural, but for mysterious reasons and against all logic it never came. There was a striking contrast between my active phases and these moments of total collapse when I felt completely alienated from my life, indifferent to my own existence.

"Even when a human child is born at full term, it's still premature. It's an aquatic creature that for nine months has been swimming about in an amniotic bubble in its mother's womb, fed through a cord that resembles a diver's breathing tube. In my opinion, the birth of a human being is by far the most violent birth there is. Wherever we are in the world, in a city, in open country, on the sea, in a forest, there's no more heartrending scream than the scream of a newborn human baby. Death is terrifyingly close, much more so than with other animals, whose newborns become relatively independent within a few hours. The child screams because it feels weak, it feels totally helpless, an aquatic animal thrown ashore in a land where it has no point of reference and can't perform any function that might make it even relatively independent. It screams because it's the hostage of its mother, and will stay that way for a long time. The life it had in the womb continues once it's outside, because it's in a state of submission to its mother. The story of man is the story of a lost paradise. And these periods of prostration that you describe are incredibly similar to the withdrawal of someone who's autistic. It's a return to silence, to a sensation of floating weightlessly, a carefree life far from the threat of annihilation that subsequently appears. I'm not saying you're autistic, Al, far from it, but any given personality demonstrates some recognizable symptoms of autism to a small extent. You withdraw because, in your mind, the terrible insecurity your mother revealed to you through her destabilizing behavior reappears in the form of a fear of death, which you fight by preparing for its imminent arrival. I know for example that your fantasies of decapitation fade when you are in that somewhat morbid state of levitation. When you're in an active phase, on the other hand, these fantasies go together with your desire to live. That may seem a bit of a contradiction, but that's how it is. It's that split that I have to try to get rid of if you're ever going to leave here in a consistent psychological state. These attacks of prostration mustn't be allowed to threaten your links with society, you have to recover some consistency in your desires. You know, Al, I've thought a lot about your fantasy, about what you call your bad thoughts. I wasn't sure at first, but I now think there may indeed be a connection with castration anxieties. Can I count on you to be really honest in your answers? All right. So tell me, are you capable of achieving orgasm other than when you imagine decapitating a woman? That means that deep down you have the feeling that your mother castrated you. Through her influence, she's destroyed your normal desire for a woman. You defend yourself against this castration by cutting off the heads of women in your dreams. It's a way of paying them back for what you suffered. I'm not yet completely certain of my conclusions but I don't think I'm far off. We'll get there, Al."

25

T hat was the last time we spoke. A Friday evening. He had just told me he thought he'd be working with me for another year or two, because he would only release me when I was able to enjoy my freedom. The following Monday we were supposed to meet early in the afternoon. When I showed up in his office, there were two grim-looking big shots from the administration in black suits and ties. They told me my therapy session was canceled until further notice and ordered me to go back to my room. I couldn't stop myself from asking them where Dr. Leitner was, but they didn't answer and I saw from their worried looks that something unusual had happened. In the afternoon, I left for school and the next day I went to my session and found a new shrink, fretting over the size of his task. He asked me to sit down and told me, without even looking at me, that he was my new therapist. He was older than Leitner.

Engrossed in my file, still without looking up, he told me Leitner was dead. To me, someone's only dead when you know how he died. I told him that and he said he had drowned while fly fishing in particularly dangerous rapids in the north of the state. The current had carried him away, and his body had been found two miles further downriver. The therapist seemed upset. You never know at times like that if the person is really moved by the death of the human being he has known or just terrified at the prospect of his own death. The news surprised me. To say it upset me would be a lie. Its effect on me was neutral on the emotional level. I'd liked Leitner. He was someone who cared about me in a way nobody ever had before, except maybe my father. He was even afraid of the risk of transference, before realizing I'm not the kind of person to transfer anything to anybody. Can I say I felt deep emotion, that tears rose in my eyes? No. You see, the curious thing, the thing I couldn't explain, was that I didn't find it any harder to imagine him dead than alive. People don't really have any experience of death. I felt kind of feverish but I'd be incapable of explaining where that feeling came from.

The new shrink's methods were nothing like Leitner's. He was grateful to me for quickly resuming the work as if nothing had happened. Other patients played up, pretending to be grief-stricken at the loss of their one link with the world. Not me, but one thing was clear in my mind, I had no intention of being treated by him. I wanted to get back on the path to freedom. You can't trust two people on the same subject. I soon realized that Welton was the complete opposite of Leitner. He needed to feel he was on safe ground by giving names to pathologies. He was fond of classifications, convinced that he was dealing with an exact science. Before ending up in this hospital, he'd been an army psychiatrist, at first given the job of sifting out the draftees who claimed to be crazy to avoid being sent to Vietnam. Later, he'd been involved in taking care of those who came back genuinely crazy. I immediately told him about my father and his role in Special Forces, and that created a connection. It didn't take me long to work out my strategy. As luck would have it, Leitner hadn't left many working notes about me. There were just a few reports about my case, including the one that had allowed me to go back to school. I realized that all this guy wanted was to be able to classify my condition and prove that I was cured. I never told him a word about my fantasies, my bad thoughts. In a few months, I got through all the books on psychiatry that were in the library. Welton was impressed by how much I knew. He even ended up using me as his assistant when he gave the other patients psychological tests. I didn't like him. I couldn't say why, but all the same I let my mustache grow like him. I think he appreciated that. I told him that when I killed my grandmother, I'd felt just as responsible as a guy in a SWAT unit who kills an attacker to save a family. That made him like me even more because it hadn't taken me long to realize that he was a soldier before he was a shrink. I would have liked him more if he hadn't tried to conceal his lack of confidence by using electric shock therapy. He wasn't sure I needed it, but sitting there in his leather armchair, he said he thought I should have the treatment as a preventive measure. He probably imagined that my brain worked at a particular voltage, and he wanted to get the current back to normal. The resemblance to the electric chair of my childhood was obvious, but I preferred not to mention that. They gave me a powerful sedative that sent me into outer space, and then zapped me like a lab rat. One of the effects of that stupid therapy is that it wipes out your memory of the actual moments when it's being done. After ten sessions, Welton must have considered I was now compatible with the U.S. power grid, and the sessions stopped.

26

They always say a plane crash is a combination of several factors. It's kind of the same with getting parole. What got me out of that hospital was the shortage of space. A lot of guys had come home from Vietnam suffering from severe mental disorders. You'd see them come in all the time, delirious, hallucinating. Some had committed rape over there and couldn't break their addiction. You also saw more and more junkies who blew up after taking massive doses of LSD, an acid that had become fashionable outside, or so I heard.

My school grades were good enough that I could go to college. If I'd played basketball, I could have gotten a scholarship, but I couldn't run. I've never done any sports and, like all outsize people, I grew up a bit lopsided. I was knock-kneed and at the medical examination I had before my release the doctor told me I was in danger of premature wear and tear of the cartilage. He advised me to lose weight, in his opinion 280 pounds was excessive, even with my height.

Between the decision to release me and my actually leaving the hospital two months passed. They tried to locate my father. But he had disappeared and there wasn't even a license number in his name anywhere in the country. They then took a while to track down my mother, because she'd moved from Montana to California. She was now a secretary at the University of Santa Cruz, south of San Francisco. The parole papers stipulated that I wasn't to live with her again, but they couldn't just let me out with no means of support. She agreed to pick me up and then immediately let me go. The probation officer would come around in three months' time to check I wasn't living under the same roof as her.

27

When I saw her in the lobby of the administration block, my first reaction was to retreat. Her body had become slightly stooped in the four years that had passed. She still looked more like a quarterback than a housewife, but she was wearing new glasses, which meant she now had a touch of the businesswoman about her. She had certainly aged, but I'd never looked at her enough to remember how she used to look. She still scared me as much as ever. The lack of affection in her eyes made me feel like a piece of plasma dragging behind her. She didn't even say hello, just started looking through my release papers. She read and reread the clauses that mentioned her, and asked for tons of explanations about certain paragraphs. All this took about three quarters of an hour, and I spent the whole time holding my breath. The outside world made me dizzy and my mother made me nauseous. My senses were going haywire. I had a strong desire to go back to my room. But she signed the last sheet of paper and turned to see if everything was there. We left, she in front, me behind. The light outside dazzled me even more than the day I was born. I looked around and saw the fields. They looked as curved as the earth. The clear blue sky was reflected on the asphalt. I felt like a little boy and was seized with a sudden desire to just take off. I thought I could grab her car keys and leave without her, but they would have immediately taken me back to the hospital and now that I had tasted a few seconds in the open air of the coast, I wanted to take advantage of it.

I sat down next to her. She reversed without saying a word. It wasn't until we reached the road that she exploded.

"What did you tell them?"

I didn't let her faze me. "That's a meaningless question. We talked about lots of things in four years."

She was tapping her fingers on the wheel as she drove but that wasn't enough, she thumped it with her closed fist like a hammer.

"Stop fucking with me, Al, what did you tell them that they should demand you keep your distance from me, huh? What is it, have I got the plague or something? What the hell did you tell them? You're worth no more than a lump of birdshit, you hear me?" She was as red as the velvet seat covers. "You gave the speech all criminals do, putting all the blame on their parents for what they did. That someone as manipulative as you could have come out of my womb makes me feel nauseous. You can't even take responsibility for your own dumb actions. Maybe I was the one who put the rifle in your hands and pulled the trigger!"

She braked abruptly, and the smoke from the tires could probably have been seen from the prison. She took a deep breath then seemed to calm down.

"Listen to me, Al. You may be my son, but there's nothing forcing me to love you, just as there's nothing forcing you to love me. I have an important job at the university, I'm the personal assistant to a dean. I don't want you to keep ruining my reputation. The reason they let you go is because they think you're cured. Now you're going to look for a job and get out of here. I'll let you stay here for three days, okay, three days and then you get out. When you killed your grandparents, you left this world, if you want to come back into it, it'll be without me."

She calmly started the car again.

"What are you planning to do?" she said, putting on a honeyed voice.

Quite honestly, I hadn't yet thought about it. I wanted to do something connected with motorcycles, or else a job in the open air, but my ambitions were no more specific than that.

"I'm planning to enlist in the army and go to Vietnam."

She found that an interesting idea, I guess because it was so drastic. "They really changed you in there. I remember you were always chicken, always pissing in your pants if there was the slightest physical threat. But can you do something like that within the terms of your parole?"

"I don't know."

"You'd better find out. Now."

We did a U-turn and went back to the office. The woman there was surprised to see us again. She didn't know much about the subject of enlisting. There were lots of guys who went from Vietnam to that hospital, but I'd be the first to do the reverse. Just then, one of her superiors put his head in through the door and she asked him. He answered in the affirmative. As long as I was in the army, I'd be considered supervised, so that didn't compromise my parole. He left me his details in case the army wanted to contact him, and he promised to reach out to the Justice Department. Before I'd even really thought about it, I'd committed myself to the war. I'd gone to a lot of trouble over the past few months to understand my reactions, my unconscious so to speak. Now I'd leaped at an opportunity that would take me, all expenses paid, as far as possible from my mother.

It was three in the afternoon by the time we got to Santa Cruz. My mother dropped me downtown. After some hesitation, she gave me a copy of her house keys, then set off for the university. I rushed and bought myself a hamburger with the few dollars she'd agreed to leave me. I ate it quickly then went straight to the army recruitment office. It was a small, cramped office and the guy on duty had a crew cut, a spotless shirt, and a grim look on his face. He jerked his head back when he saw the size of me and asked me what I wanted. Once I'd filled out a little form, he pointed me in the direction of a sergeant who was reading a comic book in an even smaller office behind his. The sergeant put on an air of self-importance mixed with a kind of calculated simplicity, and we got down to brass tacks. I didn't lie about anything. I mentioned the murder of my grandparents and that took him aback a little. He quickly changed the subject. My size, he said, would limit what I could do. He looked at my feet—the symbol of how difficult my case was. From the face he pulled, he seemed to be saying that they couldn't find shoes my size in the army. The guy looked harassed. There weren't a whole lot of people volunteering for Vietnam. At the same time, if they put a guy like me in a helicopter the damn thing would never get off the ground. He could have handled a small guy who had killed his grandparents or a giant without a criminal record. But a criminal giant was too much for him. He took my details and promised to call me if I was needed.

My mother was renting a house that looked like all the other houses on the same street. It wasn't very old, about fifteen years maybe. There wasn't much light inside. A garden about sixty feet long separated it from the neighbors. The neighborhood was so clean and respectable it felt sterile. There was a back garden, completely enclosed by a low white wall, but the door leading to it was locked. Through the window I could see she'd made it a paradise for her prize cats, who were all out there, lazing in the sun. The shaded rooms depressed me. My mother had given me a room right next to the front door. My things had to stay in my bag in case there was an unexpected visit from the probation officer. While waiting for dinner, I went for a walk around town. I couldn't believe my eyes. In four years the world had changed more than it must have done between the beginning and the end of the war. Hundreds of young people were walking around, looking unwashed, and dressed like hoboes, in shirts, long flowery dresses and sandals. The guys wore their hair long and thick like girls and had let their beards grow. They staggered about with bloodshot eyes and all kinds of charms and things on their necks and wrists. You've never seen such a bunch of raggedy people, painted from head to foot, and I thought there must be a really bad depression for there to be so many homeless young people wandering around aimlessly. They seemed to have made a decision to look ugly, and there must have been a reason for it. I was even approached a few times by girls who wanted to talk to me about all kinds of weird things, a mixture of Jesus Christ, peace in Vietnam, reincarnation and a whole heap of other bullshit all jumbled together in their drug-addled brains. There was even one who stopped in front of me with her arms folded and called me a white totem, an exterminator of Indians. I didn't need to push her to get her out of my way, she fell by herself, laughing like a half-witted little girl. I wasn't in a mood to get friendly with this bunch. All I wanted was to be left alone. There was a strong desire to bump myself off growing in my mind and I was trying to resist it. I sat down in a park where about fifty of these degenerates were bumming around on some weird kind of inner journey. I was proud of the fact that, unlike them, I was wearing a clean blue short-sleeved shirt. I was too big and impressive for anyone to try sitting down next to me. I sat there for about an hour, looking at these people and telling myself that life was meaningless. Not one of the people walking there had the slightest chance of surviving the next hundred years. The history of our species, it seemed to me, was a kind of genocide by time. Each generation struggled with its own little affairs before it filled the cemeteries. I had a real fit of the blues, I don't deny that. I could have blown my brains out, or opened fire on all those freaks or those old guys walking in the park, driven by obscure motives known only to themselves. Santa Cruz wasn't having a very good effect on me. I was furious that the fucking hospital had handed me back to my mother, and that I was as dependent on her as if I was a baby, with no money or plans. I felt hatred rising in me, hatred for all those guys who had supposedly been treating me for four years and had now abandoned me. I wanted to go back to the hospital to regain my dignity. Why the hell had they done a thing like that? They didn't know what I was capable of when I blew my top! I would have liked to see the faces of all those shrinks if they found out the next morning that I had shot twenty people walking in this park and then two or three cops before their buddies showed up and shot me down. Before they let me out, they should have found me a job. Anything, anywhere, even a job nobody wants to do, wash dead bodies in the morgue or something like that, but at least ensure my independence. Sitting there on that bench, I wept with rage.

My mother came home with just enough food for the two of us. I was lying on her couch with the mauve fringes. I stood up to avoid a comment. There was a smell of fried chicken and warm wrapping paper. The fries were separate, stuffed into cones dripping with oil. She had spent more on beer than on food. When it came to that, she hadn't changed. She kept looking either up or down but rarely straight ahead. She knocked back two bottles then muttered, "I found you a job in a gas station just outside town. And a room with an honest woman for just over a third of your salary. If you get good tips, the rent won't be any kind of a burden. What did they say about Vietnam?"

"They didn't say anything but I think they were afraid they wouldn't be able to find shoes for me."

"Is that all?"

"No, you can imagine. If I'd killed Indians, they'd have taken me, but my own grandparents . . . They didn't seem that enthusiastic. They're supposed to call me back."

"They'll never call you back. Someone capable of killing his grandparents is just as capable of shooting his army buddies in the back."

I leaped to my feet. "You can't say something like that to me!"

"Yes, I can, because it's what I think."

I sat down again. She opened another bottle of beer without offering me one. My anger deflated quickly. We ate in silence. She switched on the TV. They were showing an item about Vietnam. She switched channels to a baseball match. My mother liked baseball. I saw her fidget.

"Your sister's pregnant."

I paused before I answered. "With what?"

She looked at me in surprise. "What do you mean, with what?"

"A marine mammal?"

She pursed her lips, a sign that she was making an effort to control herself.

"I really would have liked to be proud of you, Al."

What can you say to something like that?

"I see all these students at the university and I tell myself you could have been one of them."

"What's to stop me?"

"You'll never get a scholarship, and I don't have the money to pay for you. Now that your father has vanished, you can't count on me to pay his share of anything. Anyway, I'd just be throwing money away. I don't deny you're intelligent, Al, but you have no willpower. You're a ditherer. You don't follow through on anything. Do you even know what you want to do with your life, apart from wrecking it?"

She stood up to clear and wash the dishes. I stayed where I was.

"What do you think I am, a servant?" she yelled. "Can't you get up off your ass and help me?"

I got up slowly. I took a paper and pencil to write down the addresses of the gas station and the landlady, which she dictated wearily. When she'd finished, I tore up the paper.

"What are you doing?"

"As you can see, I tore it up. I don't need a piece of paper to remember an address. But the main thing is, I don't need you to find me a job. I'm not going to that gas station and I'm not going to your landlady. I don't want to owe you anything. Not even a night here. I'm getting my bag and taking off. But not before I tell you one thing. I'm really sorry I killed my grandparents."

"You're sorry, good news!"

She couldn't give a damn. She looked around for something to light her cigarette.

"Yes, I'm sorry, I should never have killed them. It's you I should have shot."

She gave a nasty little laugh, but I could tell she was scared. My expression must have changed without my realizing it.

"Well, since I can't rely on you for the dishes, I'll finish them by myself. You can go."

She was putting on a show, but all the same she went and got herself another beer.

"If I were you, Al, I wouldn't come out with that kind of threat too often. If you do, I'll talk to your probation officer and you'll go back to the hospital pronto. That's not what I want. Take your things, vanish like your father, live your life, any kind of life, I don't care, but go."

She said all that with her back turned, and me looking at the back of her neck. I went to my room, put the few things I had taken out back in my khaki bag, and left without saying another word. I had the vague feeling I'd just saved her life. Outside, I realized how damp the house had been because the air was dry and warm. Night had fallen over the town like a curtain on a lighted stage in a theatre, but it wasn't yet pitch black. I headed back to the park where I'd been that afternoon. It's hard for me to describe the pleasure I feel, walking around when there's a vague danger in the air. Nothing might happen but you feel it wouldn't take much for the situation to descend into tragedy. It's the hour when dissatisfaction, resentment and madness are on the prowl. It's all a matter of opportunity, circumstance, and moonlight.

My exceptional memory often registers details that are insignificant to ordinary people. But it can also wipe out whole areas of my life. The hospital seemed a long way away. Leitner even further. Walking the deserted streets of Santa Cruz, I wondered if I'd really known him. I thought about my father, who'd vanished into thin air. I wanted to find him, I wanted to explain to him what I had done so that he could judge me based on a full knowledge of the facts. I could see myself moving in with him. We'd gotten along well when we lived together in Los Angeles. Women had always separated us. My mother and my sisters, whom he'd fled as if they were the plague. His second wife, who'd imagined I was ogling her. And now the new one, who I knew nothing about. But above all his mother, my grandmother. In killing her, I'd given him a strange sense of guilt. Guilt for not mourning her, because I'm sure his mother's death hadn't moved him.

Santa Cruz has the fake casualness of a university town. It was hard to imagine, but the place would be a heap of ashes if the San Andreas Fault started moving. There'd be mass destruction, the whole coast of California would be one big disaster area. Hell is never very far from heaven, but people don't want to know that, they sleep as if a good star was watching over them. They spend their time building enclosures for themselves. They accumulate possessions and don't see further than the tips of their shoes. It never occurs to them to wonder what they're doing there. If anyone gets bumped off around them, their own lives take on an unsuspected flavor. Murders don't horrify them, they give their petty existence a value they'd never hoped for.

Much to my surprise, the park was even livelier at that late hour than in the middle of the day. I had to walk around a bit to find a bench where I could sleep alone. I'd never seen such a concentration of freaks. They'd streamed in from all over, all shambling along in the same way. About a dozen groups had formed circles to play music and take up weird poses. The most stoned of them were lying on the ground with their arms outstretched, looking up at the stars. I was glad I'd had a close shave before dinner, trimmed my mustache and ironed my shirt. I sat down in the middle of a bench to mark my territory. I decided I needed a good sleep before I set off to look for a job. I could tell you lots more about those Martians and their stench of grass, but I didn't really care about them. I didn't wish them any harm, I just didn't understand where they had come from and where they were going, they seemed to be in an unreal world, floating about on transparent clouds.

Lulled by the Indian music, I was starting to fall asleep with my chin on my chest when I sensed a presence. I opened my eyes and saw a girl my age or a bit more. Her loose blonde hair fell all the way down to her lower back. She was wearing a rumpled, almost transparent white dress with lots of ruffles and a low neckline that revealed the upper part of her big breasts. She was looking at me sweetly. I replied to her greeting because I thought she was really pretty. I was just getting over the anger I'd felt since my conversation with my mother, and it hadn't completely given way to calm, which is an unusual state for me anyway.

"Are you traveling?"

She sat down at the end of the bench. Not looking at me made her confident.

"Quite the opposite. I'm trying to settle."

"Were you in Vietnam?"

"No. They didn't want me, I'm too tall."

She nodded. "It was written."

"What was written?"

"Ever since you were born, it was written that you wouldn't go out there and die because you're too much of a target. All the better. You have good karma. I have a brother over there. I feel it deep down in my belly that he's not going to come back. That's why I'm on the road. I'm from Sacramento. I don't want to be there the day men in uniform come to the door of my parents' house and tell them my brother's dead. I wanted him to desert. He didn't want to. I'm with a group of people that are forming a commune as we go along. There are already about fifteen of us. If you like the idea, you're welcome to join us."

"What kind of commune?"

"We're going to try to live according to our principles. Abolish property of goods and people."

"Some kind of a Communist thing?"

"No, nothing like that. I mean, I don't really know what Communism is. We're going north to cultivate some land and be self-sufficient. Everything we own will be shared, love will be free . . . "

"Free?"

"Yes . . . we have to get rid of all this crap about possessions, my land, my wife, my dog, my TV. We're even going to make children who'll belong to the commune. Our children will be loved the way no children have been loved in the history of the world. They won't have any more psychological problems, they won't have to deal with rivalry or competition. We're going to invent a new world without wars, where the only thing that matters is love, a world radically different from our parents' world, where material things won't matter anymore. We'll get back in harmony with nature and spend our time enjoying it."

She paused to catch her breath.

"Wanna fuck?" she said.

I couldn't have been more surprised if I'd been hit by a truck.

"Don't worry, nobody will watch. There's no jealousy with people like us. We satisfy a natural need, as natural as eating or sleeping, do you want to?"

She stood up, lifted her skirt, and sat down astride my

knees. I pushed her off, gently but firmly, and she realized it would be a bad mistake to insist.

"You're not yet ready to make the big leap into a better world. I understand that, brother. But if you want to join our commune, we're still here for two more days, time to do a little work and get some bread together. Then we're going north to Mount Shasta, you know it?"

I knew it of course but I didn't tell her that.

"If one day you want a better world, you'll always be welcome. What's your name?"

"Al."

"Mine's Lisbeth."

It was terrible to let a girl like that one go for the simple reason that you don't know what to do with her. She made me a little sign with her fingers and disappeared into the semidarkness.

I caught a glimpse of her about seven o'clock the next morning, as I was setting off to look for work. She was under a sleeping bag between two unwashed men. The thought that she had slept with them in turn or together turned my stomach. I could happily have kicked them. Without quite knowing why, I thought free love was a man's idea, even when it was women who were selling it. Anyway, that didn't matter right now, what worried me was the thought of showing up to look for work without shaving.

I walked downtown, stiff and aching from my uncomfortable night. With what was left from the few dollars I'd begged from my mother the night before I had a coffee and three doughnuts. I could feel a slight breeze from the sea on my face. I was in a state between well-being and the fear of losing it. I absolutely had to find a job before evening so that I wouldn't be forced to see my mother again. I could carry on sleeping in the park as long as the weather stayed fine but I had to eat and you don't feed bulk like mine with what I could scramble together. The proprietor of the first gas station I tried was sorry, but he couldn't offer me anything. In the second, the boss wasn't there and I didn't want to wait. With the third, a Texaco station, I hit the jackpot. The manager was a pudgy Italian who looked more like someone who sells pizzas than gas, but that's the kind of cliché that doesn't mean much. As I expected, he couldn't offer me wages, but he said I'd get plenty of tips for pumping gas, washing windshields, swelling tires and all the little maintenance jobs like checking levels. In fact, he reckoned I'd earn more than I expected. By chance, my predecessor had taken off with a customer, a woman around forty who drove the latest model Cadillac. According to Giannini, she might well have offered him more than a ride in her car, but it wouldn't last, even though he was a handsome kid, as far as he was any judge. Two hippies had come looking for work before me, but he had no intention of employing degenerates. The way he put it, the smell of gas and grease wasn't enough to cover their stench. He may have been exaggerating a little, but wops love to do that. He asked me if I knew anything about mechanics because he had a repair shop next to the gas station. He asked where I was from, but that was just a matter of form, he wasn't really interested in the answer. I told him I was from Montana. He seemed to think that was a long way to come just to pump gas or even to repair motorcycles—I'd told him that was something I knew about. As he only came up to my waist, he never looked at me when he spoke to me for fear of wearing out his cervical vertebrae. He couldn't get over how tall I was. I'm sure he must have thought I was very strong, too. He didn't know I had incredibly thin bones for a man my size.

29

Right from the first day, I was earning enough in tips to be able to rent a room. The customers, out of respect or fear of my height, never hesitated to put their hands in their pockets. My efficiency did the rest. My landlady lived in a house that was much too big for a woman on her own, at the corner of two dull streets that seemed to have no other purpose than to intersect. The concrete posts supporting the building made it look as if it was leaning forward, ready to fall at the first shake. All the rooms must have been occupied once, I could sense it. Family members dying, leaving, running away, whatever, had emptied it and the only one left was this wrinkled old woman who spent her mornings setting her hair. She had nobody to please except herself. The smell of scorched hair that came out of the few rooms she'd kept for herself caught you by the throat whenever you knocked at her door to collect your mail or pay the week's rent. She liked me from the start, after I told her I was pumping gas to work my way through college. My blue nylon shirt must have made a good impression. The first time we met, I was disturbed by her physical resemblance to my grandmother. She was the kind of woman who would have taken a husband and had children just for the pleasure of seeing them take off one by one, tired of the obsessive tidiness she must have inflicted on them. She rented three two-room apartments with kitchen for a more than reasonable price. The probation officer came to see me without warning after a month. I couldn't show him any pay slips, so I suggested he could just stand on the sidewalk opposite the gas station to check I was really working there. He was eager to know if I was living independently of my mother. I reassured him on that point but worried him too because, apart from him, nobody else was keeping an eye on me. He reminded me that I wasn't allowed to leave the state, and that the slightest infringement would lead to the withdrawal of my parole. "Where would I go? You think I'd leave the climate here in California to be a snowman in Alaska?" I could see there was something on his mind. He searched the apartment thoroughly in search of alcohol or drugs and then asked me, just when I was least expecting it, if I was all right. I told him I was, and that simple reply he somehow turned into whole paragraph, which he wrote on a sheet of paper in his file in tiny handwriting, carefully hiding it from me. The guy was about as open as a snake trying to pass its scales off as a sleeping bag. I sensed something enormous behind his lawman's veneer, the kind of burden you can never free yourself of. It was his job to provide a barrier against the triggers that lead to bad actions, and every twitch of his face or his fingers betrayed the fact that he was both repelled and attracted by that situation. I knew a lot about perverts, he could see that in my eyes, and for a split second the roles were reversed, but he quickly regained the upper hand, telling me I shouldn't expect him to forget who I was. He even got his revenge by bringing forward the dates when I had to check in with him.

30

Any enthusiasm I felt about pumping gas and washing windshields didn't last more than two months. It was the late spring of 1967 and the desire to take off was regularly nagging at me. I'd have happily hit the road in the opposite direction than all the other kids of my generation, who were flooding into Northern California. It was said they'd overrun San Francisco in their thousands and that thousands more were on their way, slowed down by a lack of money. Talking about the road, a customer who liked me worked for the Highway Administration and suggested hiring me for a fixed wage. I liked the prospect of working in the open air. Although Giannini was sorry to let me go, he was proud that a conscientious guy like me was trying to make his way in society just when so many kids were choosing to live hand to mouth. "Peace and love," those were the only words that ever came out of their mouths, like the bubbles of a perfumed soap for old ladies. Santa Cruz being between San Francisco and Monterey, these pacifist nuts were swarming around the town and in the university where my mother worked. I knew that because I sometimes took a walk on the campus to get an idea of the place where she worked. I even once had fun by paying her a visit. I knew from her boasting that she was the private secretary of the dean of psychology and I calmly climbed up to her office. To say she wasn't pleased by my unexpected visit is an understatement.

The blood drained from her face, turning it first pale then

green, as if it had oxidized. But she couldn't scream. I've never seen her looking so pathetic as she did when three other women working there came into her office to take her to lunch and looked at me in amazement as if discovering that the Empire State Building had a mother. Our faces were so alike there was no way she could deny me. She didn't even try to. But nor would she admit it. She just stayed where she was like a horse that doesn't know whether to move forward or backward. I turned to the women and said, "Hello, I'm Al, her son." They stood there transfixed and the least bright of the three said, "I thought you only had two daughters." I'd won the game. "I hope you don't want me to pull my pants down to prove it!" I said. One of the women, who I guessed didn't like my mother, screamed with laughter, making so much noise that the dean now came out of his office. The dean wasn't very tall and he was wearing a spotless shirt with a tight neck and a curious bow tie. He came in, all smiles, determined to join in the excitement. My mother introduced me as her son. He couldn't figure out what was so funny about that.

"My mother isn't very proud that I'm working to refurbish the roads of California rather than studying in a prestigious university, so she avoids introductions."

"I guess that is quite funny," the dean replied, trying hard not to cause offense to anyone. He quickly realized that his presence there was pointless. He glanced at the in-tray, just to justify having come out, and then went back in his office.

My mother, who was still not saying anything, stood up and got her bag. She was slowly getting over her terror at the thought of telling everyone the truth. She didn't show me any gratitude for that. Once outside, she said, "See you tonight, Al," as if I was in the habit of coming to her house, and disappeared with the other women. I sat down on a bench, with my arms stretched along the back of it, and watched the students walking from one building to another, alone or in groups.

Observing them told me a lot about America and how it had changed since I'd been inside. For the longest time, Communism had been the main threat hanging over the country, but now another kind of danger seemed to be eating away at it from inside. Fortunately, a majority of young people like me were still going to college and showing, by the way they dressed and behaved, both self-respect and respect for others. I felt there was a civil war brewing and it didn't take me long to choose sides. In two months, I hadn't spoken more than I needed to, and then only with Giannini, my probation officer and my landlady. It wasn't enough to get a clear idea about these things that were starting to intrigue me. I wanted to be useful to my country and help it to deal with this phenomenon of degeneracy in our youth. The result of this growing awareness was an uncontrollable urge to join the police. I suspected it would be difficult given my record, but if I played my cards right I thought I might have a chance.

When evening came, I strolled around town a little. When I started to feel hungry, I headed over to my mother's house in search of a free dinner. She opened the door and sighed wearily.

"You did say 'see you tonight' when we said goodbye at noon, didn't you?" I said. "Or did I just dream that?"

"I had to say something, Al. You can't come in now, I have company."

That suited me fine. She never took advantage of me in public and she was forced to hold her temper in check if she didn't want people to think of her as a hysterical woman. I pushed open the door to show her I had no intention of giving up. You could see she was trying to contain her anger and it was such an effort, I wondered how she was going to pull it off. Her visitor was an ageing professor. He really must be desperate for sex, I thought, to be reduced to running after a woman who was so unfeminine, with skin ruined by alcohol— including her nose, which was always red. He had never heard about me either, but he didn't seem to be offended. In nature, a male determined to mate with a female is only interested in her offspring if the latter is likely to stand in his way. My mother had made a decent meal, and she was dressed as if she was going out. This old professor ran one of the psychology departments and he was eager to show off his ability to read people. It clearly made him feel superior, but I just found him irritating. The only thing that concerned him was to know if I was going to stay on after dinner, which would have interfered with his plans.

"Your mother and I were talking about these hordes of teenagers converging on this part of California from all over America. What do you think of them, Al?"

"They call themselves pacifists but I think they're a bunch of defeatists. With people like that we might as well give the keys to America to the Soviets. And they won't even need to rape the women, they'll offer themselves up in baskets of flowers."

He thought my answer was amusing, and that broke the ice between us.

"I tried to enlist for Vietnam, but apparently I have more chance of standing and bumping my head in a helicopter than of being shot by the Vietcong. They didn't want me."

"What do you plan to do?"

"I'd like to study some more and join the police. I could help them."

"With what for example?"

"Establishing the psychological profiles of killers, investigating certain criminal circles."

"You know about psychology?"

At the thought of my answer, my mother's eyes almost burst out of their sockets.

"I've studied a lot of psychology over the last few years, and I even assisted some psychiatrists in testing patients when I was working in Atascadero. I've worked a lot on perverts. On schizophrenics too. I don't know so much about manic-depressives."

He appreciated my frankness. "Why don't you enroll in college? Ours for example?"

"I could. I have the right grades, and I don't know if my mother told you this, but they say my IQ is higher than Einstein's."

My mother confirmed this. She was about as comfortable as a bomb disposal expert handling a defective shell.

"That's impressive."

He didn't go any further. He sensed there was some mysterious thing between my mother and me, and being a patient man he was in no hurry to clear it up.

Over dinner, I laid it on thick about the role weak fathers played in the causes of perversion. He listened attentively, nodding often, and said at the end, "It'd be a pity not to let him continue his studies."

My mother pretended at first that she wasn't listening. Seeing that the professor's comment went beyond a polite formula, she turned to me. "Intelligence isn't always enough. You need other qualities like stability, perseverance . . . "

"Why, you aren't planning to turn him into a politician, are you?"

After this quip, we went on to other subjects that didn't interest me. I stood up a bit abruptly and left.

31

I didn't walk for long. I went into the first bar I found. It was full of hippies and I walked straight out again. The next one was empty and the thought of drinking alone, propped up on the counter, didn't fill me with enthusiasm. The third looked like a bar for regulars and people who were more conservative, the only kind I felt in the mood to be with. There were three gleaming Harleys parked outside, which convinced me I was in the right place. I walked around them. They must belong to a group of buddies, they were all choppers, customized from the 1960 FLH and chromium plated down to the smallest screw. Going inside, the first things I saw were the waitress, who had huge breasts, and the pool table in the middle of the room. Between the two, a whole bunch of customers, men mostly, all a little bit merry. A hippie came in just behind me, but three big guys sidled up to him, miming scissors with their fingers. It isn't easy to provoke a pacifist into a fight. The guy made a gesture of apology and went back out. The three big guys congratulated each other as if they had done something amazing and I ordered a double Jack Daniel's from the waitress, who seemed utterly bored by everything. It was like she was a victim of her big tits, as if they made it impossible for her to love. It'd have been good to inject a little life in her, just to see. I knocked back my drink and ordered another one. In her eyes I sensed that she suspected me of wanting to get drunk, so I got in first, reassuring her by telling her that a man my size took gallons to get plastered. She pretended not to hear, so I screamed over the music and ordered a bottle of wine. Whiskey burns my esophagus. Two of the bikers came and stood next to me at the bar, holding their women by the hand, one blonde and one redhead, both with big tits, not vulgar but not classy either. They greeted me, out of respect for my size. I was on the second half of the bottle of wine when we started talking. They kept serving themselves from a keg of beer that was next to them. It didn't matter because they were built solidly enough to withstand a flood. Folks come together quickly when they hate the same people. The tendency of human beings is to conform, and the best way to conform is by wearing a uniform. These four were dressed like Hell's Angels in the same way that I dressed like my father. I've always thought that the most original way to dress is to dress like everybody. We talked about bikes and they saw how much I knew about them. I told them about the Indian I'd left in Oregon. They realized that my size required one of the biggest bikes on the market unless you drove using your knees as sunglasses. They suggested introducing me to a guy who was selling a 1954 Panhead Police solo for a good price. They could vouch for him. I have to admit I really liked the idea of riding an old police bike. Buying it for 150 dollars when it had been worth a thousand new was quite a deal. I accepted, though I said I'd need some time to make enough money from my highway maintenance job. They were curious to know why I liked working in the sun surrounded by the smell of melting bitumen and the exhaust fumes of cars. I could have mentioned my childhood stuck up against a boiler, which had given me a taste for infernos. The reality was milder. We were repairing stretches of highway, that was true, but since I'd started in the job I'd been working on the coast road between San Francisco and Santa Cruz, where you were more likely to breathe sea air from the Pacific than exhaust fumes. The Hell's Angels didn't like the hippies, with their sickly pacifism and their dumb determination to be outsiders. The hippies wanted to turn the earth back into the Garden of Eden. The Hell's Angels cut straight across the hell of earth at top speed and had no desire to cool it down. Their visions were irreconcilable, I realized that straight away. I liked these guys. I imagined that joining a group and letting myself be carried along by it might free me a little from myself, even though I wasn't crazy about their long hair or their leathers, which they wore like a second skin. People said they were violent and, even though I was no pacifist, fighting scared me. They told me a pop festival was going to be held in Monterey, thousands of hippies were converging on the town, and they couldn't do anything to prevent it. At this point in the conversation, I ordered a second bottle of wine and I'm not quite sure what happened after that. I know we got along well, discovering we had similar views about a whole bunch of things. The drunker they got, the more they felt up the women who were with them. The one who was called Jeffrey even went off to bang his redhead in the toilets, I'd bet my life on it. Her friend would have liked to do the same but her guy was stuck to the bar counter like a barge in a lock. He knocked back seven or eight pints of beer and smoked one cigarette after another. His best moments in Vietnam, he admitted to me, were when he was lying on top of Vietnamese women, whether they liked it or not. If they liked it, you always had to pay them, a lot, and they did the business reluctantly, like whores. In his opinion, if they'd done the business with more conviction, there wouldn't have been so many rapes in the rice fields. He knew he was lucky to have come back in one piece, but he considered it his duty to make the whole of America share the hell he had lived through. How, he didn't say, but I could see from the angry look in his eyes that he bore a grudge against a whole lot of people. It was getting late. I paid what I owed to the waitress, who took the money without looking at me, gave the Hell's Angel, who was still talking to himself, a shy friendly tap on the shoulder, and went out. I ended the night sitting between two garbage cans, sleeping off my first big binge. I woke up just in time to catch the company bus that took us to the work site. A glorious day was rising over the Pacific, and in spite of the pounding in my skull, I had the fleeting, intense feeling that I really existed. I was glad I hadn't killed my grandparents in some wretched Midwestern state where bare plains roll on as far as the eye can see.

32

Have you found me a publisher?"

"I talked to three of them, but none of them have gone for the idea yet. They're afraid that if you tell the whole story, readers may be shocked, and if you don't, they won't be interested."

The pile of books is on the table in front of him. He pushes it away with such brutality that Susan pulls back and almost falls off her chair in the process.

"Why are you doing that?"

"I'm pissed off. I don't want to read any more fucking books to any more fucking blind people. Nobody ever does anything for me. They've written biographies about me, they stole my story for two movies, including one that's been one a huge hit around the world, and now that I ask to be published, all the doors are closed. Don't you think I need to exist for myself just a little? I'm not talking about posterity, Susan. I don't give a fuck about that. Mankind will disappear one day, that's for sure, so posterity's only temporary anyway. I'd also like to bear witness to what we are, because I'm part of this community, Susan, you hear me? I'm part of it."

"I know, Al, I know."

"Then why have you been coming to see me for years and staring at me with those big fish eyes of yours?"

Susan starts crying. He lets the wave pass in order not to add his scorn to the pain he has caused her. She recovers.

"Because you spared my life."

He says nothing at first, as if this is the stupidest thing he's ever heard in his life.

"I spared your life?" he says at last.

"It was toward the end of 1970, at the University at Santa Cruz. Darkness had fallen, and the mist made it even murkier. I'd finished my semester, and I'd stayed late to get my things together. I had to get back downtown and there was a last bus but I'd have to wait half an hour. I stood under a lamppost to hitch a ride. I wasn't feeling very confident, there were a lot of weird things going down at that time. I saw this white van come along and a guy with an honest face at the wheel. You pulled up next to me. I didn't hesitate, I just got in. There was something reassuring about the size of you. You said, 'I don't really have time to take you anywhere, but if I didn't and something happened to you, I'd never forgive myself.' I told you where I lived in town and we started talking. You asked me if I was some kind of hippie and, if I was, why I hadn't dropped out of school . . ."

He's hypermnesiac and sometimes it really bugs him, gives him migraine, that he can't forget anything. So her face can't have vanished entirely from his memory, even after forty-three years.

"Have you changed that much?" he cuts in. "Don't you have any photographs of yourself at that time?"

She takes out a snapshot taken on the campus and he recognizes her right away. Time really is pitiless. There's nothing left of the young girl she used to be apart from a few barely recognizable traces. He falls silent and lets her continue.

"You were supposed to drive me home, but on the way I told you about a commune north of San Francisco and on the spur of the moment we decided to go there. Do you remember?"

"I remember very well."

"By the time I got back to Santa Cruz a few months later, everybody was talking about you and I realized that you'd spared my life. I had only one idea, to see you again. It was the greatest act of love I'd ever seen, don't you see?"

He's dumbfounded. "An act of love?"

"I was convinced that something about me had disturbed you, even though you weren't aware of it. Am I wrong?"

"What does it matter? I could say yes, and you'd sleep easy for the next ten years. But it'd be meaningless. I never loved you and I certainly never desired you, either then or later."

"Well, I know you loved me, I know it deep down, in my flesh. If it wasn't true, I wouldn't have sacrificed all these years to you, I wouldn't have given up on the idea of living with someone. You don't know anything about the love of women, Al, but it's a superior force, a heavenly force. I've loved you for forty-three years. But I'm not crazy, I wouldn't have given in to that strength of feeling if I didn't think you paid me back a thousand times, the day you saved my life."

He thinks she's gone a little far. "Fuck this, are you crazy or what?"

She stares at him for a few moments, out of breath from chasing all these memories.

"You're crazy! I hated all hippies at the time, men and women. Of course, I wouldn't have done them any harm, but I thought you were all weak, the way you fucked, the way you did drugs, the way you hung around the street, rooting through trash cans for food because all your money had gone on buying speed or grass. You all made me nauseous, if you really want to know. It was a collective suicide. The women were particularly repulsive. Their brains leaked from the effects of dope and it was like you only needed to put a finger on the top of their skulls for them to open their legs. It made me want to throw up. I tried to understand, I studied all of you methodically when I needed to, I grasped all the ins and outs of that psychedelic experiment, and the only thing I remember is that it was all one big fuck-up. Even the music of that time, what's left of it? You ever try listening to Jefferson Airplane or the Grateful Dead without smoking a joint? And yet, that's all anyone listened to at the time. When you go back to your grandparents' house thirty years later, and you discover that the vast spaces you remember are just cramped little rooms that inspire nothing but contempt, the disappointment is overwhelming. It's the same thing."

"You can say whatever you like, but even if that experiment went bad, I don't regret it. We were following in the footsteps of Jesus Christ, two thousand years later. Society was caught off guard, and so were the radicals. Nobody before us had ever protested nonviolently . . ."

"What about Gandhi?"

"But not in our culture. We disarmed everybody. And all our prophecies turned out to be right. Our species is working toward its own destruction, which isn't so far off. Consciousness should never have been used to separate us from our environment. Now, we're really alone in the world. Money, greed and the market rule everything. We wanted to prevent that."

"You didn't prevent anything. You didn't even slow things down. The only things left from everything you did are a few oversize T-shirts for nostalgia freaks on sale in Haight Ashbury. Who listens to Joplin or Hendrix, who reads Burroughs or Ginsberg? The proof is that you've never brought them to me to read for the blind. Kerouac, the supposed inspiration, who's Kerouac, can you tell me? A guy who spends his time on the road wondering if he's really queer or if he's dreaming. But I know what's left of all that. AIDS. How do you get it? By fucking or getting high, the twin foundations of your movement. Your movement was based on a serious misunderstanding about the real nature of man. Man isn't born good, only to be corrupted by society. He's a reptile pursued by a civilization he keeps trying to escape. And your fucking sentimental crap led to the same result as the ideologies you were fighting against.

Thousands of kids who died of overdoses or threw themselves out of windows because they thought they could fly. Talking about Burroughs, you know what he did to his wife? The William Tell trick. He put her up against a tree and put an apple on her head. Instead of aiming at the apple with a crossbow, he took a colt. He shot a tad too low and the top of his wife's skull exploded instead of the apple. He got away with a reprimand. Involuntary homicide. I don't think he even did time. It happened in Mexico or somewhere like that and as he was under the influence of dope or alcohol, his responsibility didn't come into the picture. It's hardly credible. How are things outside?"

She's taken aback by the question. "What do you mean?"

"Yes, what's happening that's worth talking about? I read tons of books, but never any newspapers. I never watch TV either. The guys in here only ever watch sports. The sports reporters drive me crazy. I've never seen people talk so much and have so little to say. The other reporters are the same, they never stop. How about the black President? Is he doing a good job? Never saw a bigger show-off in my life. Are we getting out of Iraq and Afghanistan? Just as well. Even wars these days are meaningless."

He sighs.

"So, you think I loved you, or at least that I had feelings . . . No, Susan. Don't take it personally, I've never loved anyone. I can't say I don't know the feeling, but I've only ever skimmed the surface. I've felt its potential, as if a shiver went through me, followed by an immense tenderness that didn't come from inside me but from somewhere further away. Loving until even desire is gone, do you see what I mean? It's such an exciting feeling that I often remember it. But what I'm describing to you, I could never feel for long. I was defeated every time. So, how are things out there?"

"Out there, we're going under. Everything we feared has

come to pass. The earth is getting worn out like a sick old woman her husband wants to keep screwing every day. America has won. No more Communism, no more dreams either, just one model, ours. In fifty years there won't be anything left in the sea but farmed fish, we'll be breathing through masks, and water will cost more than champagne. Apart from that, everything's fine, new countries are emerging on the same model as ours. The only thing Orwell got wrong was believing that totalitarianism had a terrifying face. Not at all. As long as you accept the endless chatter of the social networks, that everything you buy will be obsolete after a year, that Sisyphus is only at rest when the sales are on, that Google knows everything about you and can possibly sell it to the cops, that you can be located at any moment with your phone, you don't run any risks. Mankind will suffer less and less and will want for nothing, but it's going to be really bored when it has to walk through the national parks in single file, looking at what's left of nature, because idiots thought that making lots of children is a good thing for the species. I have no desire to stick around for the overcrowding we're promised."

Susan breaks off and looks around. Al wonders why. She falls silent. She is only capable of speaking in waves, and when she does she can't say anything with the slightest conviction but only with a kind of resigned weariness.

"You know what, Susan? I have the impression you're manic-depressive. I'm going to be clear with you. I'm not any kind of expert on the condition, the way I am when it comes to schizophrenia or perversion, but I know enough about it to posit a diagnosis. You should see a doctor. Former junkies, and I think you're one, often have strong bipolar tendencies, problems of dissociation linked to damage to their neuronal connections. I'm not throwing any stones, after all I used to drink a lot, although that didn't last long. I really think you should see a doctor."

"I can't afford it."

"That's another matter."

Silence puts things back on an even keel.

"I don't know if we'll see each other again, Susan, I put in my request for Angola. How long it's going to take, I don't know."

"What are you going to do there if you won't read for the blind anymore?"

"I'm going to take care of the horses and the other prisoners. That'll be less boring than here, where nothing ever happens. I used to have lots of visitors, I played with them, manipulated them sometimes. I learned to hate them, because nobody ever tried to understand me. Everyone sees something of himself in me and enjoys seeing it in a dormant state. You see, Susan, nobody can deny that I do good. But I can tell you this, there isn't anything deep in my soul guiding me on that path. I've started writing my memoirs and I know there'll always be something missing, something that gives a book its flavor, whether it's obvious or not, and that's empathy. Chekhov and Carver had it. I mention those two, because Carver always claimed to be influenced by Chekhov. Even Céline or Hamsun, who were sons of bitches to judge from their biographies—Céline even more than Hamsun, you can put Hamsun's bad choices down to senility—wrote books full of deep empathy for the human race, if you look at them closely, and these books redeem their authors' personal conduct. Nothing in you touches me, Susan, nothing, but then nothing touches me anyone. If you died tomorrow, it wouldn't affect me any more than the death of any creature on this earth. For some months now, I've been having this recurring dream. It takes place somewhere I know well, the mountain road between Medford and Gold Beach in the south of Oregon. That road goes on and on, winding for miles, the forest is thick like the forest in a legend, the cliffs are sheer drops, nobody's ever traced a path along them. When the road ends at Gold Beach and you see the gray sea and the long beach in the distance, you feel as if you've been spared. Not a night goes by that I don't dream about that forest, it symbolizes what I am for my family, the end of the line. None of my sisters had a child. The younger one because she never found a man to give her one. The older one died in pregnancy, of complications linked to her obesity. My younger sister wasn't too bad. When I think back over my childhood, I remember fleeting moments of complicity, as if she'd tried to get close to me. She came to see me here a dozen times, at the beginning. She didn't know what to say, so she'd look at the ceiling as if it was going to give birth to something. She would bring me uneatable cakes covered in icing. She always seemed torn between two intentions, but I never knew what they were. She'd already stopped coming to see me before she died, for no particular reason, in her apartment in Oakland. Sometimes, I catch myself thinking that my father, who I've never been able to find a trace of, had another child late in life to wash away the insult to our bloodline."

33

I liked repairing roads but wasn't crazy about it. The days started early. We worked in teams of ten, we each had our place and nobody budged from it. As there was no specific training, I was mostly given the job of directing the traffic onto the alternate lanes. The drivers would see me from a distance, waving my orange flag. I knew I wasn't going to vegetate doing that all my life. Especially as my grandfather, the one I had killed, had spent his whole career on the highways and I had no desire to follow in his footsteps.

The smell of hot tar ended up making me nauseous. To be more specific, I have to say that at that time, my liver was being seriously weakened by alcohol. I'd started drinking a lot after every encounter with my mother and then, as the weeks passed, I drank regularly. Getting up early to go to the sites, which were always changing, required more and more effort. One morning, after a monumental bender the previous night in the bar opposite the courthouse, I decided not to get up. I deliberately stayed in bed until ten. By noon, I was in the highways office, getting the wages that were owed to me. In the middle of the afternoon, I greeted my colleagues as they got off the bus bringing them back from the site and said goodbye to them. I didn't lie, I told them the gas fumes made me nauseous and I couldn't continue. They were really nice to me. By late afternoon, I was at a Harley dealership buying a secondhand motorcycle and arranging credit. The manager must have liked me because, knowing I was looking for work, he offered me a job as a salesman on commission, which I accepted without thinking. The prospect of going back on the road on a bike gave me a real sense of joy, one I cultivate religiously in my memories. Every evening, every weekend, I was going to get back to the calm of the endless spaces and the rhythm of my twin-cylinder engine, my face numbed by the wind, reassured by the incomparable feeling that I actually existed. Deep down, I also had the idea that the prospect of those long rides would wean me off the booze. Leitner often told me that the reason alcohol had been as successful as it was among human beings was because no better tranquilizer had yet been invented. Alcohol may excite other people, but it calmed me down. I never had bad wine, far from it. After one or two bottles I entered a wonderful, calm world, the world my contemporaries searched for in drugs. A third or fourth bottle never sent me off the edge, the way I'd read about in Bukowski. But I knew the booze was getting me nowhere. I saw how it had hollowed my mother's face, and how it sometimes sent her into a stupor that never led to anything good. Alcohol made her mean, and the only way I could bear that meanness, which she spread about her with all the generosity of a female parishioner supporting children in Africa, was to drink myself.

I had nobody to share my good news with. So I went to see her at home just before dinnertime. She was already pretty much plastered, and high in a way that usually led to one of her aggressive moods. I announced proudly that I had bought a motorcycle and that the dealer had hired me.

"Am I supposed to be pleased to know that one of these days you'll kill yourself on that machine, Al? You know perfectly well you're shortsighted and you drive much too fast. As for the job, I don't see how it's better than working on the roads in a big organization that offers the possibility of promotion. I have something to tell you too, I'm moving to Aptos. I've had too many failures in this house and it's costing me too much. Why don't you go to college? Your school grades are good enough for you to enroll."

"That's new. I thought you didn't want me close by."

"I wasn't talking about Santa Cruz. There are plenty of colleges in California."

"Anyway, I'll never study anywhere near you."

She looked at me for a while with her eyes blurred by alcohol. "I don't understand why you don't like me, Al. I was hard on you as a child, but it was for your own good."

"My own good?"

For a while, we didn't say anything, didn't even look at each other either. We were like two dominant bears that meet unexpectedly in a forest and turn their heads away, distressed at the thought of tearing each other apart.

I broke the silence without thinking about what I was going to say. "If I didn't like you, I wouldn't have lied to my psychiatrist when I was in the hospital. I told him there were stairs leading down to the cellar of the house in Montana. Whereas, as you well know, it could only be reached through a trapdoor under the armchair where you used to sit."

"What difference does that make?"

"I don't know. I also didn't tell him that you used to hit me with a belt that had a buckle, a huge metal buckle that left purple marks. And I never mentioned the way you did nothing when your older daughter tried to have sex with me. I was what, eight at the time. I told you the facts and you dismissed them with the back of your hand. Nobody could touch your favorite child. I didn't want to stain your reputation more than I could bear. I want you to know that, period. I'm going to tell you another thing. You think I'm the only man who'll never leave you. That's possible. But don't count on it. I'm not my father and I'm not all those guys who've come and gone since him. You condemned yourself to a solitary life, Ma, it's your choice. I know you tell everybody you invented feminism before all those women who claim they did. I won't be your last victim."

My mother didn't like anyone to have the edge over her. "What the hell are you talking about, you pathetic loser? You think I'm finished with men and that I'm going to console myself by keeping my son around, my criminal son who never brings me any relief? You're sick, Al, and they haven't cured you yet."

"Instead of insulting me, you'd do better to introduce me to girls from your college. That would make a change from the women I meet in bars whose breath smells the same as yours."

"No girl from my college deserves to have to deal with someone like you. They're way out of your league. You think I'm going to ruin my reputation like that? 'Here, let me introduce my son, who spent five years in a mental hospital for shooting his grandparents but has a great future ahead of him, watch out, ladies, he may be the next governor of California.' I can still hear Dr. Chadwick telling me during my pregnancy: 'Don't get so agitated, Mrs. Kenner, or you'll have a miscarriage!' If I saw him now, I'd say to him: 'I'm the first woman on earth to have given birth and miscarried at the same time.' That's what I'd say to him."

34

The Jury Room is a dark, windowless bar built of perpends on the gloomy square opposite the courthouse in Santa Cruz. It looks out of place in a town that's like something in a child's coloring book. Even though the town lies right on the San Andreas Fault, nothing tragic ever seems to happen there, and there's a kind of hygienic pointlessness about the place. Sometimes I was tempted to stop a group of people on Pacific Drive and ask, "Goddammit, haven't any of you ever suffered?"

From the day my mother moved to Aptos, I never once left her house without rushing to the Jury Room and drinking until closing time. Most of the cops in Santa Cruz had also made it their favorite destination. Some out of habit, because it was so close to the courthouse. Others, forced out of their homes by domestic quarrels, came there to while away their free time surrounded by people they knew. When I bought my Harley, I thought I'd also bought myself a future. Deep inside me, the idea of becoming a cop, if possible a motorcycle cop, was growing. It wasn't about making a childhood dream come true, it was more of a compulsion, something I couldn't explain to myself. I wanted to be on the right side of the fence and take root there. For a few weeks, that illusion had the upper hand over the reality of my criminal record. I knew I was going to be asked about it at some point in the process, but I evaded the question, as if I was somehow going to find a way to carry on regardless. In the meantime, I drank with the town's cops and they really liked my company. You have to remember that at that time it was hard for them to talk to a young person my age without being called a pig. The questioning of authority was taking forms they couldn't keep up with, they didn't even know how to react anymore. My drinking impressed them because I never let myself go, which proved that I was a good guy.

When a man accepts that he'll never again see his cock unless he looks at himself in the mirror, it means he's taken the path of resignation and there's no turning back. That was the case with an old cop of Mexican descent who often stuck it out until closing time along with me. He had a belly the size of a beer barrel, which protruded over his belt and threatened to drop on the floor. He couldn't see himself piss these days, but he must have told himself he'd be retiring soon and then he'd have plenty of time to perfect his aim at the bowl. I didn't laugh at that. I suspected his wife's discontent about the subject was the reason he'd been exiled from the house. We'd have good long talks. His only son had left home to join a commune in San Francisco and he poured out his anxieties onto me. His boy had dropped out and joined the countercultural movement that was starting to gain a lot of ground, even in Santa Cruz, a town halfway between Los Angeles, where money was still king, and San Francisco, where a swarm of crazy kids thought they were inventing an alternative world. What I said reassured him. I didn't know much about the situation of these dropouts but I still came out with all these big psychological and sociological theories that left him stunned. When I told him I wanted to join the police, he was categorical that I'd never get in because of my height. He knew it was a kind of discrimination, and he felt bad about it, especially as he was convinced I would have made a good cop. When he asked me about my past, I knew I was taking a big chance, because I wouldn't be able to change my story again. I've never been crazy about either lies or the truth, but I know how close they are, and that a lie should never be too far from the truth. I had come to California to join my mother, I told him, after working as an assistant psychologist in a private mental hospital in Montana. The budgetary cuts ordered by Reagan California had forced me to change direction, which was why I was doing various jobs, the latest as a Harley-Davidson salesman. He found my story consistent and he peddled it to all his colleagues, especially to a guy named Duigan, a broad-headed Irishman who ran the homicide squad. Duigan and I became friendly because neither of us could easily find a motorcycle helmet to fit us. He owned an old Harley and went for rides on Sundays. I found myself quite drawn to him. I wanted him to like me. From the first time we met I wanted to seem like a model young man, with no vices and a firm belief in the values that had made America so attractive to the whole world. By getting close to him, I had the feeling I'd be entering an orbit where he was the center of attraction. A planet can deviate slightly from its orbit but, to the best of my knowledge, never leave it. Duigan was reserved, which was only right for a man in charge of criminal investigations. He came almost every evening to the Jury Room to have a beer before going home to have dinner. But I never saw him there afterwards, except when he was on duty in the evening or a case was keeping him busy. Although he was friendly to me, he kept that distance common to cops, who think that everyone's a potential criminal. During our first conversations, I noticed he was observing me closely and letting me speak more than he did. I was always talkative at that time, drunk or not. My need to talk was even greater than my need to drink. In four years of mental hospital, I'd only ever really talked with two psychiatrists and a perverted literature professor. Before that, I couldn't recall any real conversation with a human being, just a few long monologues to the dog.

35

T hat need to talk prompted me to buy a secondhand Ford Galaxy van, which led to a strange coincidence just as I was starting to be afraid Duigan was losing interest in me.

At the end of every afternoon, I'd come back from work and exchange my Harley for my van. I'd drive slowly along High Street in the direction of the University, which was located in the Santa Cruz hills. The faculty buildings on the sprawling campus are surrounded by tall trees. The does bring their fawns to graze on the neat lawns, oblivious to the students strolling calmly from one building to another. This concentration of studious intelligence held a real fascination for me, and I saw the colleges, up there in the woods, as branches of a single brain.

Probably because my mother thought the students were way out of my league, I felt the need to observe them, to rub shoulders with them, in order to try to understand what separated me from them. I didn't hold it against them that my mother considered me their exact antithesis, but everything intrigued me about them, their backgrounds, their dreams, their motivations. You have to realize that at the time I couldn't hold a conversation of more than a few seconds with anyone who thought they were superior to me. The only way I found to meet students and not feel they were dominating me was to give them rides when they were hitching. Their reaction to the service I rendered them could only be one of gratitude and humility, especially when they discovered what a giant I was. I wasn't guided in my choice of who to pick up by what they looked like or what they were wearing. I would drive all over the campus and, as soon as I saw someone with his thumb out, I'd give him a ride. In general, I drove them all the way home and if they offered to contribute to the price of gas, I'd generously refuse. In those years, hitchhiking was the most common way for young people to get around, and had been since the beginning of the decade. The students I gave rides to felt they owed me something and were eager to engage in conversation, which rarely lasted more than a quarter of an hour anyway, the time it took to drive all the way downtown. My aversion for hippies and those who imitated the style didn't stop me from giving rides to them in my van. On the contrary, I'd decided to find out everything I could about them. First of all because I could see how much they disturbed my cop friends at the Jury Room. I could already imagine myself becoming a specialist on their movement, overcoming my revulsion and behaving like a cross between an anthropologist and an undercover officer.

This need to talk very soon turned into an addiction. After dropping a student in town, I often went back up to the campus to reload. If I had just dropped a man, I made sure I'd pick up a girl. They were more hesitant, even though hitchhiking didn't have the bad reputation it's since gathered. But stories about rape were already circulating. The hippies who preached free love were less worried about it than the respectable girls who lived on Cliff Drive. To reassure them, I'd look at my watch like someone who's wondering if he has time to burden himself with a passenger. But then I'd always take them. The stuck-up girls from the nice neighborhoods all had the same way of creating a distance between us. Apprehension, then gratitude for the service I was offering, quickly gave way to contempt for what I represented, a working-class guy who had grown too quickly on junk food and was on his way to becoming obese. I could have lied and claimed that my mother taught in one of the faculties on campus, but I couldn't do it. Passing her off as more than she was would have required a huge effort, one that I wasn't prepared to make, even to impress a girl. They always concealed their contempt beneath a kind of polite condescension. The *wow* of feigned amazement they gave when I told them I was a motorcycle salesman sometimes made me want to smash their faces in, but I played the game by asking them lots of personal questions before I dropped them outside their homes. They had a way of putting a shine on their families that made me really angry. Not a loser in sight, just doctors of something or other, hardworking businessmen, admired sportsmen. All I could ever manage was a timid reference to my father's war record, which would earn me a furtive raising of the eyebrows before they resumed the torrent of references that had led to their birth. These pretty American girls with their fine skin and delicate nails lived in an enchanted, protected world. They seldom looked at me as if I was a human being, all they saw in me was a well-trained consumer, a natural outlet for their parents' businesses. The time it took me to drive them from the campus to their homes was about all I could stand of these stuck-up bitches. But I soon missed their superior airs because, I have to admit, there was something sexual about them that attracted me. Whether they're brunettes or blondes, girls from good families don't have the same skin or the same hair as other girls. Being in contact with them made me feel I might actually desire one of them completely one day, which would have represented a kind of achievement for me, even if I didn't go any further. I identified them with the Kennedy children, who were taught that money pardons everything, even when you've earned it dishonestly. Oswald should have been made a saint for showing these people that God is watching, even when we least expect it. That was what I told my passengers, when they praised Robert

Kennedy as if he was better than Christ himself. But even though progressive ideas were fashionable, there were still plenty of co-eds who came from staunchly Republican families. Others had fallen into the counterculture in reaction to a stifling environment at home. They'd get in my van without any hesitation. They didn't even take the trouble to put out the joint they were holding between their fingers. They'd sit down, their heads resting against the door jamb, and the first thing they asked me was to change the music. Then they'd hold out their joint, which I politely declined. Apart from a few radical militants, most of them had a blissed-out air that got on my nerves, even though I didn't show it. I'd have happily shaved their hair off and given them a shower. I said that to one of them one day when I was still angry after an argument with my mother, even though it had happened the day before. The girl, whom I'd just told about my father, commented that this kind of method was exactly what the Nazis used in the death camps and I didn't like the comparison. Their extravagant clothing irritated me. I despised them when, after five minutes, they suggested a quick fuck in the woods above the campus. What really riled me the most was that they seemed to think they'd be performing an act of charity in fucking me, because of my uptight air, my trim mustache, and my short-sleeved nylon shirts. I remember a tall girl who had got in without even looking at me and who'd started provoking me after a few minutes by making it quite clear she thought I was a closet homosexual, simply because I hadn't immediately fallen for her. This girl was a real beauty and when she offered to suck my cock in the innocent tones of a girl asking where the restroom is in a big store, I felt like strangling her. She must have sensed the bad vibes because she immediately changed the subject, asking me if I could take her on my Harley for a trip along the coast south of Carmel. I replied that I rode too fast to take a passenger and she got off soon afterwards, hardly even saying goodbye. I always told them the same things about me. I mentioned my father's war record as soon as I could, I justified my presence on the campus by talking about my mother's job, and I sometimes boasted of being employee of the month at the Harley dealership. I even beat all records for sales at the concession in Monterey even though that was located in a ritzier neighborhood, but that didn't impress anyone, the hippies any more than the stuck-up ones.

Wendy seemed impressed, though, when I reeled off my three-monthly sales figures, and so did her friend. They were neither hippies nor stuck-up. They weren't even students. I picked them up on High Street some distance from the University. Wendy could have been really pretty. Her shoulders were a little stooped and she had a bit too much of a belly for her age but her face was amazingly fresh and expressed nothing except that she was a good girl, and more intelligent than she gave herself credit for. Her friend was a similar type but really ugly, with so much acne on her face that you felt like rubbing it with sandpaper. She tagged along behind Wendy and never did anything without her agreement. For a moment, I thought they were lesbians. When I told them that, they burst out laughing. Wendy put her hand on her friend's shoulder and said, "Do you think if I were a lesbian I'd be interested in a girl like this?" That might sound mean, but it wasn't said in a mean way, which only goes to show that between people, everything's a matter of convention. They seemed to be at a bit of a loose end, not expecting anything special to happen, carried along by boredom and the slight sadness that went with it. They hadn't made up their minds where they were going. I suggested we could eat together, though I made it clear that I didn't have enough money to pay for them. We headed for the amusement park that occupies about half of Beach Street. There's a big wheel and a chamber of horrors and stores selling T-shirts. The burgers are no more expensive than anywhere else, no greasier either. They were left speechless by the amount I was able to stuff into myself. It was obvious to them that a guy who eats for three can't also be expected to pay for two girls. Wendy had a boyfriend who worked in the vegetable department of a supermarket. He wasn't in charge of the department, he just unpacked deliveries and he didn't seem to do much for Wendy. Marilyn, who'd been given that name by her parents because of the actress—they obviously hadn't realized how cruel that was—seemed happy to be a third wheel. Wendy was discreet about her life, and quite resigned to her fate for a girl her age. I soon realized that we both found it difficult to know what we really wanted. She was working as a temporary secretary in a dentist's office while wondering if she wouldn't do better to go back to school. But what would she study? She wasn't crazy about any particular subject. She described herself as passive type. If she was passive, then Marilyn was pretty much a vegetable. Our relationship developed quickly because there was nothing between us. I liked being with these two girls because they didn't feel obliged to talk when they had nothing to say. I really wanted to go for a drink at the Jury Room, but I didn't feel like taking them along. We first drove Marilyn to her house, on the road to Monterey, then I took Wendy back to her place in the hills, just above the amusement park. The apartment where she lived with her father was in a converted motel. We got out of my van just as her father was getting out of his car, which he'd just parked. I recognized Duigan's big head coming toward her. Being the kind of guy who isn't easily surprised, he didn't seem surprised to see me there, just intrigued.

"You two know each other?"

Wendy found it amusing that I should know her father.

"We sometimes have a drink together opposite the courthouse." That was all he needed to say.

*

"Your daughter was hitching on High Street," I said. "I didn't know you were related, but I thought she'd be safer with me than with anyone else."

"You did the right thing. She's the most precious person in the world to me. Feel like a last beer?"

We went up to the apartment. It was quite wide and not very deep. The window looked out on the amusement park and just a small strip of sea shrouded in mist. The noise of the machines rose laboriously from the park. The apartment was poorly furnished. We sat down on the balcony around a plastic table. Duigan took three beers from the fridge and smiled at me. Wendy rubbed her eyes like someone trying to stay awake.

"I'm sorry, I don't have any wine."

"That's okay, I only drink it at the Jury Room."

"You drink too much, I've seen you. It's just a phase."

I didn't know how he could know that but I agreed.

"Where did you two meet again?"

"On High Street, coming out of work," replied Wendy.

"I thought you always took the bus."

"Yes, but Marilyn came to pick me up, we walked a bit and we got tired."

"How about you, where were you coming from?"

I hesitated over answering but not enough to make him suspicious. Hard to admit straight off that my favorite pastime was giving rides to students, even though there was nothing reprehensible about it.

"I went to see my mother on the campus."

"Does she live around here?"

"She's secretary to the dean of psychology but she lives in Aptos. She just moved there."

"How about your father?"

"He lives in L.A. with his new wife. I don't hear from him anymore."

"Do you get along with your mother?"

"We're very different."

"You're lucky to have one, take advantage of it. Wendy lost hers when she was eleven."

Wendy didn't flinch.

"Didn't you ever remarry?" I asked without thinking.

"A woman who wants to live with a cop is a woman who thinks it's an advantage to live with a man she never sees, and I don't like that. Wendy's mother was the exception. There hasn't been any other. I hear you want to join the police."

"Yes, but Sergeant Ramirez says I'm too tall."

"Unfortunately, that's true. How tall are you?"

"Seven feet two."

"Then forget it. They take midgets but not giants. Don't ask me why. Rules are rules. Right now, you're selling Harleys, aren't you? Don't you like it?"

"I think I can do better. I took psychological tests at school, I have a higher IQ than Einstein."

"Then it's not the police you want, son." He smiled as he said it, with that sad smile he never lost after that. "What else are you interested in?"

"Psychology. I used to work in a psychiatric hospital in Montana. It's a job that's useful to society. I may take a college course."

"That'd be a good idea. But if you do criminal psychiatry, I don't know if we can keep seeing each other. I've never seen so many idiots as I have in that field. They look at cops as fossils, they think our intelligence is stuck somewhere between our holsters and our pistols."

"That's because they try to put all patients in a pigeonhole, whether they like it or not. They don't leave any leeway for individuality. In psychiatry, as far as I know, every case is unique, but they always want to pin everything down to a specific pathology. In criminal pathology, it's even worse, with the problem of responsibility and all the difficulties that entails."

There were little droplets of rain in the fog drifting in from the open sea, but the weather was still fine.

"Wendy should go back to school too. You should try to persuade her. Isn't that right, Wendy?"

"What would I study?"

"Are you planning to spend your life fixing appointments for a dentist? There must be something more exciting, don't you think so, Al?"

"For sure."

Wendy stood up to go get us some more beers. Duigan took advantage of her absence to tell me something in confidence.

"Wendy doesn't have any motivation, that's her problem. I guess it's all because of her mother's death. I'd send her to a shrink but I don't trust those guys. You should see her boyfriend. He unpacks vegetables all day. When he finishes, he goes surfing. Can you tell me the point of getting up on a board and letting yourself be pushed about by a wave? If he has any time left over, he drops by to see Wendy and they listen to music. To me it isn't music, it's noise, but what the hell, they stay there for hours without saying anything. It's like they're making a religion of depression. The guy's no good for her, I don't know if you have an IQ like Einstein's but he must have the IQ of an octopus. He isn't a bad guy or a good guy, because both of those require too much effort. At his age, I was in the Pacific, killing Japs."

"My father killed Germans."

"Where was he based?"

"Special Forces, Fort Harrison in Montana."

"What were they called again?"

"The Devil's Brigades."

"That's it. He must have seen some things. With a father like that, I'm not surprised you seem a straight-up guy."

Wendy came back with the beers and we drank calmly without doing much to keep the conversation going, like people who've known each other for ages.

"If nobody gets it into his head to kill someone, we could take a bike ride south this weekend, what do you say?"

I could have jumped for joy. Not at the thought of being with Wendy. Even though she was a great girl with nice eyes and delicate features, she didn't attract me. But knowing that her father trusted me, that was really satisfying. We called it a day after our fourth beer. I really wanted to end the evening at the Jury Room but I didn't want Duigan to find out I'd gone to get drunk after leaving his place.

36

I got back in my van and drove to Aptos, to see my mother's new house. Aptos is five minutes from Santa Cruz on the 101. I had to drive around for a while before I found the house. It was in a kind of development with buildings of different kinds. I called to a guy who was tinkering with the engine of an old Ford, trying to get it restarted. He had a lamp between his teeth. He gave me a funny look, then pointed me in the direction of 2909A. The house stood on a bend in the road, a little taller and a little less presentable than the others, and looking especially ugly with its peeling gray-blue paint. The light was on. My mother opened up. She was still dressed. Apparently she had visitors. When I went in she introduced me to Sally Enfield, a secretary like her. She looked like a whipped dog, the kind of woman who apologizes for existing. There was no way my mother would have had a friend stronger than her. She was in a good mood, probably because she had already drunk a lot, helped by her friend, who I guessed also needed it to survive. The friend seemed terrified by the size of me but she converted her fear into compliments to my mother on the handsome son she had. My mother looked at me as if she was seeing me for the first time then she made a face and poured herself a glass of wine. They must have sworn to spend the whole evening talking because that's all they did, not even bothering to ask me anything. All the staff, teachers and students in their faculty were getting hauled over the coals. My mother really thought she'd made it. She must have thought she was Elizabeth Taylor in *Who's Afraid of Virginia Woolf?* But with her height, her coarse features and her eyes like a bison's behind her big glasses, she was quite simply grotesque. I cut short her performance and asked her to lend me some money. I hadn't come with that idea in mind, but seeing the turn the evening was taking, it was the only thing I could think of.

"I'm not surprised. Sally, why else do you think he'd have come to see me?" Swaying amidst the crummy furniture in her living room she went on, "The animal never calls to find out how I am, but he still needs me. He claims I was too hard on him as a child, that's why things go bad and he only does stupid crap that I won't go into, Sally, because it's so awful you'd say it was just the wine talking. So I'll answer you, Al, and Sally will be my witness. I don't have any money to lend you. I moved here because the rent was half what I was paying before. There must be a reason for that, mustn't there?"

The black hole that's always there every day of my life, and which shrunk when I met Duigan, opened up again, a big gaping hole.

"I'm asking you for enough to fill up my Harley twice this weekend. It's yes or no, there's no need to go over the top. Oh, what the hell, I'm going!"

I stood up as I said that and crossed the living room to get to the kitchen.

"And when I think he wanted me to introduce him to my female students," I heard my mother say. "Can you tell me, Sally, what they'd do with an elephant seal who only comes to see his mother to extort money from her?"

I went into the kitchen, opened her bag, took out enough money to full up my bike twice, and left. I knew I was going to see that gray-faced Sally again. My mother always sealed her friendship with a person by insulting me in front of that person. Showing people how bad our relationship was her way of getting them on her side. As I was getting back in my van, I felt bad. Leaving like that, going back home, staying there for hours: everything seemed painful suddenly. It was always after I'd seen her that I felt most like drinking. Only drinking gave me back some of my faith in life. I'm not even talking about happiness, just the feeling that I actually existed, which was something I only felt intermittently. The sense that life has left you while you're still alive is an expression of total solitude. Nobody can understand it or share it.

The only way to bear it, to cling to the slenderest of threads still connecting you to life, is by committing an act of destruction as big as that hole. And once you've done something you can't go back on, I imagine you can expect only one thing: that, through its representatives, society will cut you off. Lee Harvey Oswald must have been in that state when he killed Kennedy. He didn't necessarily have any personal grudge against him. But to kill Kennedy, the icon of the Democrats and the whole world, was a way of filling one hell of a black hole. Robert Kennedy must have known deep down that one of these days he would cross paths with someone who was crippled by an inner emptiness. When he came to San Francisco for his campaign, I went to catch a glimpse of him. I'm not lying when I say that when I saw him, he looked like someone who'd been sentenced to death. He passed just a few yards from me in Chinatown. He was slimmer than I'd imagined him. With a thin, feverish hand, he swept back the lock of hair that had fallen over his forehead. I saw him turn pale with panic when a firecracker exploded near the official car and I thought to myself, "Man, you don't have much longer, the guy who's coming to fill the void in his life by assassinating you is on his way." I presented my theory to Duigan, and it left him bewildered. He didn't think that an event as huge as the murder of a Kennedy could ever repeat itself. When Bobby was shot in the Hotel Ambassador in L.A. on the evening of his victory in the California primaries, Duigan called me at my landlady's. He was very upset but he didn't want it to show.

The fact that I had predicted that event increased my fame among the cops who were regulars at the Jury Room.

37

One morning, my probation officer showed up at my place without warning. His unexpected arrival was like a raid and he took a sly pleasure in it. He carefully went over every square inch in search of bottles of alcohol or drugs or anything that might indicate that I was violating my parole. I never drank alone, and especially not at home. As he was about to leave again empty-handed, I asked him to recommend in his report that my parole be lifted. He said he'd see what he could do, but he had the indecisive look of someone who was afraid to lose a customer.

My pay as a Harley salesman and employee of the month wasn't enough to cover my expenses. I spent my life moving around, and moving around consumes gas. Those rides to the campus in my Ford Galaxy cost me a fortune. But so did my obsession with taking my bike out on the road on those nights when I didn't end up in the Jury Room, drinking gallons of wine. Curiously, drinking gave me the feeling that I was stopping myself from doing something really stupid. I didn't know what, but since nothing about me was small, I was afraid it'd be something huge. I was spending a fortune on drinking at the Jury Room, not to mention the beers I bought for my cop friends.

Whenever I managed to keep away, I spent the night on my bike crisscrossing the state of California, all the way to the state line and back, without ever crossing it because that would have been a violation of my parole. Driving by day made me an ordinary man. Riding at night relieved me of myself, and gave me a feeling of power and freedom. All I saw of the towns were clusters of lights. I sometimes spent the whole night riding through San Francisco. I amused myself going up and down its hills in the summer fog. Haight swarmed with hippies until late at night, and I'd stay there watching them before I zoomed off further north. I pushed myself to the limits of my strength, and I'd come back at dawn exhausted, wild and ecstatic.

I just had time to change my clothes, shave, and trim my moustache before I opened up the Harley dealership. As the months passed, the customers started getting on my nerves. Most were Hell's Angels. Always the same big guys with the same expressions, the same regulation anti-conformism, the same limited mentality. They were deliberately crude, and it wasn't so much the roar of their bikes that made them outsiders as the narrowness of their worldview. I had nothing in common with them.

The rides with Duigan took place on Sunday whenever his duties didn't keep him in Santa Cruz. He liked to go south, well past Monterey. We'd leave at dawn. I'd carry the sandwiches and beer in my buffalo-hide saddlebags, and he'd carry Wendy. Duigan sometimes let her get on behind me, after I'd invested in a passenger saddle to please him. Then he'd let me ride in front, so that he didn't have to let his daughter out of his sight.

38

From having ridden all over California by night, I only knew it under cover of darkness. L.A. was connected with my dream of living with my father. I sometimes wept when I thought about that. Further north, Atascadero reminded me that I'd been judged crazy. We seldom went further south along the coast than Big Sur, where the road rises menacingly and a few scattered houses owned by rich cranks stand defiantly, looking as if they might tip over at any moment into the depths of the Pacific. The road was magnificent, steep and winding enough that you could imagine the consequences if you took one of those bends badly. The drop was like a magnet to me, and when Wendy had rejoined her father on his bike, I imagined myself making the big leap. We sometimes stopped in Carmel on the way back. I'd never set foot in Santa Barbara in my life, or in Beverly Hills, and I had never imagined the existence of enclaves like that where the rich and powerful gather in silent communities and living's no problem, the only problem is how to grow old in a place as still as a taxidermist's. The people strolling on the little road lining the beach would look at us out of the corners of their eyes, anxiously, then go on their way, impeccably dressed, walking ridiculous little dogs in pairs, dogs with hair pruned like box trees. These people probably only made kids when they couldn't have dogs, because the young left the place as soon as they could. This little town with its neat blocks of houses and tiny gardens that looked as if they were tended with nail clippers turned its back on the world, showing it an icy indifference. All the same we parked our bikes near the beach, took a swim, and fried sausages in a sandy enclave sheltered from the wind. Duigan fell asleep on his towel after his second beer. Wendy lay down on her back, her arms crossed over her eyes. I leaned back in the shade against the stone wall and watched a few luxury sailboats maneuvering at the edge of the beach. Wendy's boyfriend hadn't been invited on our trip, which says a lot about what Duigan thought of him. It was becoming obvious that he preferred me, but I didn't know how to handle things so as not to disappoint him. He couldn't imagine anyone more suitable to protect his treasure, and we were getting friendlier every day. So was Wendy, in fact even more so.

I had feelings for Wendy, but I wasn't capable of desire. The first time she kissed me, I tensed up, though I tried not to show it, and she just put her arms around me in silence. The day she tried to go further, I refused, making the excuse that I wanted to marry her and my principles forbade me to do anything before marriage. Not being particularly obsessed with sex, she took it well. We made a nice couple, but I knew it wouldn't last because one of these days Duigan would find out that I had killed my grandparents and would take his daughter back, though I didn't want her anyway. In the meantime, the rumor went around the Jury Room that I was now almost the son-in-law of the head of the homicide squad and that was all it took for them to think of me as one of their own.

Duigan woke up, his eyes swollen with the accumulated fatigue of the week, and when he saw Wendy's head on my chest he smiled at us. Wendy rode with me on the way back and we sped across those big agricultural plains where stooped little Mexicans turn their back on the sea. At Duigan's place, we sat down on the terrace again. The noise of the amusement park won out over the Sunday evening blues that had seeped into us. We drank our beers and the sadness gently faded. The phone rang. Duigan didn't hurry to answer. When he came back he was dressed to go out and without going into any details asked me if I could give him a ride.

39

T he coast road that winds north was still full of surfers on their way back to Santa Cruz, excited by their day's exploits. Good looking guys most of them, with damp towels around their waists and pretty girls in tow. The salt had whitened their skins and brought out the brightness of their eyes. On the big houses facing the sea, I noticed two American flags flying from balconies. They hadn't been there the week before. Two rich kids had just died in Vietnam, and there was nothing else to say. We must have ridden a little beyond Santa Cruz on the 1, which runs to Half Moon Bay and on toward San Francisco. On a sandy hill planted with trees, a group had gathered. There were police cars and motorcycles barring a dirt track that descended into a wooded grove before running on toward the sea. The group had formed some distance from the road. I followed Duigan mechanically as the people stood aside for him. It was starting to get dark. On the gray sand strewn with big weeds, there was a spread of long ash-blond hair. It framed the perfect face of a young girl with big blue eyes that stared into infinity. She was naked, her legs bent under her in an unusual contortion. Her intestines lay in a disgusting heap. Duigan squatted beside her. I stood behind him. The thought of how this girl had gone from life to death started to nag at me, as if it was the only mystery worth anything on this earth. The stretcher-bearers were waiting for Duigan's permission to take her away in their ambulance. I couldn't take my eyes off her face. What struck me was less that she was dead than the irreversible nature of that death, and the power of whoever had caused it. I remembered my grandmother in that ridiculous posture my bullet had frozen him into, and the unique feeling that had followed from it, the feeling that I really existed. The killer must have felt the same thing and the idea that we had something in common made me uncomfortable. I was on his side, whether I liked it or not.

Once over the emotion, the first information came in. The girl had been on her way to San Francisco, the little backpack found near her testified to that. She had been stabbed through the heart and then disemboweled. The killer had thrown her there, no more than two hours before. A dog from an isolated house further on had discovered her, sat down next to her and barked until its master had gotten worried.

Duigan reckoned the guy had killed her in his car and disemboweled her in this spot. The way her intestines were arranged confirmed that. The order was given to set up roadblocks. They had to be on the lookout for a car with bloodstains in the interior. Duigan left his men to clean up the crime scene and asked me to give him a ride back to his office.

The station house was almost empty apart from two guards. Duigan's office was behind a glass partition that isolated him from his colleagues. He sat me down opposite him. He didn't say anything, didn't show any emotion, he was trying his best to deal with this thing as objectively as possible. Then one of his men who I knew from the Jury Room put his head in and told him that the girl was from Santa Cruz and I saw him go pale. This other cop offered to go with him when he went to break the news to the family. He declined the offer with a growl. This time we took a car from the motor pool, leaving my bike in the basement of the building. The girl's parents lived a little way back from the snazzy neighborhoods, near a small, shady park shared by three different houses. When we arrived, the father was in the garden reading a thick hardback book.

He was in his mid-fifties, with a neatly trimmed gray beard. His wife, who had opened the door to us, went to fetch him. They both seemed intrigued at the sight of this cop with his big head, accompanied by a giant. Duigan wasn't sure how to handle it and almost bawled them out when he told them he had some bad news for them. He introduced me as a police auxiliary. The father was a dignified man. He showed us in and sat us around a garden table. His wife didn't want to hear. Duigan blurted out the news like a stammerer. "Your daughter, murdered, on the coast, found in a grove by a dog." As if he couldn't stand their grief and how powerless he was to comfort them, he started questioning them at top speed. I guess he was trying to spare them by keeping things as brief as possible. We finally left them alone with their sorrow. The girl had left home to attend a concert at the Fillmore in San Francisco that Sunday evening. She had said she was going with a bunch of friends, but in fact she'd made up her mind to hitchhike, by herself. The roadblocks on the 1 didn't yield any results. Duigan was convinced the killer was from Santa Cruz.

"How do you see this guy, Al?"

My answer came instinctively. "I'd say he's just over thirty. He's a psychopath. This was a ritual crime. And the bad news, Mr. Duigan, is that he isn't going to stop there."

"How can you possibly know that?"

"I don't know it. I sense it. In committing this murder, he's discovered a whole new world, and I'm sure he'll want to reproduce that feeling. But then he'll get tired of it. After five or six deaths. You won't find any evidence of rape. He kills and then he mutilates the body. For specific reasons linked to his childhood. But he'll invent a delusion."

"A delusion?"

"Yes, a mystical justification or something like that. He wants publicity. He didn't try to hide the crime. He knew the girl was going to a concert. He had plenty of time to take the body a long way away, cut her up, and scatter the remains. In America, if you want to hide a dead girl, there's no lack of space. But not him, he wants publicity, he wants it to be known. He feels genuinely proud of his act."

"We're going to scour the psychiatric hospitals!"

The only psychiatric hospital in the state that admitted the criminally insane was Atascadero, and if the investigation led the police there, there was a danger they'd come across my file. I'd been so determined to impress Duigan that I'd been careless.

For weeks, I couldn't get the image of that lifeless girl out of my mind. The obscenity of her death haunted me. It wasn't enough for her killer to kill her, to strip her naked, he had to exhibit her innards, the interior of her body, so that the whole of her could be seen by those who found her. The image aroused my desire. Not her ravaged body, no, it was her pale, almost gray face, and especially the fixed look in her opaque eyes. I didn't feel any shame. Why was it that I didn't have any desire for Wendy but I was excited by the image of that dead girl? The only way I could answer that question was by drinking two bottles of wine in quick succession at the Jury Room, while praying that none of the cops who were there was a mind reader. By the end of the second bottle I started to have hallucinations, and I went to bed hoping that sleep would wash away those bad thoughts. In the morning, they were still there. Reluctantly, I dragged myself to the dealership. A young couple, not exactly hippies but kind of in the same style, came in looking to buy a Harley-Davidson. I advised them to start with a small model, a 1200 Sportster. They were really excited. The girl was clinging to the guy's arm like a baby chimpanzee to its mother, and the image of the two of them united like that revolted me. They were both good looking, with blond hair, blue eyes, and well-drawn features. They put the down payment on the table and almost danced away.

I hadn't seen Wendy for a while. To be honest, I was doing my best to avoid her. But that day I had the feeling I might lose her. Guys had been lining up to take her out since she'd dumped her vegetable-toting surfer boyfriend. I called her and suggested we have lunch together. I still couldn't get over the fact that I'd fallen in love with a dead girl. It was a terrible memory, and I wanted to leave it behind me. That was why I came on so strong.

"I want to marry you, Wendy."

She lifted the bun from her hamburger, suspiciously: "You want to marry me? It's just come over you like that?"

"No, I want to start a family with you, have children, buy a motorhome, forget all our cares and travel around the country."

"Is there something you're worried about?"

"No. I realize you aren't completely satisfied with our relationship."

She seemed a little weary. "What relationship, Al?" she said, without any trace of reproach in her voice. "You never kiss me, you never hold my hand, we see each other once or twice a week, usually when my father's around."

"That's what I'd like to change."

"Are you going to introduce me to your mother?"

The question hit me hard. "What for? She'll be dead by the time we get married!"

She looked at me anxiously. "Why do you say that, Al?"

"With the amount she drinks, she doesn't have much longer to live."

"I should still see her, though, shouldn't I?"

"No."

For a good long while we didn't say anything, and it wasn't until she started in on the ice cream dessert that she finally gave her consent. "When do you want to get married?"

That took me by surprise. "I don't know . . . whenever you like . . ."

"I'd like a white wedding. Do you think we can afford it?"

"I'll find the money, Wendy."

"It's a good thing we're both Catholics, that makes it easier, doesn't it?"

We didn't decide on a date.

I went back to work at the dealership and all afternoon there was a succession of time wasters, people who wanted to fantasize about owning a Harley but didn't have a single dollar to spend. By the time we closed, I wasn't feeling well and, rather than go for a drink at the Jury Room, I got on my bike and just took off. I was planning to get to Oregon and back by the next morning.

It was gradually getting cooler along the coast. I headed inland on the 101. A lot of trailer trucks glided past going north, some heading for Canada. I'd never gone further than Klamath Falls and I dreamed of riding up to Seattle, crossing the border at Olympia, discovering Vancouver and going up as far as I could toward Alaska. From having worked with asphalt, I knew how much effort a road like the 101 must have cost, how many tons of dynamite it had taken to cut a hole through the wilderness, how many men had lost their lives on it, and I felt a real pride as I sped along in the left-hand lane. I felt like I was at home. I pushed the bike as far as it would go, without worrying about the speed limit. To carry my 280-

pound bulk, I had a big Harley that weighed half a ton, with an engine powerful enough to drive a tractor. There was no fairing, so the air was like lead on my arms but I really loved that feeling that I was snatching my freedom from the elements. Around two in the morning, when I was feeling spaced out with fatigue, intoxicated by the noise of the pistons and the excess oxygen, the Oregon state line loomed on the horizon. It was time to go back. A superior force was urging me to keep going beyond that forbidden limit, but I was out of gas and was forced to leave the highway. Once I'd filled her up, I turned around and set off back home. My original desire to get to Oregon had dried up on me. All of a sudden, it seemed ridiculous. I calmed down. Fatigue wasn't the only reason for this change of mind. I rode at a reasonable speed as far as Pepperwood. From there, I got onto a road that ran through a forest of giant trees. Above the treetops, there were stars in the sky, but down below it was as dark as the cellar where I'd spent my childhood, which was why I rode for a while looking up in the air, reassured by the noise of my engine intruding into the thick silence. Then that noise turned into that of the boiler of the house in Montana and I wanted to get off the bike. I was raising my head, drawn by the starry sky, when a deer suddenly appeared in my headlights. I didn't try to avoid it. It loomed over me and just as I thought I'd gotten away, I found myself on the ground. If you've never fallen heavily, you have no real idea of your own weight. During the brief moment I spent in the air, I thought I'd either get off without a scratch or die, and both solutions were fine with me. The bike was lying on the road, the front lights shining on me like a torch. I looked along my body and saw my left arm at a right angle and my foot twisted away from my leg. Surprise had been replaced by pain, a pain made sharper by my feeling of powerlessness. The silence returned and I felt proud that I'd somehow gotten away from myself. Then my instinct for self-preservation regained the upper hand and I slid myself to the shoulder to avoid getting run over—if by some remote chance a driver decided to come along that road at such an hour. Actually nothing came until the first light of dawn. A car pulled up and a park ranger got out. His face was expressionless. He started by examining the deer, which was completely still by now. He came toward me and stood with his hands on his hips, looking down at me.

"Looks like you bumped him off."

Then he took out a pack of cigarettes and lit one with a gas lighter.

"You aren't much better, son. But at least you're alive. Anything broken?"

"An arm and a leg."

He bent over the bike.

"I'll never be able to get it out of here by myself. You sure you can't help me?"

I didn't reply, it wasn't worth the effort.

"I can't put you in my car either, can I?"

Finally he decided to go look for help about twenty miles from there.

41

I t was a huge relief being unable to move. It was like being free of myself for a few days, comfortably settled in my small hospital room in Garberville. Wendy couldn't understand how it was that, just a few hours after I'd proposed to her, I'd ended up flat on my face on a road so far upstate.

"What were you doing up there, Al?"

"I don't know, Wendy. I needed to get some air. Sometimes, I get tired of Santa Cruz, the fog, the sea. It's like the road's calling to me. But I'm also pleased when it stops. It's always been like that, Wendy."

"Will it still be like that when we're married?"

"I don't know, Wendy, I've never been married. How's your dad?"

"I hardly ever see him, he's very busy. There's been another murder."

"Another murder?"

"Yes, a girl from Aptos who was hitchhiking to Monterey. They found her at the foot of a cliff, just past Carmel. She was disemboweled like the first girl, and there was a note in her pocket."

"Saying what?"

"Something crazy. A heavenly voice ordered him to sacrifice eleven women to save northern California from earthquakes. He's only following instructions from that voice. According to him, killing eleven women to save thousands of people is an acceptable sacrifice and he asks the police to see it that way. Then some other stuff I can't remember. When are you coming back, Al?"

"In two weeks, if my mother sends me some money."

Not long after the operation they performed to put my arm and my leg back in shape, I had a visit from the sheriff. He looked worried.

"Seems like you're on parole, is that right?"

I couldn't exactly deny it.

"Were you planning to escape to Canada?"

"Why would I want to escape?"

"That's what I'm asking. Are you sure you didn't do something stupid before you took off?"

"Why do you ask that?

"Because they're talking about this guy who's killing women in your neck of the woods."

"I heard about that. I know the head of the homicide squad in Santa Cruz, I'm going to marry his daughter. In fact I'm the one who gave him a ride over to the scene of the first murder. Oh, and by the way, the day of that murder, I was motorcycling over near Carmel with him and his daughter."

That seemed to reassure him.

"You have quite a record for someone your age, you know . . ."

"I killed two people who were stifling me and I handed myself in. That's not the same as killing strangers and leaving little notes on their bodies."

He sensed that he'd annoyed me with his clumsy attempt to pin those murders on me, and that was the last time he talked about them. We saw each other again several times after that. I think he liked me. Enough anyway to tell me a few things that were on his mind. Garberville had become a real meeting point for hippies. I'd see lots of them from the window of my hospital room. They'd settled in there and were using the main street to sell stuff, some of them crap pieces of art, most of them dope. The ones who were really far gone wandered around looking like mangy dogs, laughing crazily, which didn't quite fit with their deathlike faces. Sometimes local guys would beat them up. The day before, the sheriff told me, a gang in a gray Dodge had picked up a couple of hippies, a guy and a girl. They'd shaved their heads and felt up the girl a little bit. The guy had gone to the cops about it, but the girl didn't want to have anything to do with the law. Right then and there she'd left him, and the guy had thrown himself in the river and drowned. Anyway, the little hospital where I was staying had gradually turned into a free clinic. I'd pass lots of these young people who'd been caught up by diseases people thought had disappeared, which had put a damper on their crazy, drug-soaked dreams.

Before my accident I'd been going around and around in circles, and the accident itself had been kind of a wake-up call. When I found out that the place where it had happened was called the Avenue of the Giants, I took it as a sign, even though the name only referred to the huge trees lining the road. By the time I left the hospital, the sheriff had forgotten all about my criminal record and remembered only a young man who defied his pain and dragged himself to the bathroom every morning on his crutches to have a shave. He showed up on that last day, looking as shy as a child coming to congratulate an adult. He was holding a big box and he laid it down on my knees just as they were pushing me to the ambulance in a wheelchair. I opened it immediately. In it was the head of the deer I'd killed. It had been stuffed by a local taxidermist. I was really touched by the sheriff's gesture. To me, it was another sign.

42

I was broke after my accident and had to go back and live with my mother. My boss wouldn't take me back even though he liked me. He'd said goodbye to me one afternoon, thinking he was going to see me again the next morning, and instead I'd gone speeding off into the night, which he hadn't liked at all. I called my mother from Garberville to tell her I couldn't pay my medical bill, that I'd been fired, and that I was going to give up my apartment.

"That's what happens to people like you, Al," she said, apparently calm. "A long slide down. You want me to say I'm surprised? Well, I'm not. You aren't staying with me any longer than you have to. You think I don't know what your game is? I know you dream of taking root here, becoming the only man in my life, keeping the others at a distance."

What others? It had been a long time since there'd been any man after her.

Her house in Aptos didn't give off any better vibes than the one in Montana. She'd expanded by renting the upper floor a few weeks before my accident, as if she'd had a premonition she might end her days with me. Everything was sinister in that dump, old-fashioned, tasteless. The cats had taken over and their smell was the one that dominated. A little bit of light came in through sash windows with little square panes. I found myself alone on the upper floor, which I couldn't leave as long as my leg wouldn't let me get down the outside stairs. For the month and a half my convalescence lasted, my mother simply left my food outside the door, without ever coming in to talk to me. She'd add a roll of toilet paper whenever she figured I needed a new one. Sometimes I'd wait for her at the top of the stairs, propped on my crutches. I would see her coming up, out of breath, her face red from the effort.

"It's like the alcohol in your liver has come up into the pores of your skin!"

"Shut up, Al, or I'll let you starve to death."

"You know you behave worse than the guards when I was in prison. Why don't you come and talk to me?"

She stopped halfway up the stairs. "Because I have nothing to say to you. I talked about your behavior to a young psychology teacher who's new in the department. Obviously, I didn't tell him I was talking about my son. He was very clear." She lowered her voice to avoid letting the whole neighborhood know. "He says you're a closet homosexual, Al." Then, lowering her voice even more: "A big fag who won't admit it. I told your father you'd end up like that, the way he was raising you, but he wouldn't believe me. Where is he now? Can you tell me that?"

I stayed calm and magnanimous. "Your guy is wrong. By the way, you know I'm getting married?"

She turned around to start back down. "You can always get married. I bet you'll never touch her." Then curiosity got the better of her, and she stopped for a moment. "Who's the girl?"

"She's the daughter of the head of the homicide squad in Santa Cruz."

"Does he know about your record?"

"No, but it's about to be wiped clean."

I'd given her another stick to beat me with, and it didn't take her any time at all to grab it. "You keep right on bugging me, Al, and I'm going to tell your future father-in-law the kind of model grandson you were."

She finally headed back downstairs, with a smug look on her face.

I slammed my door with a noise that must have woken the whole neighborhood. I sat down on my bed in the only room on the upper floor that she'd furnished because she didn't have enough money for the rest. I could hardly breathe. I tried to calm down by trying to remember if I'd ever desired a man in my life. As far back as I could search in my memory, I'd never felt anything like that. The hallucination that followed was very symbolic. The walls and ceiling of the room were shrinking, coming together to enclose me in a cube. I spent the night in a state of prostration. In the morning, before my mother left for the university, as a sign of peace, for the first time she threw me up the newspaper from the foot of the stairs. It hid my door with a dull thud that woke me. I was lying curled up on my bed, still fully dressed.

I didn't bother to read the whole of a long article about Vietnam and the domino theory but I caught the gist of it. If we lost over there, the writer argued, the whole of Asia was going to fall into the Communist camp and then the rest of the world would be engulfed. They were right to hold on. Damn it, I don't know what I would have given to be sent there, I'm convinced I would have done good work. On the front page, there was a photo of Duigan in front of the reporters, looking visibly annoyed. He had good reason to be. A couple of young drifters, a guy and a girl, had been found murdered by the side of a sandy track. They had both been shot in the back of the head with a high-powered rifle. There was no way they could have survived that. The girl had been disemboweled after being executed. No note this time. There was a lot of killing on the coast at that time. For a long time afterwards, I thought about the estuaries where sea water and river water mingle. They say the sharks are wild there and launch murderous attacks triggered by no known mechanism. At the beginning of the Seventies, this estuary syndrome had struck California. This is how I analyze it. We were the children of the postwar period. Our fathers had seen some tough things in the Pacific and in Europe, and there was a lot left unspoken within families, concealed behind their prosperity. The traditional family had turned into a nightmare. For the first time, you saw images of slaughter in Indochina on TV. The needle of the compass was turning madly for lots of young people who were asking themselves how to live. The only solution some found was murder, even mass murder, as if killing a single person wasn't enough.

Duigan heard about my condition from Wendy. He still liked me, she said, even though he didn't understand how it was that I'd crashed my bike in the north of the state in the middle of the night. Wendy couldn't come to see me. She didn't have a car and with the way things were at that time hitchhiking wasn't advisable. That suited me just fine. Otherwise, I would have had to tell her my mother didn't want to invite her home on the false pretext—a contradictory one, coming from her—that she didn't want to hear her son fornicating above her head in her own house.

Sally Enfield dropped by to see my mother almost every night and often stayed over. They'd become inseparable. My mother needed to talk, only not with me. She was a noisy drunk, while Sally was content to nod noiselessly. I'd hear the two of them gossiping through the floor.

"I know where my problem with men comes from, Sally."

"You're lucky if you know that."

"My first husband was a big disappointment to me. He thought I was happy to stay the wife of an electrician. No ambition, Sally. A nice quiet job, a beer with his pals in the evening after work, and nothing else . . . As if that was what I'd dreamed of. Especially as the guy had introduced himself as a war hero. Plus, and this is in confidence, he had a really small dick."

Her level of vulgarity was a clear indicator of how much she'd drunk. She'd definitely gone way past two bottles of wine.

"He had small feet for a man who was nearly seven feet tall. And that other thing was in proportion to his feet."

Sally Enfield started laughing like a woman possessed. Even if she didn't know him, it was my father she was laughing at. I could have strangled her.

"And then Al came along," my mother, who never laughed about anything, went on. "You've never had a child, so you can't know this, but when you become a mother, you get a feeling about the child you've given birth to. Let me tell you, I knew right away he was a monster. So I kept him under a tight rein, to tame him. But it wasn't enough. I failed. I almost succeeded but his father worked against me, behind my back. I don't mind admitting this, when Al killed his grandparents, I was pleased. Events had proved me right. I bet you he'll never work again. He fell off his motorbike so that he could come back here to his mother. If I'd had a Mongol son, it couldn't have been worse. What did I do to God to deserve such punishment?"

I heard a glass clinking against the neck of a bottle.

"A husband, basically, is just a husband. You know you'll never really get what you see. But a child comes out of your womb. So when you realize he's nothing like you, it's one hell of a disappointment."

With Sally Enfield, my mother had found herself a dog that answered her. I've noticed that people who buy dogs talk to them for the pleasure of never being contradicted. But the downside of this is that a dog can never agree with you. Whereas Sally always agreed with her. It was always, "You're right, Cornell, never a truer word was spoken."

She never talked about herself and, if she ever dared, my mother would stop her like a teacher stopping a pupil who strays off the subject. In a month of convalescence above the two women, I never found out anything about her beyond that inexplicable spinelessness that kept her in a state of serfdom.

43

I was finally able to support myself on my leg. My arm, which had been fractured in three places, stayed in plaster a whole month more. There was still no way I could look for work, but at least I could drive. I started taking the van out again. I needed to talk and have people talk to me. The crazed killer had slaughtered his last three victims without first picking them up as hitchhikers. Collective fears are like the terrors of horses, spectacular and quickly forgotten. The co-eds who got in my Ford Galaxy were more hesitant than two months earlier, but their apprehension didn't hold out for too long against the prospect of avoiding an exhausting two- or three-mile walk down into town.

I was now refusing to take hippie girls. I targeted respectable young girls who were as smooth and clean as pebbles in a stream. For some weird reason, they excited me a whole lot more than Wendy ever did. It wasn't her fault. Wendy was my fiancée and these girls were forbidden to me, that was probably what made the difference. I had no other opportunity to meet them outside the times I gave them rides. They didn't hang out at the Jury Room, even though there were more cops there than curls on the head of a hooker. Nor did they go to the same places as I did to eat. Sometimes I'd sit down a little bit back from the beach and admire their tanned shoulders and glossy hair. They did every sport that would help them keep their shape. The Berlin Wall must have been easier to get over than the one separating me from these creatures. When they passed me on the promenade that ran alongside the beach, they never saw me. If they ever did glance in my direction and see how big I was, the only result was an exclamation of surprise that a sequoia from Yosemite National Park had grown legs and could move. We were living in the same era, in the same places, and yet, if I hadn't taken the initiative, we would never have had the opportunity to meet. In the car, I'd ask them loads of questions about what they expected from life, their hopes, their fears. They fascinated me because they didn't have any doubts. It was as if their lives were all mapped out like railroad tracks. They never let disenchantment come anywhere near them. Any sign of pessimism was smothered in superlatives. They treated happiness like a little dog that would waste away without its mistress. It was girls like that, dozens of them, at the university and on the beach, who maintained my interest in life.

44

D uigan had lost weight. The thought of more victims to come haunted him, and his powerlessness to prevent it made him depressive. No clue had come to light on the killer since he had begun his spree. He never made any blunders. He killed at regular intervals, as if he was in no hurry to reach the objective he had set himself with all the precision of a sales manager. His field of action was limited to the coastal area, although he never threw the bodies in the sea.

"Why doesn't he do that?"

Duigan and I were sitting facing each other on his porch. Wendy was late back and that made him nervous. It was the first time I'd been to see him since my accident. I'd sometimes talked on the phone with Wendy, but we were both aware that something wasn't quite right between us. And that something was me.

"Confidences are a women's thing." That was my answer when she reproached me once. "How can I feel I trust you completely when I don't trust myself? It's my mother who's between us. I have to settle my problem with her."

"But what problem, Al? If at least you explained."

"She screws up my relations with women."

"Why don't you leave her?"

"She's the kind of woman you can't leave. How can I put this? If I move away from her, there's a risk she'll obsess me even more. When I'm near her, I feel I can control her. As soon as I put some distance between us, she has the edge on me. I know it isn't easy to understand, but I'm going to work something out."

"But how, Al?"

"I'm thinking about it, I don't have a solution yet but I'm thinking about it."

Wendy, apart from being a great girl, could be more patient than any woman ever.

A feeble wind had risen. Kids were playing on the street and their cries punctuated our silences.

"I guess he doesn't like the idea that the body might be affected by the sea. The disemboweling, which is kind of his signature, might not be so clear. He kills fast and dumps the body without hiding it, because he wants it to be found in the state he left it. That's what he know about him."

"That's not enough to establish a profile."

"He doesn't like women. He has a big problem with them. I'm sure he has a massive problem with his mother. But that's not all. There's something else, something very personal, that's hard to figure out without knowing him. May I speak freely, Mr. Duigan?"

"Of course."

"He's a closet homosexual. He can't bring himself to act on it. So he takes his revenge on women and disembowels them. The stomach isn't irrelevant, you see what I mean? The proof is that when he killed the couple, only the girl was disemboweled. He must be severely repressed. His father's fault, probably. A career soldier or a businessman, I'd say, although I'm no specialist. Let's be clear, Mr. Duigan, I have no authority to . . . "

"I know, continue."

"I'd say he's a kid who was very brilliant, very successful, up until a certain age and then all of a sudden everything collapses. You're more likely to find him in a good neighborhood than in a clapboard house. As I already said, he must have been in hospital for some kind of acute psychotic episode. I think that's probably everything. No, actually, and this is totally subjective, I insist, he must be quite short. I'd even say abnormally short . . . no, just shorter than average. Enough to have a complex about it, but not enough to make him abnormal. He isn't going to be easy to find, he's highly organized because of his superior intelligence."

Just then, Wendy came in, as casual as ever.

Duigan leaped to his feet. "Where the hell were you?"

I'd never seen him yell at his daughter before. I realized that he was really on edge and that I had to help him.

Wendy wasn't fazed. "I went for an ice cream on the wharf with Halle Norton."

Duigan kept a grip on himself. "You think now's the time to hang out?"

"That guy would never attack the daughter of the head of homicide, would he, Al?"

I put on my expert air. "I don't think so."

"Because you have a big sign on your T-shirt saying you're the daughter of the head of homicide?" Duigan retorted, but by now he was more relieved than angry. "What is there on the wharf? It's years since I set foot on it."

The wharf is like any other wharf in the world, an outgrowth made up of wooden beams on piles sunk in the sea. Below the piles, sea lions bask on the sustaining blocks and make raucous cries. Tourists take advantage of their languid poses to take photographs of them. On the wharf there are restaurants that are open at all hours of the day.

"There isn't much to do there," I said.

As we were talking about nothing, I thought about that criminal whose profile I'd sketched so precisely. I had him figured out intuitively. I could have felt his breath on my shoulder. If I'd passed him on the street, I could have picked him out, I was sure of that.

Duigan went out and I stayed with Wendy in her room listening to the radio. I was literally choking, which was the way I felt every time I was alone with her. She put her head against me but it was too heavy and I gently pushed it away. Before Wendy had time to get offended, I said, "We have to talk about the wedding."

Wendy stood up slowly, stretched, and sighed. Then she turned slowly toward me, and said, "What's wrong with you, Al? Every time you push me away you talk about marriage. Don't you realize the way you behave contradicts what you say?"

"Have you talked to your father?"

"My father? The only thing on his mind right now is that killer. And I don't walk to talk to him about it."

"Why?"

"Because it isn't going to happen, Al, you know that as well as I do. You like me but you don't really love me and you're trying to cover that up by marrying me."

My diaphragm had risen into my throat. "But I can't live without you, Wendy!"

She started wandering around the room as if she was inspecting the objects in it, then turned abruptly and looked straight at me. "You're a great guy, Al, I don't think you've ever lost your temper at me. You're very intelligent, even my father says so, you're quite a handsome boy and you can be very comforting when you try. And comforting a woman is important, Al, especially a woman like me, who's afraid her shadow is having a better time than she is. But you don't have any desire. Why? How do I know? Every time I talk to you about desire with my body you talk to me about marriage with your lips and turn as stiff as a waxwork. I'm not as stupid as I may seem, Al."

"Have you told your father about this?"

"About what?"

"All this."

"I already told you I haven't. I get the impression he matters more to you than I do. Without him, you'd forget all about me."

We spent the next hour in silence. There are girls who can make silence seem like intelligence, and then you realize it isn't. Wendy wasn't one of them. She read a few fashion magazines, calmly, as if we hadn't said anything important, while English music played on the radio. I finally left.

The streets of Santa Cruz were deserted. All those little houses lined up in rows, with their ridiculous gardens and their huge American flags, all those tiny lives, no better than animals', made me nauseous. I drove slowly through the town. The only people out and about at that hour were people who had nothing to lose, either money or honor. A few hippies were wandering around like stragglers left behind by a herd of healthier animals. The ritzy neighborhoods were only distinguished from the poorer ones by the size of the houses and the gardens. I drove as far as the Jury Room. It was a long way to closing time, but the bar was pretty lively. Mainly cops taking a quick break. The killer was on everyone's lips. I envied them for living with that adrenaline. A thought went through my mind, a not very modest one. If I'd been allowed to join the police, things would soon have been over for the killer. When I repeated his profile to one of Duigan's deputies, I felt a kind of superiority over him, because of my knowledge of homicidal urges. My pseudo-expertise in psychology irritated him a little and if I hadn't been his chief's daughter's boyfriend, I think he'd have sent me packing. I drank several glasses of wine, one after the other, then went back to my mother's to sleep.

45

She must have been asleep for a while because the window of her room, which looked out on the street, was unlighted. I climbed the stairs that led to the upper floor, filled with a fierce desire to shake her awake and question her. I was very close to doing it, before I saw reason. I lay down in that soulless room that was now mine. The wooden walls were damp, like the walls of a vacation cabin by the sea. And yet the sea was a long way away. I had only just gone to bed when the neighbor got up to tinker with the engine of his car, an old brown Pontiac as tacky as a kitchen table. Around five in the morning, he started beating on the Delco with a big hammer and my night was over. I was tempted to yell at him, but I got up, went out, and passed in front of him without saying anything, not even good morning. When I got to my van, I realized I was out of money. I had blown it all at the Jury Room. The front door was closed and my mother had never left me the keys. I took advantage of the neighbor's racket to break a windowpane in the kitchen, lift the window and slide in. For some reason, there was a nice thick wad of ten-dollar bills at the bottom of my mother's bag. I took half. I left the same way I'd got in, then had second thoughts. A normal burglar wouldn't have left half the wad at the bottom of the bag, so I went back and took it all, down to the last cent. I hesitated, then went into my mother's room. The handle creaked when I turned it. She was lying on her back in a satin nightdress that had ridden up to the top of her thighs, uncovering her legs with all those varicose veins. Her arms were stretched out and her head was on the side. Her mouth and nostrils were searching for air. There was a stench of alcohol and fetid breath. I closed the door, vowing never to see her again.

I took advantage of the first few dollars to buy two records and lunch for Wendy, who couldn't get over it. I showed up outside the building where she worked at lunchtime. I felt really bad but I hid it well. I took her to a restaurant on the corner of Beach Street and the wharf. It's a place that's popular not only with the inhabitants of Santa Cruz but also with people passing through and the atmosphere's really lively, with incredible hamburger specials. A large picture window looks out on the sea, and there's no way you can leave the place and still be hungry. I told Wendy I was going to leave my mother for good and that I'd be away for two or three days to arrange our separation. I told her about a Green Giant ad I had seen in the newspaper. I drove her back to her work and we arranged to meet up two days later, same time, same place. Wendy seemed pleased with my renewed enthusiasm and energy.

In the afternoon, it started raining. I couldn't let a chance like that pass. I put my badge allowing me access to the campus on the rearview mirror of my Ford Galaxy and drove up to the university. I pulled up in the parking lot of the science faculty. I felt as stifled as if a trailer truck was parked on my chest. I tried to catch up on the sleep I'd missed the night before but I couldn't get a wink. The rain, which had been intermittent so far, now came down more heavily, flooding my windshield and isolating me from the world. When the downpour wore off to a steady drizzle, I took off again. I was torn between going downtown for a quick drink and giving a ride to a girl, even though I wasn't in the mood to chat. I opted for a drink at the Jury Room. I knew it was the right choice because, in spite of the rain, the recent killings had dissuaded the co-eds from hitching rides. As I was about to start the big descent into town, I noticed two girls, the kind I liked, walking side by side under the same umbrella. As I drove slowly up to them, one of them turned and, seeing my face, smiled and lifted her thumb as if to say, "You can't let two pretty girls from good families get soaked."

I looked at my watch as I drew level with them and stopped.

The brunette clearly hadn't had any intention of hitching a ride but she hadn't been able to resist her friend's spontaneous impulse. The blonde had bewitchingly fine features. There wasn't a trace of vulgarity or flabbiness in her face. Her eyes were a mineral blue and I would have been surprised and disappointed if their beauty concealed coldness of any kind. The brunette got in the back, where there weren't any windows or doors. The blonde settled herself comfortably beside me and the efforts she'd been making to charm me faded abruptly. I even thought for a moment that she was trying to make me pay for that first smile. I wasn't surprised by their destination. They weren't the kind of girls who lived by the amusement park.

46

About a week earlier, I had received a letter summoning me to appear before a psychiatric panel to review my case, lift my parole and, possibly, wipe my criminal record. They were going to test me to see if I was normal. The board was meeting in San Francisco and I went there the next day. The waiting room of the prisons administration building had a great view of the city. From the window, you could see Bay Bridge in the distance over an emerald sea. I didn't really care if I was deemed rehabilitated or not. After all, who could know who I really was better than I did? All I wanted was to be able to leave the state I'd ended up in. There were three shrinks on the panel, three old guys close to retiring age. They didn't seem to be in any hurry to get back to their wives, and they studied my file meticulously, with expressionless faces. From time to time, they lifted their noses to look at me, I guess to see if my face indicated anything different than the papers. Their first question was about mother. I talked about her job at the university, how we were living together in a house with two stories and two separate entrances, the motorcycle accident that had forced me to go back to her temporarily. They seemed worried that we were together. I told them that if I was finally released and my record was wiped, I'd be able at last to get away from her.

"And do what?" asked one of the shrinks, a short bald man.

"Earn a bit of money that'll allow me to study criminology."

He smiled and turned toward his colleagues. "Interesting. Why?"

"I'm fascinated by the mechanisms of criminal behavior. To tell the truth, I'm going to marry the daughter of the head of homicide in Santa Cruz and I'm already collaborating with her father on a case. Sorry to say this, but I feel that the fact that I've killed in the past gives me a real advantage in this field, especially in understanding the phenomenon of triggers, which will always be a mystery to a novice."

The three old men nodded, one of them with a kind of self-satisfied pout.

I drove home my advantage. "Actually, in spite of my height, which theoretically disqualifies me, I even made inquiries about joining the police. It's obvious that as long as I have such a . . . substantial criminal record, that's going to be impossible. What I'd really like to do is wipe out all memory of those acts, which in my opinion were the result of a sudden schizophrenic delusion."

"Have you had any similar symptoms since?"

"Homicidal impulses, you mean?"

"That's right."

"No, never."

"Not even in relation to your mother?"

"To be quite honest, my mother hasn't changed much since I was a child, but I've come to terms with her, thanks to one basic insight: no child is obliged to love his parents if they aren't worthy of love. That does away with the question of guilt, and allows me to view her objectively. And this objectivity in relation to what she is and the harm she may have done me creates a safety barrier between us."

"How would you describe your sexual feelings these days? Do you feel any kind of embarrassment? Do you feel like the other young people of your generation or . . . excluded?"

"I'm going to be frank. I think that from time immemorial, and it's no different today, it's men who've decided things when it comes to sex. Sexual liberation, the dissociation of love and desire, are male projects, not female ones as people would have us believe. Contraception is a female aspiration invented by men who want to be able to sleep around without anything holding them back. I have quite a high opinion of women. I don't think having several partners, the way the hippies do, is one of their deepest aspirations. I don't subscribe to these false movements of emancipation, because I think their only aim is to make women slaves to the desires of men. Anyway, as far as I'm concerned, there is no dissociation of love and desire. The traditional couple has proved its worth."

"Basically, you're the true feminist," chuckled one of the three men, the one who'd been eyeing me most closely from the start.

We all laughed at that and I changed the subject. I felt euphoric but calm.

"I wouldn't want you to think that I'm trying to downplay what I did. Not a day goes by that I don't think about it. And that means I'm not an ordinary man. An absolute transgression like murder can't be easily wiped out. I sometimes meet Vietnam veterans who've taken to drink because they feel guilty about all the killing they've done. I understand how they feel, and yet in their case the country has legitimized their actions. What I did, though, isn't and never will be legitimate. It's a very deep wound and, even though I may not be obsessed with guilt, that guilt is in me all the time, and that's quite enough."

I couldn't get over how clearly I was managing to formulate my thoughts, given that they're usually so vague. The three shrinks were staring at me intently and I could see looks of genuine satisfaction forming on their faces. As they watched in amazement, the miracle of redemption was being played out right there in front of their eyes.

"I still think it's vital that you get away from your mother," said the one who seemed to be the chairman because he was in the middle.

"It's only a matter of days, doctor. My motorcycle accident drove me back to her the way the wind sweeps a shipwrecked sailboat back to shore. But there's no way I'm going to stay there. I can't keep watching her kill herself."

"Kill herself?"

"My mother's become an alcoholic. She's always been fond of the bottle but I've noticed it's been getting a lot worse later. She manages to conceal it when she's at work, but at night she drinks herself to sleep."

"How do you account for that?"

"Her failures with men. My mother hates men. Her father abused his daughters. She was never able to clear the air with him, because her parents died young in a motor accident in Montana. And since then she's never stopped making all the men she meets pay for it."

"Have you ever talked to her about that?"

"Never."

"Is it she or you that doesn't want to?"

"Both. I'm waiting for her to talk to me about it. I'm waiting for her to talk to me, period. But she never will. She's the one who ought to have been put away, not me. You know, I don't want to be her puppet anymore. When I killed my grandparents, I was her puppet in a way. I can no longer conceive of killing or doing anything illegal, I'd have the impression that she's the one who's holding my arm and I really don't want to give her the opportunity."

The chairman smiled and looked at his two colleagues. "When you come down to it," he said, "our friend is a greater danger to himself than to society. I suggest that this conclusion figures in the report. Stop riding motorcycles, Kenner, that's our advice. For the rest, you seem to me very much on the right path."

One of the men, who hadn't said much so far, and had been looking at me with the greatest objectivity of the three, now spoke up. "Do you really think your mother was abused by her father?"

"I don't know anything specific. I overheard a conversation between my parents when I was a child, that's all. But there must be an explanation. Surely a woman doesn't show such hatred toward her own son for no reason?"

He seemed to be thinking this over. "So, what do we recommend for this young man?"

The chairman gave me a broad smile. "We're going to go back to the judge and recommend a return to normality. No more parole, and a criminal record as white as snow."

47

W hy did you come back to see me, Susan?"
"Because I don't think you're going to stop reading.
Not reading for the blind anymore, that's one thing,
but not reading for yourself, no, I don't believe it."

She takes out two books and puts them on the table. A
novel by Cormac McCarthy and a new edition of Hemingway's
short stories. With writers like that, she knows she's welcome.

Susan is wearing a long dress, the kind girls used to wear in
Haight Ashbury at the end of the Sixties. He can't help thinking that the texture and design of the dress, however cheerful,
are cruel to the woman wearing it. But Susan's having a good
day, a day when she feels confident, and she wants to show it.

"How are things going with the transfer?"

"To Angola?" He starts laughing softly. "There'll never be
a transfer to Angola. I simply saw a documentary about it and
thought it would be a good place to go to kill myself. It was a
time when I was seriously thinking about taking my own life.
In any case why would they agree to transfer me to Louisiana?
No, I've changed tactics. I've put in a new request for parole.
A psychiatrist who came here and questioned me three or four
months ago has been going on TV and saying that, according
to him, I'm the only prisoner in Vacaville who isn't a danger to
society. He's ready to bet on it. But the prison administration
doesn't agree. I don't care. I don't see what I could do outside,
I've missed out on all the technological advances of the last
fifty years. Freedom wouldn't suit me any better than incarcer-

ation. Any more than life suits me better than death. I'm like a lot of people, I don't want to live but I really don't want to die. Reading is the finest human experience there is. What difference does it make whether it takes place in a cell or in the kind of room in town that I'd be able to afford? I'm in a state where everything suits me and nothing satisfies me. By the way, I thought again about our conversation last time. I've been remembering images of that commune, soothing images. I think if I'd been capable of letting myself go just a little at the time, a lot of things could have been avoided, even though the guy who owned that farm behaved later as if he was a guru. There was some good in it. But I was completely uptight. I didn't have the right sense of humor. I remember that guy who came out of nowhere and introduced himself by saying, 'Guns don't kill people, men with mustaches do.'"

"They made T-shirts that say the same thing. They sell them in Haight."

"Is that where you bought that dress?"

"Do you like it?"

"A lot."

"I have a present for you."

"I don't know if I like presents."

"It's nothing special."

From a plastic bag, Susan takes out a T-shirt with a picture of John Wayne and the words: "A man's gotta do what a man's gotta do."

He smiles and thanks her.

"I had to go to a dozen stores to find the right size but I can still change it if you want me to."

"Could you buy me a T-shirt with that thing about guns and men with mustaches?"

"For you?"

"No, to give to someone. But I need the smallest size."

"Who's it for?"

"A prisoner on my cell block. Do you remember Jeff McMullan?"

"No."

"Don't you remember that guy who killed women and disemboweled them in the late Sixties? He's serving a life sentence two cells down from me. Will you do me that favor? The smallest size you can find, okay?"

"And what about the book?"

"I'm making progress, but it's not finished. I still have the hardest part to write. I'm afraid that's where the publisher, if you find me one, will start to object. Why do you ask?"

"I've found someone who might be interested."

"Then I have to polish the style. Up until now I've been writing as if I was going to be the only reader . . ."

"Don't change a thing. I also wanted to say . . ."

She stops, overcome with that girlish embarrassment that Al knows so well and that he sometimes finds exasperating.

"If you really are serious about getting out of here . . . I'll be there. But don't wait too long. We're both in our sixties, I don't know how I'll be in ten or twenty years."

He laughs. "You think that if I get out of this prison, it'll be to put up with a woman like you, an ex-hippie, every day? I think I'd still prefer prison."

He laughs even louder. Susan joins in. It's the first time they've laughed together.

48

T he next time I saw Wendy she was again coming out of the dentist's office where she worked. I'd been suffering in silence for several days from a decayed tooth but I couldn't afford to have it seen to and I didn't dare ask. I took out the tooth myself in a highway service plaza with a pair of pliers. The blood poured out for about ten minutes then stopped. I realized soon after that I didn't miss the tooth.

Wendy wasn't in her normal state. She was usually so lethargic, but now she seemed high. She was breathing heavily and smiling broadly.

"My father wants to see you, Al." And when she saw the look of surprise on my face: "He wants to see you right away."

"Don't we even have time for lunch?"

I could see from Wendy's expression that the reason he wanted to see me wasn't to accuse me of theft, even though my mother was the kind of woman who'd happily have reported her son to the police, just so that they could back her up in her hatred of her offspring.

"What's going on, Wendy?"

"I can't tell you. Let's have lunch and then you can go see him at the station house."

"At the station house? Can't you tell me more?"

"No, I promised I wouldn't say anything. But I think you can buy me a real good lunch."

We didn't hold back. I hadn't eaten properly since the day before and all 280 pounds of me was starving. We spent about an hour in that restaurant at the corner of Beach Street and the wharf. A thick drizzle was falling. The partly gray sky and the calm sea were as one. A few students were playing volleyball on the beach, just to build up a little sweat. Wendy brought up the subject of our marriage.

"How many kids do you see yourself having, Al?"

I didn't know what to reply. I knew that a superior force would stop me having any at all, even if I'd had such a strange desire. Al Kenner III is the last of his dynasty. It's written, I don't know where but it's written.

"Four or five," I said—as I didn't believe it anyway, I thought I might as well aim high.

"Are you serious, Al? You want me to end up completely deformed."

"Tell me your figure."

"Two. A boy and a girl. What do you think?"

"That's perfect."

We didn't hang around after that. I dropped her at her work and dashed off to see Duigan, curious about what he could possibly have to tell me.

The desk sergeant at the station house seemed to be startled by my height. He phoned homicide to make sure I was expected and, when that was confirmed, he pointed the way with his hand without even looking up.

Homicide spread over one whole floor, partitioned into separate offices. I was struck by the tons of papers heaped on all the desks, and I wondered how they ever found their way through that forest of information and how it didn't fly away whenever there was a draft. All the guys I'd gotten used to seeing at the Jury Room were there. Obviously they recognized me and came up to me one by one to say hello. I don't know if they'd have done that if I hadn't been summoned there by their chief. Even his deputy, who thought I was a dreamer, came up and gave me a pat on the shoulder. Duigan was on the phone when I reached his office. It sounded like an animated conversation, but he gestured to me to come in.

"That was the mayor," he said when he hung up. Then he looked at me in a satisfied silence. "Take a seat. We've been looking for you for the last twenty-four hours. Where were you? I almost put out an APB. You look all in, don't you ever get any sleep?"

"Sometimes, but not enough."

"I wanted to see you because I have a job to offer you."

"To join the police?"

"Not exactly, but as good as. I've convinced my superiors that we weren't very strong when it came to the psychological side of things and that it could be very useful to us to take on an assistant who knew the field. I have to say that because it was you, they didn't take a lot of convincing."

"Why?"

"Don't you know?"

"Know what?"

"Didn't Wendy tell you?"

"No."

"The day before yesterday late in the afternoon our killer tried to abduct a girl near Palo Alto. But just then a car arrived, and the killer let go of his victim and drove off. The guy in the car took his license number. We've identified him. His name's Jeff McMullan."

"I'm pleased for you, Mr. Duigan, but how does that concern me?"

"This guy did a spell in a psychiatric hospital, like you said. He was committed after a psychotic attack brought on by the accidental death of his best friend. According to the shrinks, McMullan was in love with his best friend. He's definitely a closet homosexual. In the hospital, he became very dangerous and was treated for acute schizophrenia. Just as you said, he comes from a well-to-do family, a very strict Methodist family. He's never been back to see his parents since he came out."

"Have you arrested him?"

"Not yet. He hasn't set foot in his apartment, which is in a nice residential area on the coast near San Francisco. He must be wandering the roads. What worries me is that he's never had a job as far as we know and we don't know what he's living on. I think he's very mobile and good at hiding himself. But it's only a matter of time before we get him. The point is, you were pretty damn right about his psychological profile."

"That's not what helped you to identify him."

"No, but it proves how accurate you were. And that's enough for me to offer you work as an investigator. As far as McMullan is concerned, we can manage by ourselves, though of course if you have any idea what he might try now, it'd be a great help. But there have been several disappearances locally, disappearances we can't explain to the families. We think they're runaways. It couldn't have been McMullan, he doesn't like to hide the bodies. No, I think they really are just runaways. For example, a girl who disappeared a month ago came back yesterday. She had run off with a hippie. When she'd had enough of hitchhiking and eating out of trash cans, the dream turned sour and she came home. Now we've had a report about two co-eds who disappeared yesterday afternoon. They were last seen on the campus in Santa Cruz. Given that McMullan was identified at about four in the afternoon in Palo Alto, about to abduct a young girl, I don't think he could have been in Santa Cruz at the same time. If you agree to start work tomorrow morning, I'll take you to see the parents of one of the girls and then hand the case over to you. You'll have to decide whether or not you think they're the kind of girls who are likely to run away. What you often find is that parents have an image of their children that doesn't correspond to reality. They're convinced they have a perfect relationship with their kids when in fact the kids have only one thought in their minds: to get as far away from their family as they can. It's a modern thing, I don't know where it'll all lead, but right now we have to deal with it. Talking about your salary and all the paperwork connected with it, you can go see Debbie Watson. She's the nice little gray-haired lady who has an office near the entrance downstairs. And there you have it!"

He stood up and walked me to the door. Before he opened it, he said in a low voice, "I'm taking you because I think you're good, Al. So, if you're really serious about my daughter, don't boast about it to my men, they'd think my hiring you was nepotism and that isn't my thing, right?"

"Right."

"Something wrong, Al?"

A storm had risen without any warning inside my skull, and I guess it showed.

"Yesterday afternoon," I said, "I gave a ride to two girls who were hitching from the campus. I often do that to avoid them falling into the wrong hands. But I left them on the edge of the campus, it wasn't convenient for me to take them all the way downtown."

"That makes you our prime suspect," Duigan said, bursting into laughter. Then, more seriously: "If they are the same girls we're talking about, did you notice anything unusual about them?"

"No, they were normal, respectable girls. I do remember they never stopped talking."

"Do you think someone might have taken advantage of their weakness?"

"Who knows?"

49

It was quite late in the afternoon by now. I set off for the campus to see my mother. I wanted to make one more attempt to get her to talk to me. I didn't want only to hear her when she was under the influence of the booze, which made her babble on like an actor doomed to always play the same part in some crummy theater. She never drank during the day, her fear of being caught out was stronger than her addiction. But when she got back home, she got down to some serious drinking and she would continue until sleep interrupted the binge she'd planned. The pain of waking in the morning and reconnecting with reality must have been intense. I imagine there was about fifteen minutes every morning when she thought about killing herself before she made up her mind to live another day. Her job at the university and the pride she took in throwing everyone off the scent kept her on her feet for the rest of the day. But once she was alone, there was nothing to hold her back.

I waited in the parking lot for her to leave the building. A hairless deer came and grazed in front of my fender with all the native's contempt for the immigrant. It lifted its head whenever there was a suspicious noise, but didn't seem to believe there was any real threat. I got out of my van to stretch my legs. The office staff came out on time but my mother wasn't among them. As I was getting ready to leave, I heard steps behind me. Sally Enfield, who had seen me from the offices, was coming toward me with her strange walk.

"Looking for your mother?"

The question wasn't worth an answer.

"She's in bed."

"Since when?"

"Since a large sum of money disappeared from her bag." She was looking at her feet. "It was money she owed. They may seize her salary. And as long as that threat is hanging over her, she doesn't dare show her face here. You don't have any idea who might have done this to her?"

"Whoever sells her booze," I replied curtly. "With the amount the two of you drink, she must have run up quite a tab."

She wasn't the kind of person to think of a quick comeback.

"Has she reported it to the police?"

"She can't, but she's in big trouble. It wasn't you, was it?"

"I've just joined the police, now's not the time I'd have chosen to steal money from my mother."

"Maybe you ought to drop by and say hello. It'd cheer her up."

I burst out laughing. "She might use me as her doormat, but I don't think I'd cheer her up . . . You're her best friend, haven't you noticed that she's never either cheerful or depressed? Ashamed, now that's possible, but being depressed is a concept that doesn't suit her. I never want to go anywhere near her again."

"Why?"

"Tell her I've found a new job, I'll be staying at her house for a couple of weeks more, just long enough to get back on my feet financially, and then she'll never hear from me again. I have a job, and I'm planning to get married. I'm going to lead a normal life. She'll die soon, from the booze and the cigarettes. You can see that by her complexion. Next to her, a dug-up corpse would look like it's just come from a vacation by the sea. My mother doesn't like solitude, so she'll take you with her. She would have preferred it to be me, but she's out of luck, I'm stronger than she thinks."

I got back in my Ford without another word. I'd already

said enough. I was in such a state of nerves I could easily have gotten carried away. I started driving slowly. I felt something powerful rising inside me. I hadn't reached the slope that descends toward the town when I saw a girl holding her thumb up uncertainly, ready to take it down if she had the slightest doubt. She was wearing a short skirt, though she seemed to regret it. I looked at my watch and pulled up level with her. I opened the passenger door and said, "I hope you're not going far, I don't have much time, I have to be at the station house in fifteen minutes."

Mentioning the station house reassured her. She was Oriental looking and quite short—she had to make two attempts to climb in the van. Once she was seated, she gave me that antiseptic smile typical of girls from her background. I smiled in response without looking at her. I could feel myself getting back to normal. I asked her where she wanted to go, then started the conversation.

"Where are you studying?"

"The science faculty."

"What are you planning to do?"

"Aeronautics. Actually I've finished my cycle here, I'm leaving for Stanford tomorrow. I'm doing a PhD."

"You're young to be doing a doctorate."

"I'm not as young as all that, I'm twenty-two."

"You really don't look it."

"How about you?"

"Have you heard this one? Somebody told Alfred Hitchcock that he wasn't getting any older, and he said, 'That's only natural, when I was twenty I already looked as if I was eighty.' It's rather the same with me."

She laughed, but then said politely, "No, you look young."

"Are you Vietnamese?"

"Oh no, my father's Hong Kong Chinese and my mother's American."

"The Chinese came here to build the Pacific railroad, didn't they?"

"Yes, but my father came a long time after that."

I'd suspected as much.

"Any brothers or sisters?"

"No, I'm an only child."

"Your parents must be proud of you."

"I don't know, they don't express it much."

"Don't they give you lots of love?"

"Kind of, yes, but they aren't demonstrative."

"That's bad, we should always show our children we love them."

"Everyone does it in his own way. Why, didn't your parents love you?"

"My father, yes. My mother in her way. One made up for the other, so it balanced out. Do you want children?"

"Yes, but I'm in no hurry. I have to finish my studies, find a job, with Boeing in Seattle I hope, and then meet someone suitable to make them with."

"An Oriental or a typical American?"

"I don't have a preference. Appearance doesn't really matter to me."

"Do you think you could like me?"

My question made her ill at ease.

"I don't know, we don't know each other. I think you said you were with the police, I don't think that's the kind of area where I'd look for a man."

"Why not?"

"I guess a policeman's always busy, right?"

"That's true. I asked you the question to make conversation, but actually I'm getting married soon, to the daughter of a cop as it happens."

I sensed she was relieved. She looked out the window. We were almost there.

50

Of the two missing girls whose file Duigan entrusted me with, one was from Santa Cruz, the other from Sacramento. The parents of the first lived three houses along from McMullan's first victim, going toward the sea. Duigan drove slowly. He was on the verge of exhaustion, and only his solid Irish constitution was keeping him on his feet. I hadn't slept for thirty-six hours and was taking caffeine capsules to keep going. That was something truck drivers took in those days, and with it they could go for two whole days without sleep. Duigan took the photographs of the two missing girls from his jacket pocket and spread them on my lap.

"You did tell me you gave two co-eds a ride that day, didn't you?"

I didn't look at them for a long time. "These aren't them, nothing like them. They were a blonde and a brunette too, but different. Much prettier actually."

"A pity, we might have made more progress. I don't have much time to waste on these two. I'll introduce you to the parents and leave you with them. I still have to catch that son of a bitch McMullan. If he kills again before we arrest him, I could get fired by the mayor. Not to mention that I'd feel responsible for not preventing another murder. You think he might start again?"

"I think he's going to lie low and hope we forget about him. He did what he did to defy his father. Now that his name is everywhere, he must be pleased he's brought shame on the family."

"Lie low where?"

"Where's he from?"

"Salinas."

"Too small. He's already headed south to L.A. or north to San Francisco. At a guess, I'd say San Francisco."

"We learned this morning that he'd emptied his bank account in Salinas. That was a fair amount of money."

"You should investigate in the gay community. It's possible his murders are helping him to accept what he is. At least for a while, because he's a real madman, and one of these days he'll have more hallucinations. I don't think he'll start killing girls again one after the other. He might decide to bow out with a mass murder."

The Dahls' house must have cost its owners a small fortune and there was no attempt to hide the fact. Big plate-glass windows on the upper floor looked out on the sea. That's where the living room was, all decked out like a big cabin on a ship. Seeing the hostile gray expanse out there, I remembered that I'd never been to sea in my life. I'd never even bathed in it. Not on the beach, not even in an isolated creek. The thought of displaying my body to other people had never crossed my mind. I couldn't understand how anyone could pay that much just to have a view of nothing.

Duigan introduced me to the Dahls as a detective paid by the local police to investigate missing persons cases. The father was a tall guy, still young. His daughter's disappearance hadn't dented his self-confidence. The mother was a determined optimist who rejected the possibility of anything bad having happened to her daughter. In that sense, she was right, because nothing bad had happened yet. I guess nobody as big as me had ever set foot in their living room, because for a while they weren't sure what seat to offer me, before pointing out the whole of the couch. The wood in the room didn't smell like the wood in my mother's house, which smelled more like a cheap coffin than the inside of a yacht. Some forests of sequoias have that aroma, and it makes you feel bigger.

I have to admit that it was stimulating to match wits with these people. The father was a born decision-maker and you sensed that, whatever you might say, he gave other people only limited credit.

"You think my daughter ran away, captain, but that goes completely against the grain of how she thinks."

Duigan wasn't in a mood to argue. He stood up, saying that he was handing them over to me but that he would follow the case closely. Dahl must have had a connection with the mayor to have such resources allocated to the search for his daughter.

Before Duigan left the house, he said, "Whatever we find, I can guarantee your daughter's disappearance has nothing to do with the killer we're hunting for. Physically, there's no way he could have been on the campus at the time your daughter and her friend disappeared. There's no reason to suppose there are several killers operating on this coast at the same time. There's never been anything like that in the history of Santa Cruz. In spite of everything, this is a peaceful town. All the same, we won't rule out anything, you can rest assured of that."

Mrs. Dahl served us coffee in little cups. I'd never drunk anything like it, it must have come straight from South America. I swallowed this marvel in one go and got straight to the point.

"My training is basically psychological, even psychiatric. I don't want to boast, but I produced a very exact profile of Jeff McMullan, the killer who's on the run right now."

They thought I was five or six years older than I really was, an overestimate that was essential to my credibility.

"I spent several years studying criminals in a psychiatric hospital in Montana before I joined the missing persons department here, but that doesn't stop me being fascinated by the victims . . . I mean, the presumed victims. I always go by intuition, and then I try to prove that this intuition is the right one. But I'm always willing to accept that I can be wrong. As far as your daughter is concerned, the likelihood that anything terrible has happened to her seems to me very remote, for the reasons the captain just mentioned. The two of you are absolutely certain that your daughter isn't the type of girl who'd run away from home. I can quite understand that. But the fact remains that it's much more likely she ran away than that she's been abducted or murdered. So if you don't mind, I'd like to tackle that possibility first. What's your daughter's name again?"

"Janis."

"If it turns out that Janis can't have run away, then we'll follow another line."

"But it'll be too late," Dahl retorted, still suspicious.

"Not at all, Mr. Dahl. Investigating this as if it's a kidnapping won't give us any more latitude than for a runaway, believe me. I'm going to handle the search for her personally and, wherever she is, I'll find her. To do that, I'll need your help. And the best way for you to help me is to let go of your preconceptions. Can we begin?"

Mrs. Dahl gave her husband a questioning look. Clearly he was the one who made all the decisions. She had abdicated any personal opinion. She only had eyes for this man who had proved himself over and over. There was no need to ask him for his service record, he certainly hadn't gone sick during the war. I did a quick inspection of the room and saw photographs of groups in uniform. There was also a small display case with medals in it. I lingered over them long enough for Dahl to notice my interest.

"My father was in Special Forces in Italy," I said.

He opened his eyes wide as a mark of respect but didn't say anything.

"How can you be so sure your daughter hasn't run away?"

Dahl shook his head slightly, before his nervousness drove him to stand up. "It'd be so unlike her!"

"You feel you know her that well?"

Mrs. Dahl said nothing, just nodded.

"Who knows a child better than her father and mother?" Dahl said, stunned by my question.

"Couples who are as close as you seem to be sometimes don't give their children enough room to breathe. Hasn't it ever occurred to you that she might break the pattern?"

Dahl seemed outraged.

"Forgive me for saying this, sir, but even though you're try-ing to hold it back, I can see how strong your reaction is to my question. That tells me you never imagined she could ever want to be different, be something other than a model student . . . By the way, what is she studying?"

"Architecture."

"And if you don't mind my asking, sir, what's your profes-sion?"

"I'm a property developer."

Instead of making a comment, I was silent for a moment or two, which I think was more effective, then went on, "Can you remember the day she decided on that course?"

Dahl quickly racked his brains. "She was coming up to her eighteenth birthday. Her brother, who's much more brilliant than she is, was doing medicine and we talked about who'd take over from me one day. I suggested to her that she study architecture. Architects have always been a thorn in my side. She liked the idea."

"The path was all marked out for her. She'd be following in her father's footsteps, and she had a solid couple—if my first impression is the right one— to take as a model. Where was there room in all that for her to develop her own personality?"

Dahl was ready to send me packing but he was restraining

himself, less for fear of upsetting me than from a desire to put on a bold front.

"Did your daughter have a boyfriend?" I asked.

"Not as far as we know," Mrs. Dahl replied, after first glancing at her husband for permission to speak.

"Are you both sure she wasn't having a relationship with any young man her age?"

"Quite sure," Dahl said. "Janis is an open book, she'd never hide something like that."

"She never brought any male friends to the house?"

"Yes, sometimes, boys she played sports with. Janis had quite a traditional conception of love. She didn't want to burden herself with a boyfriend before she'd finished school. She wanted to meet just one man, marry and have children."

"Then how do you explain that she was on the pill?"

The couple looked at me, stunned. I now also stood up and walked to the window. The swell had risen, and an oblique drizzle pattered on the windowpanes.

"This is all still just guesswork. But I think that if Mrs. Dahl takes the trouble to search your daughter's room, she'll find a box of pills there. It's important for our investigation."

My size protected me against a hostile reaction from Dahl, who finally motioned to his wife to go upstairs. As her footsteps echoed above our heads, he sat down and poured himself more coffee. He didn't offer me any.

"I think you're going to be disappointed, detective."

He was somber and weary.

Some time went by before Mrs. Dahl reappeared. She was behind me but I could see from Dahl's face that I'd been right. I downplayed the discovery.

"I wouldn't like you to think your daughter was hiding something from you. But she had her own life, the life of a girl her age. It's often scientific and technological advances that determine evolution more than ideas do. Your daughter belongs to the generation of the pill and the transistor even if you don't think so. I'm not jumping to conclusions, just speculating, but the friend she disappeared with was in conflict with her parents. They admitted that to me on the phone. She may have dragged Janis into trying something new. Unless Janis had a relationship with a young man, a member of the counterculture, and wanted to join him. She's already a long way from here, and she's still alive. Lots of young people Janis's age want to experiment with living in communes. The strongest personalities are those who take the experiment furthest. Your daughter wants to know. She's intrigued. I don't think she's involved with any movements, but she's intrigued by what's happening to her generation."

A sailboat stood out on the horizon like a floating prison, an illusion of total freedom that was just another form of incarceration.

"What's better? Realizing that your daughter isn't the girl you thought she was or losing her completely?"

The Dahls, still trying to absorb the discovery that their daughter might have a sex life, couldn't grasp the significance of what I was trying to tell them.

"I'm going to track her down. Once I've located her, you can decide what you're going to do."

"How will you go about it?" Dahl asked, recovering his composure.

"These young people are like sheep, they follow the flock. Most head for particular communes, generally to the north of San Francisco."

"But what drives them?" Mrs. Dahl asked.

"Your generation stood out because of the war. Some young people of our generation don't want that, so they've invented a cocktail of stupid ideas they think will lead to a better world. It's a return to the origins of Christianity, but with drugs added. Because the main obstacle to Christianity is reality, and with drugs they think they can take the experiment further. Has your daughter ever taken drugs?"

"She wasn't even supposed to be taking the pill," Dahl said.

He had lost a little of his arrogance. I sensed that, in spite of the relevance of my approach, he didn't like me an awful lot.

"How do you know so much about these people, Mr. Kenner?" Mrs. Dahl asked anxiously.

"I did a big sociological study that took me several months. I gave rides to a thousand student hitchhikers. The interior of a car soon becomes a place to talk. They know they probably won't see me again, so they open up as if I were some kind of harmless confidant. I'm not like them, and without my car I wouldn't have had the opportunity to get to know them."

I walked toward them to say goodbye. "Within two weeks, I will have found your daughter!"

"Keep us informed of your progress," Dahl replied. He didn't seem happy, as if knowing that his daughter was almost certainly alive wasn't enough for him.

51

I followed the coast road back to town. Once the Dahls' door had closed behind me, I'd felt incredibly empty. I couldn't become myself again. The true Al Kenner struggled to come back to the surface as I walked with big martial strides along Beach Street. I walked like that for about an hour to calm down before going back to the station house to make my report to Duigan. The thing about the pill really impressed him.

"How could you have known that, Al?"

"It just came to me suddenly. I had a one in two chance of being right and I thought it was worth the risk."

Duigan looked outside for a long time. Everything out there seemed still.

"But if she ran away," he resumed, "don't you think she'd have taken her box of pills with her?"

"No, I don't think that at the time she left the university, which was when the last witness saw her arm in arm with her friend, she'd yet made up her mind to run away. Don't forget she's a very conservative girl. She longs for adventure, but I don't think she'd plan to run away. On the other hand, seeing her photo, I think she's capricious enough to decide to leave on the spur of the moment. All it took was for a woman to offer them a ride, a woman who said she was on her way to San Francisco, and in a split second the decision was taken. It's the old question of the trigger yet again. As we speak, I can just see her, drunk with freedom and at the same time full of guilt. But she can't just pick up a phone and let her parents know she's okay, you know why?"

"No."

"The pleasure she gets from knowing they're worried is even stronger than the guilt she occasionally feels. I'm convinced she's tempted to break with them for good."

"But why?"

"The Dahls are a very conventional couple. On one hand, the wife is subservient to her husband to such an extent that she's afraid he'll disapprove if she shows her children too much love. Janis is excluded from her parents' relationship. On the other hand, they chain her to them. She's studying the subject her father wanted her to study. These two contradictory forces are explosive. What was the trigger? We'll know soon enough. I think I can find her. Janis is a girl with character, she'll go a long way in questioning the model her family represents. And then one of these days she'll suddenly come back."

"If she did run away, then I'm not sure this is really a case for us, but Dahl's a friend of the mayor. I'll give you ten days to track her down. Go by the office and get the money for your expenses." Then, without looking at me, he asked, "Are you serious about marrying my daughter?"

"Yes. I was just waiting until I found a steady job."

"Find Janis Dahl and you'll have a steady job. I hope you're honest, Al. My daughter is more fragile than she seems. She's a good girl, straight, a bit sluggish sometimes, but I know her mother's death has a lot to do with that. She finds it hard to believe in life."

"When I was working at the mental hospital in Montana, I had a boss who influenced me a lot. He used to say that all our problems start the day we come out of our mother's womb, and that the child screams because it's angry at having to move from a world of amniotic weightlessness to a world of gravity where you must never forget to breathe. If in addition the mother then dies, the sense of disappointment is overwhelming."

"You make her feel good about herself, Al. Much more than I can. The other day, when I asked her what she thought of you, she said, 'He's like a cast-iron locomotive and I'm like a wooden wagon.' She added that you're good toward her, and that you respect her. These days, young people sleep together before they've even talked, but you're not like that, Al. Let's get this straight, I'm not forcing you into marrying my daughter, I just want to know if the two of you are on the same wavelength."

"We are, Mr. Duigan."

"You can call me Pat."

52

After leaving the station house, I went into the first bar I found. Now that I had become their colleague, I didn't particularly want to see any cops, which was why I didn't go to the Jury Room. The St. James, which wasn't any classier, was next door to a McDonald's and a smell of greasy fries hung over the doorway, making your stomach turn. Three Harley choppers were parked at the curb. As someone who'd handled bikes professionally, I could see they'd been decorated in really bad taste. Their owners were playing pool and smoking, a bottle of whiskey and some beers to hand. The girl who was tending bar was quite attractive. In spite of all her efforts to look tarty, she didn't quite succeed. I ordered a glass of wine and we talked a little while the bikers carried on with their racket. She was from the Sierra Nevada, she'd been born in Bass Lake a few miles from North Fork. Like me, she'd turned her back on the sea. All that salt water and those dumb surfers didn't fill her with enthusiasm. She was dreaming of going back to the Sierra Nevada. She had a chance for a little job in Yosemite National Park. It was a nothing job, just keeping a shop selling sandwiches and souvenirs but at least up there in the mountains the air was cool and dry. With the money she made during the tourist season she'd be able to spend the winter as snug as a bug.

Natural light only entered the bar when a customer opened the door. The subdued lighting gave the floor a brownish hue. The lamps over the pool table distorted the players' faces into disturbing shapes. The waitress could see I was drinking a lot and to reassure her I put a few dollars down on the bar counter as I went. She asked me if I was unhappy in love. I replied that it was a lot worse. One of the bikers swayed up to the counter, grabbed the waitress and touched her breasts. He started pressing on them and yelling, "Stick your tongue out and I'll let go of you." Without the help of alcohol, I would never have had the courage to butt in. The guy reacted angrily but I put my hand behind my back, as if reaching for a gun in my belt.

"That's no way to treat a woman. I'm a cop, don't make me take out my gun."

The threat, added to my size, was enough to calm him down, though all the while I was trying to stop my teeth from chattering. I put my hand back on the counter, quite pleased that I hadn't been forced to show a gun I didn't have. The three bikers finally left without making any trouble. I was left alone with the waitress. She had someone in her life but she wasn't averse to getting better acquainted, far from it. She even added that she was ready to wait a little. So this was the kind of girl I was meant for, one who lived on the margins of respectability. By the time I left I was drunker than I'd ever been before. I clambered into my Ford and drove carefully to Aptos. I parked a hundred yards from the house, behind a clapboard garden shed. My room smelled musty, but I didn't have the courage to open the blinds. In my heavy, fuzzy sleep I heard the voices of my mother and Sally Enfield in the distance. My mother couldn't have been in much better shape than I was, because for once that damned Sally was fully launched on her monologue, passing comments on all kinds of people. When she saw my mother dozing off, she started in on me.

"You know your son scares me, Cornell? I've never been scared of anyone but when he comes and stands there in front of us, he's terrifying. It's the way he stares, I think. If he said something threatening, I wouldn't be so scared of him, but he just stands there like a statue. I'd bet my bottom dollar that's the look he had when he killed his grandparents. Do you realize that's the last thing they ever saw?"

I listened hard and heard my mother say, "They didn't see him, he shot them in the back."

"I hope I die instantaneously, don't you, Cornell?"

"Definitely not," my mother replied. "My life was stolen from me, I want to make sure my death isn't too. I want to have time to see it coming, to savor it."

Then she started coughing like an old woman with TB. She coughed like that for at least ten minutes. I fell asleep just as she was finishing. The sound of metal beating on metal woke me up at sunrise.

I went off to get breakfast at the amusement park near the beach. The big wheel was sleeping off the previous night's efforts. The coffee was as big as it was bad and the doughnuts were soggy. Then from there I went up to the Duigans' place. I waited patiently for Wendy to come out. She was surprised and happy to see me. She was wearing a nice blue dress that made her look unusually feminine. I drove her to work. She thought my van had a strange smell, which surprised me. I opened the windows wide, and as she was early we drove up into the hills a little.

"My father told me you have a lot to do."

"Yes, that's why I wanted to spend a little time with you this morning. I'm investigating the disappearance of a couple of co-eds. I'll be going up north."

"Why north?"

"I don't know, everyone has a compass in their heads, mine's pointing north these days."

"Do you think they were murdered?"

"No, I think they ran away. They'll come back under their own steam eventually, but as one of them's the daughter of a friend of the mayor's, your father has asked me to track them down."

"How are you going to do that?"

"I have kind of an idea."

We smiled at each other and she laid her head on my shoulder. Right then, I'd have given anything to be like everybody else.

"My father says you make a really good detective. He'd really like to have you join the police for good when you've proved yourself. When are we getting married, Al?"

"How about in two months? You know I can't afford a big wedding."

"I know, Al. How many people would you invite on your side?"

I think I laughed. "Nobody."

"I thought I'd invite Marilyn and my boss."

"And your father will invite the whole station house, that's for sure."

"Yes, that's for sure, but he won't let you pay. When will you be back?"

"In a week or two."

"Is it going to take that long?"

"Maybe less."

She got out and turned to give me a little wave. I was weirdly relieved to be alone again. As I watched her walk away in her loose blue dress, I wanted her to disappear, to dissolve, I wanted it to be as if we'd never met.

53

I sat there for a while without moving, feeling as if I was falling to pieces, disintegrating. I imagined my grandparents in the top-of-the-range coffin my father had had to pay for. The Sunday best they'd been buried in must have looked better than they did now. I set off again and my sad thoughts faded away. When I got to the station house, I went to the office to get an advance on my expenses and salary. Duigan had arranged everything, but all the same I spent about an hour filling out forms.

When I came out, a pack of photographers and reporters were standing around the square in front of the building. I asked one of them what was going on.

"They've arrested McMullan."

I waited with them for a short while and saw a short, bald, gray-looking man about my age dragged out of an unmarked police car by two triumphant cops. Duigan got out of the front seat of the vehicle and started an impromptu press conference, although it wasn't really impromptu, while the prisoner was led inside. The mayor, who had showed up out of nowhere the way politicians often do, had joined him.

"The arrest of Jeffrey McMullan is a great relief to our police force. For months now, this monster has been defying and terrifying our community. He attacked the weakest among us. We're overjoyed to see him behind bars, but that shouldn't make us forget the grief felt by the families of the victims."

When the mayor stepped up to speak, I slipped away quietly to the St. James.

I could see it in the waitress's eyes that she thought I'd come back for her. I put some music on the jukebox, an old Elvis song. I've never been interested in music, as I may have mentioned before, but it's useful when you don't want to talk. The waitress didn't dare say anything to me and she was wise not to. What might have been bearable to hear the night before wasn't bearable anymore, you don't give bullshit like that a second chance. I drank steadily, without any hurry. I left early in the afternoon without eating anything and set off for the campus. I was feeling bad, the way I always felt when I was stuck too long with my own thoughts. I needed someone to talk to.

The first girl I saw thumbing a ride was fairly nondescript. The second one looked like a die-hard Republican, and this wasn't the day for them. The third was Susan. She already had that shifty look behind her round Janis Joplin style glasses, damaged red hair and moist little blue eyes. Her body was concealed beneath brightly-colored but rumpled clothes. She was wearing an incredible amount of cheap jewelry that jingled like cowbells as she moved. There was a lingering smell of sweat that she'd tried to conceal with patchouli. I asked her which way she was going and she hesitated then asked the same question back at me.

"I'd like to take off somewhere, anywhere," I said, "but I haven't made up my mind yet. I've been told about a commune north of here. I'm tempted to try it."

"When I saw you I'd have bet on anything except that," she replied, gravely.

She'd said the right thing, if she hadn't I'd have thrown her out of the moving car without hesitation.

"If I dropped by my place to pick up a few things," she went on, "would you wait for me?"

"I don't think so."

She changed her mind. "Maybe I don't need anything after all. Will we have to share the gas?"

"No need."

She went red with joy. "Not a day goes by that I don't tell myself I'm going to drop out and join a commune, and then the day I finish my exams you show up. You're Father Christmas!"

Her happiness struck me as obscene.

"Don't you think there's something not quite right about this? A big guy with short hair, a short-sleeved blue shirt and a mustache?"

She replied with an embarrassed no.

"You know you can't open the door on your side?" I continued in the same neutral tone.

She smiled weakly and tried to look at me.

"Didn't you hear about McMullan, the guy who's been killing girls and ripping them open?"

She'd stopped smiling. "Yes."

"He was arrested this morning."

She relaxed immediately.

"At least that's what they think," I said.

"Why?"

"Only kidding."

"No, tell me, you're not some kind of sex maniac, are you?"

"If I was, I don't think I'd be interested in a girl like you."

It was time to change the subject.

"Do you know a particular commune?" I asked.

"Yes, I have a friend who dropped out of school to join it and she hasn't been back for five months, which means it must be really cool there."

"Then let's go. Which way is it?"

"If I remember correctly, it's on the 1, above San Francisco."

"How far from San Francisco?"

"I'd say a couple of hours along the coast."

"What's the name of the place?"

"I can't remember exactly, but as soon as I see it written somewhere, it'll come back to me."

54

I took the 101, heading in the direction of San Francisco. Susan was all excited, that was obvious from her sighs of joy and the way she kept jumping in her seat. Chuck Berry was playing on the radio and she asked me to change stations, but I refused. She came back to the business of the door.

"Why doesn't it open on my side?"

I was in no hurry to answer. "The mechanism is blocked, I suppose, this van's getting old."

"It's strange, I get the impression you're forcing yourself not to be nice."

"I never force myself to do anything. That's my problem."

As we got closer to San Francisco the traffic grew denser and we slowed to a crawl. Susan took advantage of that to look at me closely.

"Why do you want to join a commune? You look more of a loner to me. Do you really like other people?"

"No, but I'd like to learn."

"I get the feeling you're at a stage where you don't have any choice. Will it bother you if I roll a joint?"

"Until now this van has been a nonsmoking area."

"Does that mean I can smoke?"

I answered with a categorical no and she retreated into her shell. Then she had a fierce urge to take a leak. We were approaching Bay Bridge on a highway packed with traffic, and I couldn't see any place to stop.

"You'll have to hold it in until we've crossed the Golden Gate."

"When will that be?"

"If it carries on like this, I'd say an hour."

"That's really impossible!"

She begged me to pull up on the berm and I had to walk around to the other side of the car to open the door for her. She relieved herself behind the van where nobody could see her. I thought I might leave her there, after all I knew as much as she did about the location of the commune. Then I realized it was in my own interest to have her tag along. Without her, I'd arouse suspicion in the commune and that wasn't what I wanted. Mist was falling over San Francisco, so damp it was like rain, and the stream of cars was taking its time to clear.

"I don't think I'll ever go back to civilization," she said solemnly.

"How can you know that?"

"Because it's meaningless. Look, we're packed in like a herd of cows for slaughter. We're here to consume, period. I can just see myself with a little house and a garden and the neighbors coming and bringing me an apple pie with cream to welcome me while they look inside the house to see if there's any clue about what religion I am. There've never been so many bad people claiming they're Christians as there are in this fucking country. But Jesus Christ is nowhere to be found. Either he's dead for good, in other words the resurrection failed, or he's so pissed about things he's given up. What I like about what our generation is doing is that we're returning to his basic principles and showing all those imposters that Christ's message of love is still topical."

"You're going to fall flat on your face."

"Why?"

"Because man is bad. Evil is in him from birth. Look at a schoolyard, it's not much better than a prison yard."

"Were you ever in prison?"

"That's neither here nor there."

The guy in front of us braked abruptly and I knocked his car without causing any damage. But he got out, looking as if he wanted to kill me.

"Why don't you look where you're going, asshole?"

He came running toward me. When I got out he was stunned to see all seven feet of me rising up in front of him. He might have held his ground except that I had a 9mm pistol in my hand. He turned straight around and walked back to his car as if nothing had happened. Susan was slumped against the door on her side.

"You pulled a gun on him. Are you crazy or what?"

"I'm not crazy, I just don't like it when people show a lack of respect."

We set off again. Two miles further on, having calmed down by now, I said, "I don't regret it. When I was a kid, I used to be terrified whenever I was insulted, but that's all over now. If you don't want to keep riding with me, I'll drop you wherever you want."

"That's not cool, it's really not cool."

She repeated this phrase several times, but she stayed put. Then she asked me to get rid of my gun. "It's illegal anyway."

"Then let's get things straight, both of us," I said. "I'm a cop. It's my service weapon. I'm searching for two missing girls. I hope I find them in that commune, if I don't it means they've been murdered. You keep that to yourself, okay? I don't mean your brothers any harm, I'm even prepared to understand them, but I'll never be one of you, I don't like beards, or long hair, or smoke, or love, or people who don't wash."

The rain started beating down on the car, making the silence that had fallen between us more bearable. Susan sat wedged against the door, with her knees pulled up to her stomach. Her sudden attachment to me was like a victim's to his executioner. I could say whatever I liked, brutalize her verbally, nothing could dissuade her from staying with me. The situation disgusted me.

"Why do you want to join a commune?" I asked. "Is it so you can sleep around?"

"Why do you say that?"

"Because free love is great for ugly girls. A pretty girl can have whoever she likes anyway."

"Why are you so mean to me? Where does that get you?"

"I don't think I like you. There's something about you that bugs me."

"That's because you aren't attracted to me, isn't it? You'd have liked to combine business with pleasure but I don't turn you on, right? Didn't you see what I looked like when I got in?"

This conversation wasn't going anywhere because neither of us knew where it had come from.

"What do you know about this commune?"

"My friend only called me once. They don't have phones and using a booth costs a fortune. She said the people there were really cool, that they still didn't have enough food but they were on the right track. I think we should take them something."

"Like for a birthday party? We could take wine."

"I don't think wine's their thing, they prefer grass or tabs."

"What are tabs?"

"LSD."

For a while we didn't say anything. The Golden Gate was drenched. The cars were going at a snail's pace. Below, the muddy sea was watching us like a shark observing its prey gesticulating on the surface. Susan suddenly retaliated.

"Even the ugliest woman can find someone to have sex with. It isn't always the same for men."

I didn't reply, it wasn't worth it and I wasn't in the mood. I realized that crossing San Francisco had taken a while because she wanted to take another leak. I left 101 at Sausalito, a little coastal town filled with rich bohemians that's going to tip into the sea one of these days, and took the 1, which winds its way through really luxuriant country. I dropped Susan on a dirt track. She didn't think she was out of sight enough. I got a bit riled and asked her what she had to hide that was so amazing. I should have suspected that she was the kind of woman who'd fall in love with a guy that mistreats her. I told her that and all she could say was: "But I don't feel like you're mistreating me, Al."

The road was winding so much it made you nauseous. Susan got her box of pills out of her bag.

"I didn't know you had a man in your life."

"I don't have anyone," she said gravely, "but I don't like being caught by surprise. This thing is the invention of the century, lots of tragedies are going to be avoided. The poorer people are, the more kids they make, the more they argue, the more kids they make, it's like having kids is the cure for everything. I don't know why my mother had me. She didn't love my father. Any more than she loved me. She became pregnant, and she kept me, without asking herself if she was doing the right thing. And as far back as I can remember, I don't think I ever wanted to live."

"That's disappointing," I joked. "Here was I wanting to cut your throat, and now you've taken away my motivation. You can't kill someone who wants to be killed. Where's the pleasure in that?"

"I swear to you that for a moment, when you first picked me up, the thought did cross my mind that you might be a murderer and then I told myself, 'Hey, that'd be great if he was.' I had this whole fantasy about someone who takes life meeting someone who doesn't care about losing it."

"I can't believe you don't want to live."

"When I'm out in the country, my life seems valid, but in the city I sometimes think about killing myself."

"Did you ever try?"

"No, I don't love myself enough for that. But tell me, who are these two missing girls?"

"Two architecture students."

"I'm studying literature, so I don't suppose we ever met. Are they hippies?"

"You mean in the way they dress?"

"Yes."

"No, they're quite conservative."

"I know lots of girls like them who've gone over to the other side. It's a matter of survival. The family is the place where there's the least oxygen, so they need to get away. Just because our parents fought the war and won it, they think their way of doing things can't be challenged. I don't give a fuck about the model they've set down. Work, religion, family, country! Pride in being American! How can you be proud of being American with all the terrible things we're doing in Vietnam and South America and Africa? Whenever anyone tries to share out the wealth a little better, they're killed. Supposedly because they're Communists. America is a paradise for hypocrites . . ."

"If you don't shut up, you walk the rest of the way."

She had gotten a little overexcited and she realized it. "You're just back from Vietnam, aren't you?"

"Why do you say that?"

"I can tell when a man has killed and when he hasn't. You're tense, like a man who's been forced to kill and who'll never get over it, who'll carry that guilt with him for the rest of his life. I understand you, you know, our fathers killed but they had morality on their side, whereas we can't justify killing people in Vietnam. And you don't like people like us, because we don't help you to justify what you've done, we don't glorify you for doing it. But I forgive you, you know?"

I could have killed her. With men like Duigan or Dahl, I was a different person. I used all my intelligence to impress them as if I they were my father. But sluts like this Susan brought me back to the real Al Kenner. I could have killed her in a second and thrown her in the bushes that lined the road and not even a dog would have picked up her scent. But that urge to kill was the kind you never do anything about. She sensed that I wanted it, that I was capable of doing it and she was enjoying it because she didn't care about her wretched life. A man who'd like to kill but doesn't dare and a woman who'd like to die but doesn't dare, that was the situation we were in when the sea appeared around a bend. Honestly, who would want to kill a depressive like her?

55

A little road to our left, deliberately badly maintained to discourage speed, led to the sea. I drove along it and came to a parking lot specially set up for campers. I pulled up, got out without a word to her, and started walking toward the beach. She understood that I wanted to be left alone. There was a wooden bridge over a clear stream. I walked across it to the white sand dunes that were like the sea's rampart against civilization. At this late hour, a few people were walking away from the beach and back inland, a mixture of families and barefoot hippies. There was still the odd person on the beach, which was a semi circular creek from which you could see the houses of Stinson. I sat down in the sand, hoping to find a little peace. But the tingle of unease wouldn't let go of me, as if something in me was constantly reminding me of my own peculiarity. Susan finally joined me. She stripped down to her panties and her bra.

"Aren't you going for a swim?"

"No, I scare the animals."

She smiled. I found it strange that a girl with so much vitality could care so little about life. It had to be a pose, something to do with her awareness that men didn't find her attractive. Her graceless figure got smaller and smaller until she entered the water, where the cold made her jump. The thought crossed my mind of taking her clothes and leaving her on that deserted beach in that ridiculous getup, but I didn't want to hurt her any more than I already had. She came back frozen by the wind.

She shivered as she dressed, then started crying. I pretended I hadn't seen anything and got up and walked back to the car.

Just as I was putting the key in the ignition, I felt really bad. I could see a time coming when I wouldn't be able to keep going, when I'd have to be taken to a psychiatric hospital. I tried to think positive. Maybe I felt so bad because I was hypoglycemic. Susan didn't see any of this, but she could tell from the way I started the engine that there was an urgency in me. We drove to the main street and I parked outside the general store. It was run by a smiling, overweight black woman and, even though she was just about to close, she waited patiently while I looked around the drinks shelves. I picked out four bottles of wine, and just the fact of clutching them in my arms comforted me. Susan was waiting for me, leaning on the van, smoking a huge joint. I got in the back so I could drink without anybody seeing me. I knocked back two bottles straight off even though I really wasn't thirsty. Susan also got in, high as a kite. She'd remembered the town where the commune was. The name didn't mean anything to me, but it didn't me take long to find it on the map. It was just two hours' drive further north, near the sea. You just had to follow the coast road, and that's what we did. The animosity between us faded. There was no risk of running across any cops on this road and I opened a third bottle and sipped it slowly, looking out at the landscape. At regular intervals along the coast there were little lagoons where the sea was motionless, protected from the wind and the tides. The people who'd ended up on this coast had strewn it with wooden cabins where they lived out their dreams of solitude.

A wave of optimism rose in my head and I started thinking about Wendy, the house we could buy together, the old bike I could restore in the garage while she baked cookies, and then as the road left the sea and rolled past verdant meadows I started crying at the thought that I had no future. Don't take that for sentimentality, I've never felt any kind of self-pity and I have to be really wasted for that kind of emotion to break through. Susan didn't notice this passing fit of blues at all. She'd put her feet up on the dashboard and her dress rode up her legs, which looked thinner because of the position. The joint had plunged her into a wonderful world, a world without anxiety, where she didn't feel shy or awkward.

"We're the first generation in history to raise human consciousness to such a level, and that's the truth."

I didn't answer because I wasn't listening.

"Our parents came out victorious from the last war, but they also came out blind. They didn't realize that humanity had showed its darkest face in all that killing. There were no good guys and bad guys. Just a species that had lost its place on this earth. America always says she's fighting for her principles when in fact she's only doing it for her own interests. We're going to undermine this society from inside, peacefully. We're going to put an end to consumption, production and all that bullshit that's stifling us."

She came to an abrupt halt, like an electric mower running out of power. Then she concluded, "I hope they'll take us in their commune."

"Take *you*," I said. "I'm only passing through."

"You say that, but you don't know anything about it. Don't close yourself off from the experience, it might save your life."

"Save my life? No way. Save other people's lives maybe."

She didn't understand what I meant.

"There aren't enough communes for the thousands of young people who'd like to join them."

"Why don't they start new ones?"

"It isn't so easy to find land."

The drinking had made me hungry.

56

After driving miles along a road that ran close to the ocean at times and at other times far from it, we discovered a big log cabin that was used as a restaurant. All they served there was fried fish and I'd never eaten fish in my life. When she found out, Susan asked me why, but I had no idea. Because it was fried, the fish didn't taste so bad. Also for the first time in my life, I had wine in a place that wasn't a bar or my room or my car. Susan smiled between every mouthful, which I soon found tiresome. There was a salt water lake below the restaurant and the water was as still as ice. Some fishing boats were moored to a landing stage that led to a little wooden house on piles. A man was living in that house. From the restaurant, you could see him bustling about in his little kitchen. Then he came out wearing high plastic boots. He was completely bald, but made up for it with a long white beard that went down as far as his chest. In a flash, the thought came to me that it might be good to swap my life for his. I dreamed for a short moment that nature might trap me in a place I couldn't leave, where relations with other people would be limited to a polite nod of the head when I went to buy matches from the corner store and nobody would ever ask me the slightest question. The dream was shattered when the waitress brought the check. I had never seen such a big one. It was a major chunk out of my expenses, and I wondered how I could justify Susan's meal. Then I told myself that as far as I was concerned she was a kind of informant, and that was how I'd present her. In the car, I rinsed my mouth clean of the smell of fish by drinking the last bottle straight down. Susan fell asleep before I set off and the journey continued in silence. I drove slowly because it was the hour of the day when the deer think they own the place. Not so long ago, just a hundred years, the men and women who had won the West had ended up here, next to this unfriendly sea, and I imagined them, exhausted but happy to be at the end of the trail. Then they'd had to retreat inland, toward more fertile land. The coast unrolling in front of my yellow headlights seemed strangely deserted. Sometimes we drove for miles without seeing a house or passing another car. I thought about my family leaving Germany for New York. I didn't know what had driven peaceable farmers to leave their lands and set sail on a ship full of wild-eyed emigrants. We'd never talked about it, on either side of the family—my forebears on my mother's side had left their native Bavaria at the same time as my father's grandparents. Neither family had been driven by starvation, I'd have bet my life on it. There must have been a few skeletons in their closets, not the kind of thing you boast about to your children, sitting by the fire as night falls on an isolated farm in Montana or the Sierra Nevada. It's the kind of secret that blows up in your face eventually, and the explosive is me. I'm the American nightmare of those two families, the dead end their adventures led to. With each generation, by a tragic chance that nobody can explain, there was only one person left to continue the line. I'm the last of the Kenners just as my father was and my grandfather before him. I'm also the last of the Hasslers. My mother's two sisters died without leaving any children. My older sister died in pregnancy. She was too fat to get any bigger, her heart gave out in the third month. My other sister also died, but I don't really remember how even though I preferred her to the other one. Preferring her doesn't mean I loved her.

The road wound too much for a tired man who had

knocked back four bottles of wine, but I was still clearheaded. I vowed that when I got back from this escapade I'd look for my father again. He must have been somewhere. I couldn't imagine him out east, let alone in the southeast. He couldn't stand Texans. Florida, with all those old people who came there to get a tan, scared him even more than the cemetery. Louisiana was like a laundry. He hated the climate, and even though he wasn't a racist, he claimed that the blacks there had too many children. I should point out that he'd never actually set foot in any of these states, it was just the idea he had of them. He certainly hadn't gone back to Montana. I had the premonition he wasn't living very far from me with his new wife, who wasn't so new anymore. When the sign saying we were entering Tomales showed up in my headlights, Susan was fast asleep with her head on her chest. I shook her. For a moment or two it was obvious she didn't know where she was or what she was doing there. I parked outside a hotel, under a street lamp. At that late hour, the citizens were sleeping behind their thick curtains. I got out of the van and walked up and down the nearby streets in the hope of meeting someone. A car suddenly appeared out of nowhere and drew up near us, and an old guy got out and walked to his house, which was on a corner. He gave us a funny look but didn't seem scared. I went up to him and he turned to face me and tipped his hat back over his ears.

"Excuse me, sir, we're looking for a commune around here."

He didn't seem pleased about that. "You planning to join those degenerates?"

"Oh, no, we're just looking for someone."

He liked that answer. He pointed to a street going off to the left. "That's Ocean Avenue and as you'd guess from the name it leads to the ocean. After three miles the country changes completely, it's like the Highlands of Scotland."

I had no idea what the Highlands of Scotland looked like, and it was dark anyway, as I pointed out to him.

"O.K., let's just say that after three miles that are pretty flat, the road suddenly turns hilly and there are big bends. Keep going like that for two miles and then on the left, if you're lucky and there's a moon—mind you, even if there is a moon the fog hides it—you'll see a farm, quite an impressive one, though the first few buildings are dilapidated."

Susan had joined us and she made a bad impression on him. He didn't respond to her greeting.

"That's where they live and breed. They copulate like rabbits in there, so I'm told. You often see the women roaming around here, and they're always pregnant. We don't like them, but we don't do them any harm. Now, if you get to a village made of little wooden houses, that's Dillon Beach, and you'll have gone too far."

All at once, realizing I wasn't one of those people, he turned pensive.

"Look, I don't have anything against these poor kids, but I'm from a generation that worked hard to get somewhere. When I see them using firewood for heating and oil lamps for light, that's kind of an insult to people like us. Seems they don't wash in hot water, and in spite of that they swap their women. You got to understand, we try to be tolerant, but it isn't always easy. I'll give them this, though, they have guts. It's two years now since they took over that land. It's some of the worst soil in the county and they've somehow made a go of it. If you want to criticize the bad things, you have to admit the good things. But I don't like them and there's nothing I can do about that."

Then he said goodnight and went into his house.

We set off again, driving slowly. The night was dark, and the drizzle made for poor visibility. Then we hit some fog patches, which slowed us down even more. We drove at a crawl without finding the entrance to the farm. We came to something that looked like a toy village, about twenty clapboard houses surrounded by tiny gardens on a sandy ridge, each one with a pickup truck and a small boat. We couldn't go any further and there was no point turning back. I decided to wait there until daybreak. Susan fell asleep and I sat there thinking. Drink and drugs are the only way to get away from yourself a little. Otherwise you're always with yourself and that can weigh you down, especially for people who find it hard to get to sleep. I thought about Wendy.

Wendy was a good sleeper. She'd have liked for us to sleep together, but I couldn't see myself sleeping with her in her father's house or taking her to my mother's and having my mother tell her all about my past. She had suggested I take her to a hotel but I'd never set foot in a hotel in my life and I'd have felt as if I was treating her like a whore. I couldn't understand why she didn't get tired of me.

57

Day was just breaking when I finally got to sleep. Susan was still asleep, with her thumb in her mouth. The noise of the engine woke her and for a long time she stretched and shook herself. She was hungry and didn't want to get to the commune on an empty stomach. We did a U-turn and had to wait another hour before the only general store in Tomales opened its doors. It was run by a great guy with a beard and hair like General Custer. A small store like that wasn't enough to channel all his energy, and he kept wandering nervously from shelf to shelf. I bought a few doughnuts wrapped in plastic, a big bottle of Pepsi and a case of wine. There was no reason to think I'd need it, the wine I mean, but it was best to be on the safe side. He asked us where we were going and we talked about the commune.

"Have you been invited?" he asked.

Susan and I looked at each other in surprise.

"Why, don't they let you in without an invite?"

"No, but there are lots of requests. We see dozens of young people come past here every week." He laughed like someone who's just told a good joke. "I mean, it isn't like a convent or a monastery, people don't go there to live a life of chastity. My God!"—he opened his eyes wide—"free love, that must be something. No, I'm joking, I'm sure these young people have other reasons to go there. I know they've taken in a few draft dodgers. There's going to be a police raid one of these days. But there're good kids, well behaved. Are you going there to join them?"

I gestured toward Susan. "She is. I'm just driving her."

We set off again in the other direction. I held the wheel with one hand and a doughnut with the other. By now the fog had lifted and the farm appeared after a bend. It backed on to these big bare meadows that rose toward the sea. The first buildings looked like ruins from an Indian raid. One of them had even burned and the roof had collapsed like a game of jackstraws. Two houses had survived the effects of time. We drove in through a rusty gate that dated from the end of the last century, left the Ford outside one of the barns, and headed for the first house. We passed several people who smiled at us in greeting without asking us anything. A guy came toward us, looking a little more suspicious than the others.

"Can I help you?"

Susan got in first with her answer. "I'm here to see a friend, and Al drove me. He's searching for two girls."

He didn't like the sound of that. "We never give out information about people who come here. Never, that's the rule. Are you police?"

"Oh, no! I'm working on behalf of two families that are looking for their daughters. We have reason to believe they came here."

"Did they say that when they left?"

"No, but your commune has the reputation of attracting lots of people."

"Far too many. But that's no reason to give out information about anyone who's been here."

"Then try to imagine this. Some guy has killed and mutilated a whole bunch of girls in a particular area and your daughter has disappeared in that same area. I think you'd be really pleased to know where she was, don't you?"

He wouldn't give in. "What if these girls don't want their parents to know where they are?"

I took out two photos and held them up in front of him. He reacted very calmly.

"Pretty average-looking girls. But I don't recall seeing anyone like them. Anyway, they aren't here. If they were, I wouldn't let you in."

He gestured to us to follow him. From the way Susan looked at him, I guess he was a good-looking guy. But his slightly evasive eyes made him seem less manly, and his hair was tied in a ponytail behind his back. Apart from that, he seemed pretty average, I'd even say he looked like a science student. He led us straight into the big communal room where they had their meals. About fifteen men and women were busy eating. The place was as silent as a cathedral. Even the children, who were just normal, snotty-nosed kids, weren't making very much noise. A smell of tea and freshly baked bread filled the room. A man of around twenty-five, who'd been sitting next to a stunning blonde, stood up and came over to us. At the same time, Susan's friend Linda recognized her and they were all smiles of joy, which seemed excessive to me. The guy who had been the first to speak to us made the introductions. The new guy looked at us for the longest time and, just as I was expecting a question, he motioned to me to sit down and serve myself, then went back to the blonde. She really was out of this world. I could understand why he was completely absorbed with her. Any normal man would be. I sat down on a bench, while Susan and Linda continued getting reacquainted. Nobody said a word to me. But every time I met someone's eyes, they smiled. Nobody spoke aloud, everybody was whispering like in a confession box. I had a little look around. You didn't have to be a genius to spot the draft dodgers. There were three of them. They looked out of place with their shifty looks and their pale, worried faces. Looking at me, they could never have imagined that just two years earlier I'd wanted to enlist. The world was upside down. Susan couldn't stop herself from repeating our conversation with the proprietor of the general store. They must have been aware that everybody knew the commune was sheltering draft dodgers. When the gorgeous blonde stood up, the guy with her also stood up and came over to me. He sat down on the bench opposite me with kind of a mocking look on his face and sipped his coffee out of a clay container. He seemed very sure of himself, the kind of person who wouldn't say anything until the other person had started a conversation. But I held out. That was when he said, "Do you really think the cops'll come looking for them here?"

I played dumb. "Who are you talking about?"

"The conscientious objectors, of course."

"Objectors or draft dodgers?"

"O.K., draft dodgers, if you insist. I guess that's worse, isn't it?"

"I don't know."

"So why do you ask?"

"Because that may be worse. If it's worse, the cops have a better reason to come here."

"That makes sense. What's your job with the cops?"

He had a row of perfect white teeth, and I guess he thought that displaying them was enough to excuse his attitude.

"Who told you I'm a cop?"

"Nobody. If you aren't, you probably want to be one. But you aren't interested in draft dodgers, that's not your thing, your thing is missing girls from good families, who've swapped their Republican world for real life, isn't it? It's kind of the same thing when you come down to it, these guys deserting their country, the girls leaving their families, it's all part of the same movement."

I looked at him for the longest time, trying to get him a little scared. But nothing scared him.

"I'm not really a cop, I've been hired by the families to find their daughters. If they weren't in danger of being murdered, I wouldn't be here."

"I understand that, but it's absolutely against our principles to inform anyone about what one of our brothers or sisters is doing. We just don't do it." He jutted his head forward. "I can assure you, my friend, we can't do it. But you're welcome here all the same. You can stay as long as you like."

He stood up and stretched, and his shirt lifted to reveal his hairy belly. Then he turned to me suddenly and held out his hand across the table. "I'm Ted Woolf."

The room was slowly emptying. He sat down again.

"This property belongs to my family and I've made a gift of it to the commune. Twenty people can live here and be reasonably self-sufficient. We raise sheep. We swap lamb's meat for vegetables. We even manage to grow a few starchy foods. Three of our brothers fish from a boat moored at Dillon Beach, which is just along the coast. And the rest of the commune weaves lamb's wool. We take turns in going out to sell our products, which gives people a chance to leave here for a while from time to time. We also take turns teaching the children. For the moment we have six children. None of them is school age but we play educational games. What else? Well, everything I've just told you concerns the material organization of the commune. We also have a very intense spiritual life. We can talk about that later if you like. But for now, I have to go to work. Everyone living here has to give his time in exchange for the food we provide. If you don't want to work, you can go to the village and buy mass-produced food, we won't stop you eating it, we aren't sectarian."

I thought about leaving then and there, but my curiosity was stronger than my desire to get back on the road.

58

B rian, the first guy who'd spoken to us, led me to a barn where this big brawny guy was busy doing something, and left us alone. Paul, that was his name, behaved toward me as if we'd known each other forever. His long hair and beard made him look older than he was. He complained, though without any rancor, that he was the only guy in the commune with a bit of muscle, which meant that he was given most of the physical chores. He looked me up and down and tapped me on the shoulder.

"You're a godsend. I have a mile of fencing to put up to keep the sheep in. And they've bought these really high posts. I have to get up on a crate to hammer them in. That's the problem with barter, you swap what you have for something you don't necessarily want."

The posts came up to my waist. We loaded them, along with the wire netting, a crowbar and a sledgehammer, onto a two-wheeled cart pulled by a docile-looking horse. Placid as it was, it recoiled for a moment when it saw me. The human beings it was used to obviously weren't as big as me. Paul immediately realized I had farm experience. I told him about my early years in Montana, and all the school vacations when my mother had stuck me on a ranch with people who had lost the habit of talking because they lived so far from anywhere. We set off for a huge meadow from where you could see the ocean in the distance, gray with white flecks, flinging itself at the deserted beach. The ocean air reached us and mixed with the smell of the joint Paul had rolled while we were talking. As often happened when I'd spent a day in a state of uncontrollable nervousness, the following day I felt strangely calm. I was breathing normally, thinking normally. I was determined to take advantage because I knew this sense of peace never lasted more than a day or two, and that was the time limit I'd set myself to stay here. We got to work. Paul would make the hole and hold the pole while I drove it in. After a while, we took a break. He rolled another joint, lit it and offered it to me. I refused, saying I never touched the stuff.

"You're right, nobody knows where it leads. Apparently in people who smoke a lot, there have been cases of dissociation. You know what that means?"

"Yes, I do," I replied. "I used to work in a psychiatric hospital."

"Fuck, man, you've sure done some jobs. All I ever did was two things: study math, and kill people for two years."

I let him just keep on talking.

"Imagine we're both here, laying our fence, and we hear the noise of a plane along in the distance. A minute later, this plane empties its load over us, and we're turned to dust. A dust even thinner than the one we're promised in the Bible. There's nothing left. It's the Apocalypse. Not a single living soul, not a flower. I spent two years in those planes as a navigator. Of course, I'm not responsible. That's what I tell myself whenever I think about it. And I think about it all the time. But I can't convince myself, so I light a joint to get away from the memories. Two years of war without seeing a corpse, can you imagine that? But I know we burned thousands of men, women and children to cinders, and I never even knew what they had against us. I contributed to a statistic, my friend. And with all the goodwill in the world, I can't get over it. Were you in Vietnam?"

"I tried, but they didn't want me because of my height."

"Fuck it, man, you were lucky! Don't feel sorry about not going, we're not doing any good over there even though the people in Washington say the opposite. It's like the end of the world, it really is. I came here when my time was up. I never had the guts to desert. If this commune hadn't taken me in, I'd be on the road. Ted's a good guy. He really helps the others. He has theories that add up. He says the source of all problems, the thing that's leading us to disaster, is that we want what other people have. Nobody thinks about anything except extending their own territory and grabbing other people's money and women. He's some kind of Taoist. I don't know exactly what that means, but I think it has something to do with getting away from your own ego, your own past, your own upbringing and just going back to nature. And that's fine with me. We're working hard to get somewhere. It's a race against the system. The cops have their eyes on us, but apparently the worst thing is the IRS, which is demanding a ridiculous amount of back taxes on our barter. You planning to stay?"

"No, I just came to drop off a girl who wants to try it out, and to find out about two co-eds who may have come through here in the past two weeks."

To underline what I was saying, I took the photos from my pocket. He looked at them for the longest time, then sighed.

"I'm high so much of the time I couldn't swear it, but the blonde looks familiar. The other's more ordinary. They look like model students. Why are you looking for them?"

I rehashed the same old story. "They disappeared from the campus in Santa Cruz. And as there was a killer on the prowl around the same time, their parents are worried."

"I can understand that. They may well have come through here. But one thing's for sure, they didn't stay. And if they didn't stay, where would they have gone?" He laughed. "My God, when I think about all those cops in California who must be after that killer of yours. I mean, rightfully so. But I pulverized thousands of Vietcong and I have a medal for it. I should have thrown that fucking medal in the toilet at my parents' house. My poor parents thought they'd welcomed back a hero. Sometimes I tell myself I would have preferred to kill those Vietcong in hand to hand fighting. Then at least I could have claimed it was self-defense. But from up there in the sky, Jesus, man . . ."

Paul wasn't a bad guy, but he was starting to make my head spin. I picked up the sledgehammer and one of the posts to signal that we were starting again. The lunch break wasn't a long one. A little soup in the communal room. I wasn't used to having a meal without meat. I thought for a moment about going out and buying myself a hamburger. Work resumed after an hour, and an hour and a half later we hit an area where there was a layer of stone under the topsoil and even when I hit the poles with all the strength I had they wouldn't go in more than an inch. That riled Paul, but it wasn't my problem anymore. It meant the shape of the pasture was all wrong and the fenced-in space was smaller than it should have been, but it was better than nothing.

That evening—they'd already lighted the oil lamps—Paul was so full of praise for my work that Ted suggested I stay. I replied that I wasn't ready to live in a commune, that I didn't like other people enough, and that I thought their utopia would melt away like spring snow one of these days. As we were talking, I could sense everyone getting excited. It was time to decide who was going to sleep with who. I realized it was kind of an obligation. One of the unwritten rules of the commune was that it didn't accept people who were already in couples, and that it was forbidden to form long-term couples while there. According to Ted, that was the only way to ensure they wouldn't fall back into the mistakes of the traditional possessive family model. I talked with Ted for a good part of the night. I saw Susan move away, followed closely by a not very handsome guy, and I told myself she was finally going to do what she'd been itching to do. Ted explained his whole philosophy to me as if he was trying to sum it up for himself and reassure himself that he was on the right track. The stunning blonde was waiting for him. It was obvious she didn't dare go to bed alone for fear someone other than Ted would slip in beside her. I wasn't too bothered about the way they'd dropped out, or their threadbare philosophy, or the fact that they were doomed to extinction. What made me nauseous was how they treated women, making them pregnant without really knowing who the father. That struck me as really disgusting. There weren't as many women in the commune as men and, every evening, there were always two guys who didn't make the grade, like two men who have to keep watch when the rest of the crew of a ship are asleep down below. So that night, there were three poor solitary guys surrounded by moaning coming from every direction. Not many couples closed their doors and sometimes they swapped in the middle of the night. And the reason the two guys who were keeping me company were there was because they wanted to be. A girl came and joined us, it wasn't a good day for her, her period had started and she'd only just realized. All these people who were trying to escape man's primitive instincts ended up with even fewer taboos than primitive man himself, which made them real savages when it came to sex. They didn't give a damn because they were all off their heads with drugs. Around two in the morning, I saw Susan come out, stark naked, dragging a little woolen blanket along behind her like a floor cloth. She asked me if I wanted to join her. I wasn't obliged to sleep with her, she said, there were other girls in the room. That was when I decided to leave. I pretended I was just going into the fields to relieve myself, and that was the last they saw of me.

In the van, I knocked back two of the bottles of wine and set off. I was relieved to be alone again. For no particular reason, I thought about Charles Manson and his gang who had murdered Sharon Tate. I could have done the same thing in that commune. All I had to do was take out my 9 mm pistol and start shooting, just as if it was the shooting range at the fair. But why? There's no logic to these things. You either want to or you don't. I didn't feel the need, even though those people disgusted me. When I got to the village, I left the coast road on the right and drove straight on in order to get back onto the 101.

When I got back to my room I drank two more bottles to help me get to sleep. It's unusual for day to break before I've slept.

59

I woke up at dawn with a terrible migraine and a craving for a cheeseburger. I carefully showered and shaved, ironed one of my short-sleeved blue shirts, put on one of the only two pairs of pants I had, and left the house. My mother had settled in a strange kind of area. It wouldn't have taken much to make it a well-off neighborhood and even less to make it an area for the destitute. I'd been obsessed with talking to her ever since I'd woken up. The obsession was worse than ever. But it was impossible to talk to her in the morning. Even though she hadn't starting drinking yet, her brain was still fuddled from the previous night's binge. I made up my mind to get home quite early that evening and catch her when she was still in a state to think clearly. What did I want to talk to her about? I had no idea yet, I just knew I had to talk to her.

Beach Street was only just waking up at this hour. A few people were starting to leave home. I walked along the wharf to a restaurant that opened early to serve the fishermen who ate there. I ordered a huge cheeseburger with fries and emptied a bottle of ketchup over it. At that moment, I felt a kind of well-being. I drank two big cups of coffee and set off calmly for the Dahls' house. I wanted to catch them as they were waking up. There was less chance they'd be high and mighty toward me. I walked along the cliff, where there were all these little memorials to intrepid young people who'd drowned thinking they could brave the sea with impunity. It was unfortunate, of course, but not sad. The mist was lifting, and the rising sun shone through it. The sea breeze seemed to be there specifically to calm down anyone walking at that hour. When I rang the bell it wasn't yet eight. Dahl opened the door in his dressing gown.

"I wasn't expecting you so early in the morning. Come in."

He looked at me closely, but didn't dare to ask me the result of my search, he preferred to see it on my face rather than hear it. But I remained perfectly inscrutable. We went upstairs to the living room. In passing, Dahl knocked at the door of his wife's room and told her I was there. Then he opened the glass doors and we sat down on the terrace.

"Well?"

I took my time. I didn't want to encourage that arrogant attitude he tended to assume, even when his daughter's life was at stake.

"I located her."

He stood up abruptly, pulled his dressing gown around him, and rushed to his wife, who had just appeared, dressed as if it was Thanksgiving Day.

"He's found her, Beth," he said, in a loud but contained voice. "He's found her."

I savored the effect I was making. "What I mean to say is, I have an idea where she's been."

"Where?"

"In a commune on the Pacific coast north of San Francisco. Don't ask me where, the people who cooperated with my investigation made me promise to keep quiet about their location. Anyway, she's not there anymore. She must have gone further north."

Relief gave way to annoyance on their faces.

"To be honest with you, Mr. Kenner, I never doubted that my daughter is alive. Especially as the killer who's just been arrested has confessed to his crimes. I spoke with Duigan on the phone yesterday, and he says the man is so proud of what he's done, he's admitted every single murder he's committed. Tell me about this commune, you say she isn't there anymore?"

It was obvious that now Dahl was convinced his daughter was alive, he felt justified in emphasizing the narrow-minded Republican morality that ruled his life.

"She wasn't there when I passed through, but it may be that she left it for a few days and was planning to come back. The members of the commune weren't very cooperative. That's because they're sheltering a few draft dodgers."

"Of course!" Dahl said sharply. "What do they actually do in this commune?"

He'd started treating me like one of his employees. He looked at his watch. He was back in business.

"They raise sheep on a big farm that belongs to one of the members, they smoke a lot of marijuana, and they practice free love. Couples are frowned on. They're vegetarians and obtain fruit and vegetables by bartering their animals. They also weave lamb's wool. From a spiritual point of view, they're Taoists."

"What the hell's that?"

"From what I was able to understand, it's a way of redefining your place in nature and the universe, fleeing your primitive instincts, of which the most harmful is apparently possession, and rejecting all forms of material and spiritual alienation. They also reject the Bible, which they see as an anti-spiritual text that creates an unbelievable God in the service of men and their petty interests. But they praise the goodness of Christ."

"You hear that, darling?"

Mrs. Dahl heard very well. She had been holding her hand over her mouth as she listened to me. "About . . . about free love, you mean they . . ."

I kept it as factual as I could. "In the evening, couples form depending on what individual people want. They split up the next morning. Sometimes, they change partners in the middle of the night or couples decide to regroup, the idea being that early in the morning these arrangements are dissolved, and everybody goes back to work with plenty of memories but no rights at all over that night's partner."

Dahl stood up. "Goddammit, Kenner, don't tell me my daughter is mixed up in all that?"

"I didn't see her with my own eyes but I think it's likely she followed the rules of the commune. Or maybe she left because she didn't approve of things like that. A lot of other communes are based on the traditional couple, and they don't go in for swapping."

Dahl walked up and down the terrace for a few seconds without saying anything but looking at his wife as if preparing her to hear something terrible.

"My daughter has ceased to be of interest to me. As of today, she's no longer my concern. I invested a lot of hope in the bond we had. She might well have taken over the family business eventually. But now that's out of the question. Even if she comes back tomorrow. Even if she swears to high heaven that she never took drugs or took part in these orgies, even if she expresses remorse for running away and for the suffering she's caused us. Do you agree, Beth?"

Mrs. Dahl started crying but her husband had no intention of letting the situation turn emotional, and the glare he gave her dried her tears immediately. He went back into the living room, opened a drawer, took out a wad of banknotes and handed them to me.

"For your trouble."

I raised my hand as a sign of refusal. "I'm paid by the police to do my job, Mr. Dahl. If I accepted that money, there'd be a conflict of interests."

He walked me to the door without another word and as we took our leave of each other I could see in his eyes that as far as he was concerned his daughter was dead, and nothing could ever make up for his disappointment. I allowed myself the last word.

"Forgive me for saying this, Mr. Dahl, but I don't see what could be more important than the joy of knowing that your daughter is alive."

60

On the way back, the promenade was full of dogs and their owners in sports gear, plus a few young people jogging. I picked up my car, which was parked on Beach Street, and drove to the station house. Duigan had just arrived. He was clean-shaven and looking a lot more relaxed since the arrest of McMullan. But he was genuinely worried by how tired I seemed.

"I'm not sleeping much," I said. "That must be why."

"Is there any reason for that?"

"Maybe not. That's just how it is."

He patted me on the shoulder. "When you sleep with my daughter every night, you'll sleep soundly again. There's nothing better than a woman to improve your sleep. Now tell me about your investigation."

"The girls had been in a commune I visited, north of San Francisco. Either they didn't stay there, or they left it temporarily. It wasn't easy asking questions in a place like that, they're sheltering a whole bunch of draft dodgers so they clammed up. And when they saw me coming, they knew right away I wasn't one of them."

"So now you're a specialist on missing co-eds. Did you reassure the Dahls?"

"Yes. If you can call it that. They didn't take it well. They'd always thought their daughter was like them."

"That's understandable. At least the father will stop calling the mayor, and the mayor will get off my back. I don't know how I'd take it if my daughter got involved with hippies. With you as a husband, there's no risk of that. Talking about that, Al, we never mentioned this before, but what religion are you?"

"Catholic."

Duigan smiled broadly. "Catholic? God, that's a relief. I mean, I'm not fanatical about these things. Not sure how much I believe, although I go to church. Still, my grandparents were from the south of Ireland and it would have bothered me if . . . Anyway, you're a Catholic, and I'm relieved."

"Didn't Wendy tell you? We did talk about it."

"No, Wendy doesn't tell me much about you. By the way, we've had reports of more co-eds running away . . ."

He searched on his desk, which looked like the Temple after it had been destroyed. He picked out three sheets of paper and handed them to me.

"Nothing too worrying. But if you can take care of it . . . "

He put his feet up on his desk, which faced the window.

"I questioned McMullan. My God, Al, I've never seen such a crackpot in my life. And I talked with his mother. According to him, he was a brilliant, well-balanced young man until his best friend died. That was when he started to withdraw and go off the rails, and his parents decided to have him committed. He was treated and then released when they decided he wasn't dangerous. But you realize when you talk to him that the guy's completely crazy. The victims' families won't even have the consolation of seeing him fry in the electric chair."

"Why not?

"California has declared a moratorium on the death penalty. Tell me, do you think someone like McMullan is born a killer?"

It was a good question, and I thought about it for a while. "The percentage of born killers is very small. All the others are just paying back society for the harm that's been done to them. And when I say society, I mean the family in particular. Just as most crimes take place within the family, the family is the main breeding ground of criminal behavior. Instead of talking to you about her son as a perfectly normal boy, McMullan's mother would have done better to tell you about what was wrong with him, what had led him to develop homosexual drives, how they were severely repressed in his family circle, to the point where he needed to take it out on poor girls by ripping open their stomachs as if it was his own mother's stomach he was attacking. Out of every hundred men suffering from the same psychological disorder, sixty deal with it by drinking or smoking dope. Thirty-eight kill themselves. The last two become murderers. It's no more complicated than that."

"I just hope the one that's left will go do his dirty work in another county, and if possible in another state."

Duigan was called away on an ordinary homicide. A battered wife had put five bullets in her husband's head, which proved he'd been battering her for a long time, otherwise one bullet would have been enough. Before Duigan left, he invited me to dinner at his house the following Saturday night.

61

I had kind of a panic attack when I left the station house and the only way I could think of to get over it was to go see my mother. I drove to the campus, thinking I'd catch her at lunchtime. She was alone in her office with a lousy sandwich and a homemade salad, her big glasses low on her nose, looking pretty rough from the previous night's binge and her gigantic efforts to hide it from her colleagues. Seeing me, she recoiled.

"What are you doing here, Al?" she said in a deliberately muffled voice. "I've told you a hundred times never to disturb me at work. I hope you haven't come to ask me for money after robbing me?"

"At least you have less to spend on booze."

I went and stood at the window with my hands behind my back, and all at once the room darkened like a stormy day. She stood up to go out. I went and barred her way to the door. Now that I'd come away from the window, daylight had returned.

"I came to hear you talk to me."

"Talk to you?"

"Don't you feel like you have something to say to me? Think carefully."

"What do you mean, Al? This isn't the place, you know that."

"It's the only place you can't scream, that's why I came."

"I have nothing to tell you except what a disappointment you've been to me."

"Is that all?"

"Yes, that's all."

You should have seen the expression of disgust on her face.

"I came to tell you I've found a job with the police."

She sighed. "Will you be able to leave the house and rent somewhere else?"

"I told you, Ma, I'm getting married soon. I'll be moving somewhere with my wife."

"Does she know what you did?"

"No."

"You have to tell her. If her father's a cop, he'll get hold of your record one of these days."

"My record is clean. I appeared before a psychiatric panel and they said I was fit to lead a normal life. That's why I need you to talk to me, to explain, don't you see?"

"Explain what? The evil you have inside you? That's life, Al, we're born good or bad. You can play at being good, but you'll always be bad, you'll always be the little boy who cut the head off his mother's cat, you'll always be the teenager who shot his grandparents in the back. It's not your fault, Al, you were born like that. You were born without empathy for other people. You don't care about other people's pain, or about mine. You can see I'm suffering. Why do you think I drink? I drink to console myself for your lack of empathy for me. You don't realize the harm you've done. You can't imagine what it means to a mother to lose a daughter and have a criminal for a son. So what do you want me to do? Jump for joy and introduce you to my students as the ideal son-in-law? You can survive, Al, but as for living? Forget it. You lost the thing that gives a man value, you lost your honor. Does your father want to see you again? No, we never hear from him. Total silence. He's wiped you out. Because of you, he doesn't even know his daughter is dead. So what do you want me to talk to you about?"

She slumped on her chair in an attitude of complete disillusion, chewing slowly in a circular movement. Once she'd swallowed her mouthful, she went on, "The only question is whether I'm going to let you screw up the life of an innocent girl who sees you as just a nice young man. I don't think that'd be the proper thing for me to do. If anything happens, the law could hold me responsible, Al, and they'd be right."

She put the half-eaten remains of her sandwich in the trash bin under her desk.

"I haven't decided yet. I could just as easily say nothing, Al. So do me a favor and get out of here."

I'd never imagined anger could fill me to the roots of my hair, but that's what happened. Some kind of subterranean creature burrowed its way into me, urging me to destroy that office, that building, that faculty, and leave only a few atoms as if they were all that survived from a nuclear war. But none of my tempers ever spilled over into violence. This time, yet again, my anger faded, and I was alone with my mother, who had resumed her work. It took me about fifteen minutes to summon up the strength to get back in the van, ready to drive away. I opened a bottle of wine and drank it down in one go, without taking a breath. I didn't really feel any better after that but I couldn't be bothered to open another. I set off, driving slowly. I switched on the radio to take my mind off things. A man with a strange, soft, high-pitched voice was singing a song where these words kept coming back: "I'd rather be the devil than to be that woman's man." At the end the presenter mentioned the singer's name, Skip James. When the song was over, there was a commercial: "Do you have a problem with excess sweat?" These people who have things to sell don't respect anything. I started feeling bad again. I knew very well why I couldn't sleep, my dreams had left me

62

You leave the campus in a big curve that descends toward Santa Cruz. From there you can see a strip of ocean in the distance and, with a bit of luck, Monterey. There's even a bench that's been put there so you can sit and look at the landscape, but, curiously, it's separated from the road by a barbed wire fence. That was where the two girls had stopped to thumb a ride. I wondered if I should pick them up, I didn't know if I was calm enough to bear their chatter. I slowed down without indicating that I intended to stop. I finally looked at my watch and drew up alongside them. They didn't hesitate to get in. If a whole farmyard had attacked my van, my eardrums wouldn't have suffered more than they did. The two girls had no manners at all, they just continued their conversation as if I wasn't there. I braked abruptly in the middle of the descent. The one who was sitting next to me banged her head on the glove compartment and the other one hit her nose on the back of her friend's seat. The noise stopped abruptly and you could almost hear the ocean, even though it was at least three or four miles away. They didn't hurt themselves, but they realized right away who was boss.

"Sorry," I said, "I take size 14 shoes, and sometimes I hit the brake pedal without meaning to."

They believed me but they stayed silent after that.

"Where can I take you?"

They were going to Aptos. I told them I lived there too. They didn't know the area where my house was, but it didn't matter. I told them I had shopping to do. I wanted to buy a record player and a particular record. They liked the idea and we headed for the Santa Cruz exit, because they knew of two stores in a shopping mall in Santa Cruz that might have what I wanted. They thought I was an electrician, which annoyed me a bit even though it was my father's last known job. When I told them I was a cop, they apologized, although it didn't seem to make much difference to them. The record salesman wasn't sure they had any Skip James but after a good search he found an album from the thirties. The girls went with me. They kept laughing all the time, and I got the impression they were running away from something. Not me, anyway. They got back in the van and resumed their chatter, which was full of private references only they could understand. Then we headed for Aptos.

63

I didn't get back to my mother's until the evening of the next day with my record player and the Skip James album under my arm. Sally Enfield's car was parked in my spot, so I parked in front of it. I went upstairs to lie down for a while. I heard them having their usual alcoholic conversation but didn't quite catch what they were saying. I wanted to sleep, that was all. I was starting to have blurred vision, and I kept wanting to cry for no reason. I had to keep breathing in to fill my lungs and my body weighed a ton. I had never before known such tiredness. I looked for a long time at the photo of Skip James on the album sleeve. I would never have imagined I could be moved by music, let alone music by a black man. Not that I had anything against black people—I hadn't met many of them in my life, except in Los Angeles when I lived briefly with my father. My father used to say, "The blues is like the soul gradually emptying," and now for the first time I understood what he meant. So, contrary to what my mother claimed, I was capable of a kind of empathy for other people. She was hardly the one to lecture me about that, she never felt sorry for anyone. I fell asleep for half an hour before I was woken by the two women's laughter. They were obviously at the height of their drunkenness. I could hear their vocal cords vibrating, obscured by booze and cigarettes, their alcoholic voices that made even laughter sound like a dirge. I switched on the record player and played the Skip James disc once. Then again, louder. The laughter had subsided. The third time,

I raised the volume to maximum. I heard knocking on my floor with a broom. My mother started yelling. So I went down. The door was locked. I knocked. Neither of them came and opened up. I knocked louder. In desperation, I put my fist through one of the panes of glass and turned the key. They were both standing there with glasses in their hands, and the low table was covered in empty bottles.

"What the hell are you doing here, Al, can't you see I'm with friends?"

I stared at her friend. "I know her. I know she only comes here to get plastered with you." I pointed my finger at the woman. "What a petty little life that is, the life of Sally Enfield. When she's dead, there'll be nothing left of it, not even a dog to piss on her grave. Just like you, Ma."

My mother's features were distorted with rage. "If you don't leave this room in one minute, Al, I'll call the cops and tell them all about your past!"

Instead of leaving I went and sat down on the couch. I looked at Sally Enfield. "It's past your bedtime, so go. I won't say it again."

"Stay!" my mother ordered.

"Didn't you hear me, Sally? This is family business and you're not family, the only ties you have with her are ties of booze, not ties of blood, so go back to your room before I lose my temper."

"Don't move, Sally!" my mother yelled.

"What I have to say to you doesn't concern her," I went on in a soft voice. "Unless you want me to reveal certain family secrets."

She lowered her arms, and Sally Enfield headed for the guest room like a little girl who's being punished. My mother took advantage of her departure to pour herself a drink and light one of her long menthol cigarettes. She didn't know how to regain the edge.

"You'll never again get the better of me, Ma, never. Now that we're both here, talk to me. I know you're going to tell me you have nothing to say, but I suspect that if you make the effort, I might start to understand you a little. I'm not talking about forgiveness, Ma, you don't forgive your mother in return for words, you forgive her because she's your mother and that's all. But talk to me."

For a while she didn't say anything, just sipped at her drink and took such deep drags on her cigarette that her lungs must have been completely black. Her jaw was trembling, and so was the hand holding the glass. The ice cubes knocked against the sides of the glass, making a noise like hail.

"Why don't you tell me about your father?"

"My father? What do you want me to say?"

"I don't know. Think carefully."

"There's nothing to think about."

"When you made me sleep below your room in Montana, you told Dad one day that your father used to feel you up."

She started laughing, pleased with herself. "I must have made it up, Al. Because it suited me. Sometimes when you live with somebody, you spice it up with something dramatic. I made it all up."

"Are you sure your father didn't abuse you?"

She laughed even louder. "Hell, no. My father would never have been capable of something like that. No, Al, you're wrong, nothing like that ever happened. I swear on your dead sister's grave."

From my experience in the psychiatric hospital, I remembered that when you harped on about something that was really fundamental to a person's life, that person changed color. The blotchy scarlet of her face hadn't changed at all. Every gesture she made told me that she wasn't lying.

"So talk to me."

She looked at me, laughed like a madwoman, stopped

abruptly, then said, "Don't look elsewhere for what's inside you, Al."

She said that without much conviction but she said it several times, then, too exhausted to continue, she staggered to her room and closed the door without turning around in order not to meet my eyes. Just when I was least expecting it, she half opened the door again and said, "I have to put a stop to all this, Al, I have to tell them what kind of monster you are. The worst thing that could happen to me would be if you had a child. I don't want to be responsible for the proliferation of evil. You understand what I mean, don't you?"

64

S usan has been sitting in the usual little visiting room. Al arrives late. He apologizes.

"I just gave a speech against firearms to a class of high school kids in Sacramento."

He sits down and stretches his legs sideways in order not to get in Susan's way.

"They should confiscate all the weapons that aren't in the hands of professionals. But Americans don't want that. They'd have the feeling they were walking naked, with their dicks exposed."

He has started laughing. He's in a cheerful mood. Then he sighs. "I've been remembering our trip to Tomales. When did you leave there?"

"A long time after you, I told you. I fell in love with a guy from Mississippi, and I didn't like the idea of him sleeping with other women. Ted said we were withdrawing into ourselves, and he didn't like that. After a while, he asked us to leave, saying we were going against the spirit of the commune. Some claimed he was only keeping the commune going so that he could sleep with all the girls. I don't think so. I think he was genuinely convinced that returning to conventional practices would drive us back to society. I met him again twenty years later, in San Francisco. We talked a little. He was working for Apple. He seemed to be a success. But you could see from his face how bitter he was that our experiment had failed. Are you writing that section?"

"I already did. Right now I'm getting to the last part of the book. And I'm not sure yet how to handle it. I'm afraid even readers who've been with me up until then will reject the book at that point. Could I discuss it with the publisher who's interested?"

"They want a finished manuscript. We can still fix it later."

"Leave it to me, I'll work it out. It's all a question of knowing how far to go with reality. Fiction is reality. Why would people read novels if they didn't bring us closer to real life? But if you use too much reality in fiction, you get further away from it because reality isn't reality. It's a chicken and egg situation. I appeared before the parole board, by the way."

"And what happened?"

"Once again, they said I was perfectly sane and posed no danger to society. In spite of that and my model behavior, the warden wasn't in favor of letting me go. He told me that personally. I admitted to him that I'd put in the parole request just to keep myself occupied but that basically I don't really want to be outside again. Here, at least, I'm fed and housed and my clothes get laundered. And they respect me. No prisoner has ever dared disrespect me. Except McMullan who called me a "killer whale," which I didn't really like. McMullan is a short thin guy, probably doesn't weigh more than 120 pounds. He was sitting in the canteen. I went up to him, pulled his chair away from the table, sat down on his knees and placed my tray over his. I took my time eating. By the time he walked out, his legs were purple. That was the last time he called me a killer whale."

He smiles before continuing.

"I'm a little bit bored. I don't have any personal experience of life anymore. It's kind of sad but that's the way it is. How could it be any other way? That wouldn't make any sense. So, it seems the country's on the verge of bankruptcy?"

"So they say."

"People are spending more than they earn. That's impossible in here, nobody gives you anything on credit. Money, friendship, love, anything. I'd just like to want something. The punishment for having wants you can't suppress is that after you've satisfied them you don't have them anymore. It's a strange mechanism, the mechanism of desire. Do you still sleep with guys?"

Susan blushes like a farm girl. "The only man I'd like to sleep with is you."

Al laughs. "Even if they got me out of here, I wouldn't sleep with you. Ex-convicts aren't so desperate they sleep with even the ugliest women. Hell, no!"

Susan starts sobbing, in a dignified manner. "You can be real mean sometimes."

"I'm not being mean, Susan, I'm teasing you."

65

It was a Saturday morning. Every Saturday morning our neighbor got ready to go out to sea. His boat was more like a bathtub than a yacht, but he probably couldn't afford to buy a better one. It spent all week on the trailer like a soul in torment and I wondered where the guy found calm enough water to risk his life on a boat like that. He and I had never spoken. The more developed a country is, the less neighbors speak to each other. At least that's what they say. If there's ever been a day in my life when I wanted someone to really talk to me, that day was it. I went out and locked the door behind me. The neighbor was checking that his boat was secured to his trailer and his trailer was secured to his car. He looked too old for these expeditions, and in fact that was the first thing he said to me.

"I'm too old for these expeditions."

Maybe he was expecting me to either agree wholeheartedly or contradict him. My silence surprised him, and I could see from his face that he was sorry now that he'd started talking to me. It was obvious he'd realized that I was Cornell Kenner's son, the boy they said had killed his grandparents. They said that because she'd boasted about it. I could even date the day of her boasting because, from that point, I saw that the neighbors didn't look at me the same way they had before.

"But I'm afraid if I stop I'll be too old to do anything at all," he hastened to continue. "Oh, I never go far but the fog comes down so quickly in the Bay. I got caught in it last year. And the sea had risen too. I thought I was done for."

I had no intention of making conversation. When I got in my Galaxy, he said with an embarrassed smile, "Say hi to your mother for me."

I replied without thinking, "I already did."

He stood there speechless, arms dangling, and I started the engine.

66

I'd never experienced such tiredness before. I swallowed two caffeine tablets and headed north. I could feel a buzzing in my head. Something in me was going to explode, I was sure of it. My legs were turning to stone, my blood was flowing like lava. I got back onto the 101, moved onto the left-hand lane and put my foot down. My reflexes were all shot. I knew that if another driver took too long to get out of my way, I wouldn't be able to brake or avoid him. Fortunately my van couldn't do more than eighty miles an hour on the downward slopes. I could see myself ending up in the back of a trailer truck filled with Minnesota chickens. My anger was like the temperature of a kid struck by meningitis, it wouldn't go away. Nothing worked. I was going to kill myself, I was sure of it. It wasn't a supposition, it wasn't a desire, it was an inevitability. I could see looks of horror on the faces of the drivers I overtook. They too sensed that I was going to kill myself. All at once, near Vacaville, a town between San Francisco and Sacramento that has more inhabitants locked up than free because of the penitentiary there, I realized that if I carried on like this the cops would arrest me and put an end to my plans, even though I didn't know what they were yet. I took the exit and pulled into a parking lot. I was overexcited. I went into a roadside diner and drank a gallon of coffee. Then I spent at least fifteen minutes with my head under the faucet in the ladies' bathroom. A woman yelled at me that I shouldn't be there, but she regretted it when I rose to my full height and she saw my eyes. I had another gallon of coffee, and then the idea came to me to steal a convertible, so I could get some air. It had become an obsession. I wanted to drive with my head in the open in order not to fall asleep. I hung around for an hour in the suburbs of Vacaville looking for a suitable car. A 1967 Mustang convertible was parked by the curb, top down. I got the engine going in a couple of minutes. I went back to my van to get my things, which consisted of my 9mm pistol and some rope. I looked all through the van to make sure I hadn't forgotten anything and I found a strip of contraceptive pills. I took that too. Luck was on my side, the driver had left his papers in the glove box. I sat down behind the wheel. There, I realized that I really had to drive with the top down, otherwise my head would get stuck in the hood and the Mustang would look like a dromedary. The designer had probably never imagined that a guy my size would ever drive that car. I folded the hood in three seconds. Not that this solved all my problems. The top of the windshield was exactly at the level of my eyes. And since I couldn't lower myself I was forced to crane my neck to see the road over the top. All these details bothered me. I got back on the 101. Rain started falling and mixed with my tears. I thought about my father. I'd have given anything to find him again. Why had he never gotten in touch with me? When I was little, I was his favorite. He called me the Kid. I walked in his shoes, which were too big for me, and made them clank on the floor. Damn it, I was crying and couldn't stop, I would have liked everything to start all over again from zero, for everything to be wiped out, blank page. He should never have abandoned me. I really didn't deserve it. If I had to explain it all one day, I knew what I would have to say. No, I'm not crazy. No, I don't have psychosis. I had no other choice than to use a perverted defense mechanism in order not to sink into madness. I always stopped myself on the verge of madness because I was strong enough to do so. Don't ask me the impossible, goddammit, don't ask a guy who's driven to madness not to defend himself. The rain was falling more and more heavily. It hit my glasses at high speed and I couldn't see any more than if I was at the bottom of a pond covered with water lilies. All the same, I didn't want to die there, so I slowed down and moved into the right-hand lane, but without intending to stop. If I died, nobody would ever understand anything about this story. And then my life would have been pointless. It was that pointlessness I couldn't bear. But at the same time I had the desire to put a bullet in my head as I drove and put an end to this fucking wretched life of suffering. Had I ever experienced pleasure? Could anyone tell me that? Since pleasures were forbidden to me, I had made my own. Weirdly, I have to admit. But we do what we can. Hell, I stopped in time. In time, even if it was too late. It wasn't too late for everybody. Nobody stopped me. Who stopped me, huh? Nobody. I stopped myself, because my intelligence allowed me to. I don't have a higher IQ than Einstein for nothing. They burned my emotional brain, there's no doubt of that. But I can still reason for myself. The rain was coming down harder. I'd stopped bothering to wipe my glasses. I was driving by following the lights of the trucks in front of me. The people in the other cars were watching me aghast. I was pretending to be impassive, as if the rain couldn't reach me. My shirt and my skin had become one. There was no risk of falling asleep, that was the main thing, nothing else mattered. I finally pulled up at a fast food joint and had another coffee.

67

I asked the girl for a strong coffee. I was dripping onto the floor and she was watching the water run down me. She offered to sell me a towel for a quarter, because she didn't have one of her own. My banknotes were dripping too. I felt totally drained. After drying my hair, she told me she recognized me, she had served me, not last night, but the night before that. She seemed to be begging me to recognize her, but I couldn't place her, even though it was true I had been around there the night she said. I drank her coffee and went outside. The rain had stopped. I sat down in the Mustang and burst into tears. I called to my father. I wanted him to come and get me, to take me home. I was crying so much I was all choked up. Then the tears also stopped dead. I set off again after filling her up, realizing that I had just enough money to finish my journey. Of course, with the help of a loaded 9 mm, I could get more supplies, but I didn't want to end up as just another young punk. As I drove through Eureka, I thought maybe I'd blow my brains out, an honorable end to a life that wasn't completely honorable, although that's debatable, and I'm serious when I say that. I've never managed to take control of my own life, that's the reality of it. I remember all my efforts to chase away my bad thoughts. There was only one thing I only needed to do to get rid of them. Just one thing. And I did it in the end. I did it too late. My intelligence let me down. The long version of Einstein's brain couldn't solve a trivial equation, and now I'm full of regrets. Not for the harm I did. My mother was right

about that. I don't have empathy, the harm I did remains the-
oretical. I inflicted collateral damage. You don't mourn collateral damage, you regret it, at best you apologize but you don't
spend the rest of your life begging forgiveness. Not everybody
has the gift of empathy. Soldiers and politicians don't have it
and nobody blames them. Power is in the hands of men and
women without empathy, they are my brothers in a way and if
you look into it, we may have the same excuses. I too wanted
to be acknowledged by my family, and by people in general. I
too wanted to draw attention to myself, even though I'm not a
narcissistic pervert. Or a pervert, period. I have a perverted
defense mechanism. Which is going to fall apart now. Just
when my brain is as clear again as a newborn baby's, I'll be
dead. Yes, they're going to kill me. They should kill me. It's
what I'd do if I were them. That's why I've been struggling
since the beginning of this journey with the idea of blowing my
brains out. Because I want to leave that to them. But they can't
execute me before I've explained myself. This society has to
understand once and for all that I wasn't born to kill.

68

As I neared the Avenue of the Giants, it started raining again, just as my shirt had almost dried. I was starting to get pissed off at all this rain, which kept coming without warning, and by now I was tired of getting wet, I'd had enough of it. A service station reached out to me from below the highway. I filled her up again, that Mustang was a real gas guzzler. An old man served me. His wife kept the cash register and a little bar that served a few hot dishes. These people looked too old to be working still, but I guess they had no choice. I ordered six fried eggs with bacon and coffee. The old lady crept away to make them. A woman of about thirty came in. She was wearing a gray raincoat over a short skirt that revealed her nice legs. She sat down on one of the two remaining seats, took out a cigarette, and started smoking nervously. I sensed that she wanted to talk to me but couldn't make up her mind. I didn't exactly encourage her. I was staring at the black oil in the fryer, on the verge of collapse. At last she took the plunge.

"You going north?"

I didn't answer straight away. I finally turned to her. "Yes."

"Could you give me a ride? I'm going to Eugene, Oregon."

"I'm going to Oregon too, but I'm stopping just over the state line, in Gold Beach."

"At least that's something, if you agree to take me."

"Yes, but there's a problem. I'm driving a convertible and, because of my size, I can't close the hood. So when it rains, I can't guarantee you'll stay dry."

"But why did you buy a convertible?"

"I didn't buy it, I stole it. But it's like when you steal shoes from the cloakroom of a stadium, you don't know if they'll fit your feet."

I didn't turn my head to see her reaction. The old lady came back. The fries were still hot. The woman ordered a Pepsi.

"So will you take me?"

"You'd be taking your life in your hands. I haven't slept for three days. It might be better if you waited for someone else."

"I don't have time to wait."

Her life didn't interest me. I told her that.

"O.K., I'll take you, but I don't want to know anything about you and I don't feel obliged to hold a conversation with you. I'll drop you near Reading if we get there alive."

Suddenly doubt struck her. "You're serious, right? You haven't slept for three days?"

I swallowed my mouthful. "I'm serious."

"Okay, then I'm going to wait for someone else."

I finished eating then said, "Your problems aren't so bad that you should risk your life. You just realized it, and that's a good thing."

I stood up and went back to my convertible under an almost brazen blue sky. I looked westward. No sign of rain. I got in the car and just as I was about to leave I dozed off. I must have slept at least an hour. When I woke up, the girl was standing in front of the car with her case in her hand and her raincoat tied around her waist. Seeing me open my eyes, she walked up to me.

"Now you've slept, maybe you can take me."

I turned the key in the ignition and slowly pulled up level with her.

"Now I've slept, I don't feel like it."

I sped away, memories stirring my blood. Sleeping hadn't refreshed me. Fatigue continued to weigh on me like cow's milk on a baby's stomach. The traffic on the 101 made me feel dizzy. I left it and drove along the coast road as far as Gold Beach, at the mouth of the Rogue River. I found myself in Oregon without realizing it. I didn't really care, I wasn't particularly trying to get out of California. Gold Beach was the last town I had to drive through before I hit the forest. I had driven the last hundred miles without going back on my decision. I was going to climb up to the mountains and blow my brains out near the tree that had been struck by lightning. Not directly underneath it. I didn't want to cause offense. Gold Beach was wearing its most conventional face. The darkening gray sky melted into a menacing sea. The big deserted beach seemed to despise the town, which had no reason for being there. There were three motels there, one of them with an Irish theme. I immediately thought of Duigan. Then of Wendy. I hadn't had the time or the calm to think about them up until now. Wendy had talked to me about her mother one day. When her mother had learned that her cancer was incurable, there had been several days when she couldn't believe it. She had told Wendy that there was no greater suffering in life than to know that you were going to die within a fixed period of time. Those words stirred so many memories of all the bad stuff I'd done that I walked back to my car, which I had left along the 1. I had to hurry up and be done with it. What the hell was I doing, running around like this? All at once, just when I was least expecting it, an obvious idea came into my mind and wouldn't go away. I had to do something good. I'd never ducked out of things in my life. But if I was going crazy because of the guilt that was growing in my head like a brain tumor, then I had to tell Duigan everything. I owed him the truth. The poor guy was going to be in enough trouble anyway. No, I wasn't the kind of son of a bitch who'd let down the people who trusted him. I couldn't. I really couldn't. But instead of calming me down, that decision made me twice as nervous.

I carried on along the Rogue River for about ten miles. There, at the foot of the mountain, I knew a place. Nobody lived there apart from an old guy who kept the only gas station for miles around. There it stood, a big dirt yard in the middle of all those steep roads. That gas station meant more to desperate drivers than a shrine means to pilgrims. His house was ridiculously small. Almost as small as the phone booth that sat in the middle of that yard. Apart from a few deadbeats, the area was deserted, surrounded by conifers, but with the Rogue River flowing past to the sea. The old man recognized me. He was a nice old guy with no teeth. This was the third time he'd seen me. I had never met anyone as cheerful as he was. He subscribed to a wine club, and was very proud of his bottles. Unfortunately, as he told me himself, he only liked beer. So he was very generous to wine lovers, to make up for the exorbitant prices he charged for gas. "Have you ever seen a guy dying of thirst after crossing the Mojave Desert on foot arguing about the price of water?" He offered me some wine. I drank a bottle to calm down. He offered me another, telling me he had to empty his cellar. They'd just found a nasty tumor in one lung—he'd been systematically filling his lungs with smoke for fifty years.

"I'm not sure I'll be here next time you come. They want to operate on me. If they don't operate on me, I'll die. If they operate on me, I haven't a cent to pay them. I'm going to be forced to die to escape my debts. That's how life is, everything's fine and dandy and then suddenly you're screwed by fate. But I'm not complaining."

He opened the second bottle then sniffed the cork.

"It's a wine that should be kept, but who's going to keep it? If you like, you can take the bottles that are left. I don't have any family."

"That's a pity but I won't be able to keep it either."

"Why's that?"

"I'm not sure I have long to live."

He looked at me, deeply shocked. "At your age, son, that isn't natural."

Before I could satisfy his curiosity, which was quite understandable for an old man living alone without any distractions, I stood up.

"Is the phone working?"

"It was working this morning. I saw a guy in there, making these big gestures like he was trying to convince somebody at the other end."

I walked nervously to the booth and I was shaking as I picked up the receiver. I was hoping, though I wouldn't admit it to myself, that I wouldn't be able to get through. At last I heard ringing at the other end, which lasted so long I was going to hang up. But then a breathless young woman's voice said, "Santa Cruz Police Department, homicide squad, how may I help you?"

She must have run from the coffee machine. I asked to speak with Captain Duigan.

"He isn't on duty today," she replied smoothly.

"Then put me through to whoever *is* on duty."

"That's Lieutenant Carlson."

I remembered Carlson, a sandy-haired cop with eyes that were too close together. He came to the Jury Room from time to time but didn't drink. He only came there because he was afraid of missing something. He'd never particularly liked me.

"Who should I say is calling?"

"Al Kenner."

"Can you tell me what it's about?"

"No."

"Okay, I'll go see if he wants to speak with you."

"Tell him I'm Duigan's ex-future son-in-law."

The concept of ex-future son-in-law brought her up short.

"Yes, I was supposed to be marrying his daughter next month."

"Isn't that going to happen now?"

"There's some doubt about it."

"Okay, I'll put you through to Lieutenant Carlson."

I was left waiting for quite a while. I was starting to fear I'd run out of coins.

Carlson finally picked up.

"You want to speak with Duigan? He left for the weekend."

"You have to find him wherever he is."

"Why?"

"I killed my mother and her friend."

The pause didn't last long.

"I noticed you were quite fond of your drink at the Jury Room, Kenner, but I don't have time for this kind of bullshit, I'm the only person on duty."

"I tell you it's the truth. I'm in a phone booth and I don't have a lot of coins. I'll give you the number, tell Duigan to call me back. Please do it because I'm going completely crazy here and I have a 9mm pistol with me."

I started dictating the number but I was cut off. I was so angry, I thought I was going to knock down the booth. I only had one coin on me, plus a banknote. I went back to see the old man and asked him to help me out. He had just enough change.

In the meantime a woman had stopped next to the booth. She had a scarf on her hair. As I walked toward the booth, she closed the door. In the twilight silence of the valley, I could hear everything.

"I don't give a damn about your wife, Sean, I don't give a damn. I got dressed to come and see you, and I'll be there in twenty minutes. No, Sean, it's her or me now, and when I show up I think it'll be me. Open a bottle of chilled white wine, throw your wife out, and before you have time to take a shower, I'll be there."

The guy at the other end must have said something in reply.

"What do you think, Sean, I'm going to let you enjoy Saturday night with your wife in your house with a view of the sea while I have a hamburger in my car, parked under a lamp-post? I'll be there in twenty minutes, Sean."

She hung up and came out of the booth.

"Did you listen to all that?"

"No, but I heard it."

She was having second thoughts. "No, I'm going to give him an hour to get rid of his wife, what do you think? Poor dear, he's so helpless when there's a problem."

"You can call him afterwards. I have an urgent call to make."

She just stood there and didn't move.

This time I got hold of old Ramirez, with whom I'd shared dozens of rounds at the Jury Room.

"What is all this crap, Al? You know perfectly well you aren't capable of doing something like that."

"Yes, I am."

"What's going on? Have you flipped or what?"

"No, I assure you I haven't. I'll give you the address." I dictated it. "It's a two-story gray house on a bend. They're both there. My mother and her friend, Sally Enfield."

"How did you kill them?"

"It isn't a pretty sight. I smashed their heads in with a hammer."

"O.K., I'll send a patrol car, Al, but if this is all a joke . . . I can't believe it. You're one of us, Al, you've done good work. What are you doing, making creepy jokes like that?"

"I assure you it's true. I have to go, I'm running out of coins. I'll give you the number. Tell Duigan to call me. Don't take too long, I have a 9mm pistol with me and a really strong urge to blow my brains out. I'm staying alive for Duigan."

I read out the number, then said, "I'll be waiting next to the phone booth," and hung up.

The girl had heard everything. She stood there with her back to the glass side of the booth.

"What are you waiting for? You can call now."

She was paralyzed with fear.

"Make your call, but make it quick, I'm waiting for them to call me back. And not a word to anybody, or I'll come looking for you."

I ended with a smile, but that wasn't enough to relax her. She got in her car without turning back. I knew she wouldn't say anything, she was too eager for a night with her lover, and, after all, she was a witness to the fact that I'd given myself up. I sat there with my back against the booth most of the evening, thinking about my miserable life. I wasn't the Incredible Hulk. I'd never had the strength to break my chains, escape my prison, prevent my predestined fate. I fell asleep. Just as a stray dog sniffed my face and woke me, the phone rang.

70

I knew it was Duigan by the way he didn't say anything. But then I didn't say anything either, so he finally opened his mouth. "We just came back from the house, Al," he said wearily. "What have you done, Goddammit, what have you done?"

I took a deep breath. "I know it's upsetting, Mr. Duigan, but I can explain."

"Your mother's head cut off, darts in her face. Can you explain that, Al?"

I sensed that he wanted to cry and I didn't want to hear his sobs.

"Let's not make it more dramatic than it is, Mr. Duigan."

"And her friend . . . Al, where are you?"

"In Oregon. In a parking lot between Reading and Gold Beach, ten miles from Gold Beach maybe, on the road that runs along the Rogue River."

"Why Oregon?"

"I have to explain. I want to give myself up to you, Mr. Duigan, and nobody else. If you send one of those dumb local cops, I'll take him out and then put a bullet in my own head."

"I'm on my way, Al. Can you promise me you'll be there?"

"I can't promise anything. The only reason I'm still alive is because I owe you an explanation. You're the only man in this world who ever treated me well, better than my father or my psychiatrist in Atascadero. I know you may get into a lot of trouble, not to mention your disappointment, and I don't want to leave you in the lurch. Believe me, though, I'm struggling to stay alive because I really don't have anything to expect from life anymore. Whatever happens they're going to fry me. But I'm not afraid. The only thing I care about, Mr. Duigan, is that you don't think I'm completely crazy."

"You're asking a lot of me, Al. Don't move from where you are. I'm getting in my car with a deputy, I'll be there by sunrise."

"I only hope there's going to be a sunrise, Mr. Duigan."

"Why do you say that?"

"No reason. I'm waiting for you, don't forget, you follow the Rogue River from Golden Beach to the first gas station on the left, that's where I'll be."

"Don't you want to come a little closer to home, Al?"

"No, I don't have the strength, and besides I have some things to show you around here."

71

The old man had gone back inside his house. I knocked but he didn't answer. I opened the door. His house was only one room with a kitchenette filled with cans of food. I was fifty years younger than him, but I didn't have any more of a future ahead of me than he did and that made me warm to him. His life had also amounted to nothing, or not very much. He had fallen asleep, sitting on his couch, with an empty beer glass in his hand. I was seized with a sudden desire to take off and drive all the way to Alaska, but I didn't have the guts. All I wanted was to give myself up.

I closed the door again softly and went and sat in the convertible. I tipped the seat back into a horizontal position. It was bitterly cold, and I was forced to put the top down. I thought back over those last minutes.

I had gone back up to my room after the last words my mother and I had exchanged. I couldn't get to sleep and I had the premonition that my unconscious was leading me to do something serious, something I couldn't resist. I waited until I couldn't stand it anymore, then went back downstairs. The living room was deserted. I knocked at her door but she didn't answer. I went in. She had fallen on the bed with her arms outstretched, fully dressed, overcome by the booze. I tapped her on the arm. I couldn't remember how long it was since I'd last touched her. Her skin was warm and flabby. I pinched her. She looked at me as if she wasn't surprised to see me there and sighed. "What do you want now?" I sat down next to her on the bed, with my back against the wall. "I'd like you to talk to me, Ma." She looked straight at me. "You know you're start-ing to piss me off, Al. It's pathetic, a big lump like you begging for attention. Let me sleep." "Talk to me, Ma," I repeated, just once." She sat up. "I'm serious, Al, leave me alone or I'll call your cop friends and I'll tell them all I know." When I didn't move, she screamed, "When the hell are you going to make up your mind to get out of my life, to disappear? Don't you see you're killing me, Al? You're killing me." I heaved a big sigh and seeing that she was calming down I stood up and left her room. I carefully closed the door behind me, taking care not to slam it. I couldn't stand violence of any kind. I went back to my room and lay down. I played Skip James until four in the morning without thinking about anything. They say music soothes the savage breast, I must be the exception that proves the rule. At four-fifteen, I was ready to go. You can be hyper-mnesic and still have memory gaps. Why there was a hammer in my room, I have no idea. It was no use to me. But it was there, as if it had come through the wall and ended up on my night table. I picked it up, without any hatred but with all the determination of a Sunday handyman who's made his mind to get down to a chore he's been putting off for a long time. I went downstairs. My mother hadn't got up to close the door. I headed for her room. She was asleep again, but this time she had had time to put on a nightdress. She was sleeping on her back, with her arms still spread. At that moment, it seemed to me that I had no other solution. I did what I had to do, with-out any anger. I hit her three times with the hammer, very hard. Sally Enfield must have had a sixth sense because, I can assure you, those hammer blows didn't make much of a sound. She came out of her room, in a ridiculous blue nightie, the kind of blue you only find in dish soap. I was in the corridor, thinking about washing my hammer. I had no intention of doing anything to her but in her dumb twittery little voice she asked me if I was all right. "I'm fine," I said, "I've just killed my mother." She gasped, as if it was all too much for her, and turned to go back into her room, where I guess she hoped I'd forget about her. I hit her with the hammer before she'd gotten through the door. She wasn't worth another blow, and anyway she died immediately. I won't dwell on what happened next. I made love to my mother. It didn't take long. Then I went back in the kitchen to get what I needed and cut her head off. I placed her head on the shelf above the tacky false fireplace in the living room and threw darts at it, singing her a rhyme I'd put together: "There's a hole in my head, dear Liza, dear Liza, There's a hole in your head, dear Liza, a hole." All that blood running all over the place finally pissed me off. I've never felt as alive as I did during the minutes that followed. But exhaustion spoiled that moment of calm.

72

It was getting colder and colder. I switched the engine on and started the heating. When I turned it off, the noises of the valley took me by surprise. I could hear the sound of the Rogue River as it rushed to the sea. I fell asleep. I was woken by a little black bear sniffing at my door, attracted by the smell of a box of crackers. It gave up after a while. Daylight rose in an arc over the mountain. I thought about the Avenue of the Giants, where I'd had my motorcycle accident. Without that accident, I wouldn't have gone back to my mother's and things might have been different. It wasn't so far from there and yet these trees were nothing like those. There weren't any sequoias here, just conifers, thousands of conifers, packed close together as if they didn't want to let anything through.

The light still hadn't quite reached the mountaintops when a car came along, moving slowly. It bounced over a rut in the road and drew up in a cloud of dust. Two men got out. I recognized Duigan from his big square head. I knew the other cop by sight. He was a bit taller than Duigan, with very short fair hair and a twitch that made him look like a hoodlum. He hadn't been in Santa Cruz very long. I got out of the Mustang and walked toward them, holding my head high. I wasn't as exhausted as the day before and the confident way I was coming toward them must have gotten the fair-haired cop worried, because he put his hand on his holster. It was like being in a Western. I raised my arms in the air and turned my hands like a child to show the idiot that I wasn't armed. Things had gotten off to a bad start between us.

"Do you think I brought you here to kill you?" I said. Then, to Duigan: "They let just anyone in the police force these days."

Duigan was a terrible sight. He looked as haggard as if he'd just come from a funeral. We stood there without saying anything while Carter, the new guy, lit a cigarette. Then he asked me if the car was mine. I replied that I'd stolen it and that I didn't have anything in it except a 9mm pistol they were going to need.

"Need why?" Carter said, breathing out smoke from his nose like a dragon.

I didn't reply. During our exchange I could see Duigan looking at me with a distressed expression. Carter went to the Mustang to look for my gun, leaving us alone. The only thing I could find to say was: "It's going to be cold in the mountains."

He said nothing.

"I think you're going to need the Oregon police."

He started talking in a voice that wasn't his. "California isn't so far, we'll say we arrested you there."

I shook my head slowly from side to side. "No, Mr. Duigan, you're going to need their state police."

"Why, Al?"

I'd never seen him look so weary.

"I can't tell you, but I'm going to take you." As Carter was on his way back, looking more like a hit man than ever, I said, "I'm sorry, Mr. Duigan, I was going to blow my brains out. The only reason I didn't was because I owe you an explanation, but now I'm afraid I'm going to put you in a really difficult situation."

He looked at me, intrigued. I turned my back on Carter and lowered my voice.

"I have something to show you, but I'd prefer the two of us

to go there alone. Then you can decide what you want to do. I assure you, it's in your own interest." I turned to Carter. "I have to show the captain something, but alone."

Carter, who made up for his lack of intelligence with a sense of discipline, twisted his neck and gave Duigan a questioning look.

Duigan seemed doubtful. At last he made up his mind. "Stay here, Carter." Then to me: "Will it take long?"

"The whole morning." I turned back to Carter. "If you need the Mustang, you just have to touch the wires under the dashboard together."

We left without further ado. Duigan couldn't find the words to start a conversation. At the intersection, which was the last we'd come to for hours, we turned south to cross the mountains. I opened my window, letting the smell of damp pine needles into the car. The road was narrow and steep, with sharp bends. An army of conifers obstructed the view. It was dark under the trees even though the sky was blue. Climbing like this, we soon found ourselves way up at the top of some high cliffs. That didn't bother Duigan. He still hadn't said anything. But I was in no mood to keep quiet.

"You looked at my record, Mr. Duigan."

He nodded.

"Obviously there's nothing in it. The psychiatric panel wiped it all clean, and said I was perfectly normal. But I killed both my grandparents in '63. The day JFK was assassinated. I spent five years in a mental hospital. They said I wasn't responsible for my actions. Which I question. Responsibility is the number one question in life. Who's responsible and who isn't? I'd argue that mankind in general isn't responsible. But I am."

Duigan turned to me. "Why did you kill your mother, Al?"

"Because I had no choice. It was the only way I could survive. If I'd killed her in '63, I'd have had a normal life. I'm sorry I didn't have the guts to do it before. I dropped out of her womb like a crate falling off a truck, but she was my mother all the same. It takes time to come to the right decision."

"What about her friend?"

"I didn't like her. But she doesn't matter. She was an alcoholic, and in my opinion she didn't have long to live. I did her a favor."

Duigan jammed on the brakes, appalled. "But Al, you're completely crazy." He raised his voice. "Do you realize what you did? You killed your mother and cut off her head . . ."

"I raped her too."

I thought he was going to throw up. I didn't give him time. "It's a perverted defense mechanism, Mr. Duigan," I went on quickly. "It was either that or go crazy."

"But you are crazy, Al, you're raving mad."

"I don't like to contradict you, but to be honest, I don't think so. I used a perverted defense mechanism in order not to become a pervert, even though everything was driving me in that direction. I don't have any established psychosis, the experts agreed with me about that. You don't know my mother. I never planned to introduce her to you anyway. But if you'd known her—when she was alive, I mean—you'd have understood that she gave birth to a son thinking there wasn't room for the two of us in this world. She lived fifty years, including twenty-one during which she stopped me from breathing. I had to come up for air one day. As far as the rest of it goes, I know it's upsetting, but you don't kill your own mother just like that, there has to be a least some kind of ritual. I had things to exorcize symbolically. Cutting her head off so she could give me back my head, and fucking her . . . well, that was a tribute if you like. Or maybe I was trying to give her back the fucking seed which gave me my fucking life in the first place. As for the darts, well, I had to deny her, the way she denied me."

Duigan got out of the car. "You're fucking crazy, Al, a fucking nut," he yelled. "Don't you feel any remorse?"

I also got out, to take a leak and to answer him.

"For killing her? None at all. For putting you in this situation, when you trusted me, I can't deny I really hate myself for that."

The forest stretched as far as the eye could see. We got back in the car. The altitude was making my head and legs heavy.

"Is it still a long way?" Duigan asked.

There was still another hour's drive ahead of us. I was worried by the fact that he didn't seem at all curious about the place where I was taking him. He seemed paralyzed. He just sat there brooding. He must have been seeing his whole career pass in front of him, and wondering why he'd ever risked it on a guy like me, a guy he knew almost nothing about.

The road became a dusty dirt track then turned back to asphalt. The bends were tighter now, the cliffs steeper and steeper. Duigan was getting worried.

"Where are you taking me, Al? Do you even know where we are?"

"Don't worry, we're nearly there."

73

After a bend, we saw below us a tree that had been struck by lightning. It looked like a man who'd been crucified, with his head and hands torn off and just a few shreds of flesh hanging from him. The dead tree was alone, surrounded by healthy trees on an impressively steep slope. I gestured to Duigan to stop the car.

"You brought me all this way to show me a dead tree?"

I felt very embarrassed. I knew I was going to hurt him a hell of a lot. When he found out, he might well take out his service pistol and shoot me in the head. He knew he wasn't going to be getting any good news in this place. He seemed resigned, though, ready to face the reality of the situation.

"So, Al, what's so special about this dead tree?"

I hesitated for a while then said, "It's as dead as the girls I threw down there."

Duigan leaned against the car. He wasn't sure he wanted to hear the rest, but he made a huge effort to control himself and said, "What girls, Al?"

"The missing girls. Six co-eds from Santa Cruz."

He came and stood in front of me. "Like the Dahls' daughter, you mean?"

I nodded. He started crying and I felt genuinely sorry for him. Then he stopped abruptly.

"Oh my God, you killed the Dahls' daughter?"

I tried to regain the initiative. "That's why I brought you here. It's for you to decide. There probably isn't much of them left. The bears, the coyotes, the wolves, the birds of prey . . . "

"Stop with the fucking zoo, Al! How did you kill them? With a hammer?"

"Oh, no, with my 9mm pistol, a bullet just under the breast. And I made sure they couldn't be identified. I cut off their heads and hands."

"And what did you do with them?"

"I threw the hands away in the forest. I kept the heads. I just couldn't bring myself to get rid of them. You won't believe this, but the day I appeared before the psychiatric panel that wiped my record clean, I had two heads in the trunk of my car. But then . . ."

"Then what?"

"Sorry to go into these details. Even when I put them in the refrigerator, I had to throw them out after two or three days."

"What did you do with them?"

"I put them in the garbage. You know, people imagine things about heads. Even a big head isn't so heavy. There you are, Mr. Duigan, now it's for you to decide. I'm not trying to apologize for anything, but you have to know that I picked up hundreds of girls. But with these girls, I couldn't stop myself, even with alcohol. And then three days ago, bringing the last two girls here, I realized it wasn't their fault at all. It took me two more days to make up my mind to kill my mother. Now, I feel as if the evil has gone out of me. I feel as if I've been exorcised. I know I'll never harm anybody again."

Duigan was silent, not daring to look any further than the tips of his toes. If we'd been in a movie, the cry of a sparrow hawk would have pierced the silence of the forest. But in that place, all the sounds seemed to have been sucked down into the bowels of the earth. Duigan walked to the edge of the precipice and tried to make out something below.

"You won't see anything. They're a long way down.

Nobody will ever find them by accident. Not even hunters. I almost got noticed one night. I was just tipping a body over the edge when a guy pulled up in a pickup, a surfer type with white teeth, a little drunk. He was surprised to see me there in the middle of the night, and asked me if everything was all right. I went up to him and smiled. He left without suspecting a thing. So, what's it going to be?"

"I'm going to call the Oregon police, and then, when I get back to Santa Cruz, I'm going to hand in my resignation."

"I'm sorry, Mr. Duigan. You know, I did everything I could to resist. I could have killed so many more."

He'd stopped listening to me. The only thing he was thinking about was his decision to quit, and almost certainly to leave the region of Santa Cruz—to do what, I wouldn't have dared to ask him.

"Tell Wendy that . . . that I'm sorry too."

74

We set off again in the opposite direction. Duigan was less tense than on the way there. But there was something on his mind and it took him a while to come out with it.

"Could you have killed my daughter too?"

The question shocked me. "Oh, no! How could you suspect me of something like that? The idea never crossed my mind. I liked you too much, and her too. You were my only family. It would have had to stop anyway. Wendy would have found out in the end that I could never really touch her, if you see what I mean . . ."

From that point on, I sensed that the gratitude Duigan felt toward me for not killing his daughter was stronger than his resentment over his lost career.

"Did you rape the girls too?"

"Yes, just after killing them, when they were still warm. But that wasn't why I killed them, although I guess that's hard to believe. I wanted to see the transition from life to death with my own eyes. That's the one moment you live for. Of course, it's hard to imagine, but when they realized that nothing could save them, they stared at me without saying anything and I could see love in their eyes. I gave it back to them by penetrating them. I owed them that at least, didn't I?"

Duigan was eating up the miles, getting as far away as possible from that carnage.

"All that to make love seven times in my miserable life," I said.

There was still something I hadn't been able to explain to myself.

"I have to confess something to you, Mr. Duigan."

He jerked his head around. "You aren't going to show me any more corpses, are you?"

"No, no. Just something that doesn't really matter. I'd put the girls' heads on the pillow next to mine, then I'd lie down beside them and pull the blanket up to our chins. We'd watch TV like that. And then I'd fall into a deep sleep until late the next day. I've never felt so calm in my life. But the weird thing is, it upsets me to talk about it now."

There was a long silence after that. When we got to the bottom of the descent, I tried to make a joke.

"I only killed the daughters of Republicans, do you think Reagan will hate me for that?"

"Why? Is it true you only killed the daughters of conservatives?"

"Yes. I wasn't interested in all those liberal girls, let alone the hippie girls. I met some pretty ones but they disgusted me. I think I dreamed of marrying one of those girls who despised me even though I was intellectually capable of doing better than them or their families."

Duigan didn't answer right away. It wasn't until we got to the intersection with the road that crossed the plain that he said, "Reagan won't even kill you, Al. California still hasn't repealed the moratorium on the death penalty."

"I'm going to demand to be executed."

"You aren't going to demand anything. From now on, society will decide everything for you."

We reached the gas station. Carter was standing in the wind, smoking nervously.

The last thing I said to Duigan was, "All those girls are believed to be runaways. Their bodies will never be found. Carter doesn't know why we went up there. You can decide to stick with the story that they ran away, it'll be less painful for their parents. We have to think of them too."

He stared at me. "You can actually say that?"

"Yes, and you won't have to resign. We can make time stand still. I'll never kill again, Mr. Duigan, I don't have any reason now that my mother's dead. Why throw away your life, and Wendy's life, and the girls' parents', why make a mess of everything when we could live together and start a family? They'll say I wasn't responsible for the murder of my mother and Sally Enfield, and in five years I'll be back, completely cured . . ."

"Shut up, Al, I beg you, shut up."

75

I don't know if I'm going to spend my life designing and building apartment blocks like my father. It does pay well, though. You just have to see the way we live." She opens her hands to the sky as if to underline the obvious. "My plan is to become a world famous architect. I want to be asked to build museums, huge stadiums, houses for intellectuals, I want to give interviews in *Architectural Digest*. Will you work with me, Jamie?"

"Of course I will."

"We should go to Europe sometime and study classical architecture. It's incredible, the heritage those Italians and French have over there."

"I love their food."

"Oh, me too, just love it. I'm going to ask my father if I can do a semester in Paris. Though they say Frenchmen are weird."

"How do you mean, weird?"

"Apparently when you ask them how they are, they're quite likely to answer, 'Not bad.' Can you imagine? 'Not bad.' They're not as handsome as American guys either."

"But in bed, they go crazy. I swear to you. I have a friend who did art history for a semester in Paris. She went out with a Frenchman who was always in a bad mood. But in bed he did . . . you know . . . five times a day."

"Five times a day, Jamie? That has to be an exaggeration, right?"

"Must be great going out with a Frenchman. But living with him, marrying him?"

"They spend their time criticizing everything. Apparently they're all Communists. They had a revolution two years ago. And they don't really like us. But then we are very different. How about you? Do you know France?"

"Only by name."

"Haven't you ever been abroad?"

"No. I've never been further than Montana in the east or the sea in the west."

"Don't you miss it? Do you realize, Jamie, he's never been outside the United States. I already did the whole of South America with my parents, and Japan. My father says Japan is the future. My next trip is to Europe, Jamie, you come with me, I don't want us to be separated."

"I'll follow you, Janis."

"Aren't you afraid of flying?"

"No, I love it."

"How about you, are you afraid of flying?"

"I've never been on a plane."

"You should, trust me, it's a great feeling, I don't understand how people can be scared. But . . . where are you going? If we go this way, we're off our route."

"Just as I intended."

"But what's going on?"

"Nothing's going on. I've decided to take you where I want."

"You're joking, right? What do you want to do? Rape us? Kill us?"

"Both. But not in that order . . . No, no . . . only joking."

AUTHOR'S NOTE

To put a real person into a novel is to betray him, all the better to reveal what we perceive as his reality.

From his prison in Vacaville, Ed Kemper may understand why I appropriated his life. So might Stéphane Bourgoin, whose documentary on Kemper for the Planète channel first aroused my desire to involve myself with this complex character.

MARC DUGAIN

ABOUT THE AUTHOR

Born in Senegal in 1957, Marc Dugain is the author of numerous successful novels. His novel *The Officers' Ward* recounts his grandfather's experiences in World War I and was made into a 2001 film of the same name.